STILL THE ONE

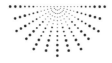

CARRIE ELKS

 *an, aged 6*

IT WAS A TEN-MINUTE WALK, and she knew it by heart, even though it was her first day of school. She needed to go out the front door, turn on her kicking foot, and walk toward the tree whose leaves were as red as her mom's favorite lipstick. Past the DeBoone's house, whose porch was always sparkling thanks to Marnie DeBoone's constant scrubbing, then along the sidewalk until she reached the corner.

This was the part where Van always ran. All the kids said that Old Mr. Shawson's house was haunted by his long-dead wife who had wanted children and would steal any who stepped on the lawn. Last year, Richie had pushed her onto the grass there, and she'd wet herself. Only a little, but she'd hated it just the same.

Only babies wet themselves, and she was six-years-old, too old to be a baby. But she ran anyway, not wanting Mrs. Shawson's ghost to stop her from getting to school on time.

The gates to the elementary school were open, the yard full of small children clinging to their parents' hands, oversized backpacks stuck to their spines like turtle shells. Van walked inside, pushing past legs and bags and sniffing children until she reached the door where Mrs. Mason was standing, talking to parents as she held a large brass bell loosely in her hands.

"Hello," Mrs. Mason said, frowning as she looked down. "Savannah, isn't it?"

Van nodded.

"Where's your mommy? She's allowed in the school yard on the first day of school. Why don't you go and get her?"

"My mom's sick." Van shrugged, as though it didn't matter one bit.

Mrs. Mason blinked. "Oh. Okay." It took her a moment to find a smile. "We'll be going inside in a moment. In the meantime, why don't you wait here." She turned back to the mother she'd been talking to. "Tanner looks so much like Grayson. Is he as much trouble as his big brother?"

The pretty mom laughed. "Not yet. Though Cam and Logan keep egging him on. I know you had your hands full with them last year."

"Well, at least I'll get a break before Rebecca starts school."

The lady smiled. "You'll probably need it."

"Speaking of breaks, I need to ring the bell and take the children in." Mrs. Mason checked her watch then lifted the brass bell up, clanging it three times. A group of boys who were shouting and playing in the corner of the yard ran over, one of them barging straight into Van.

She stumbled, clutching onto the stained rucksack she'd found in the bottom of her mom's closet a few days earlier. Two warm, small hands reached out to stop her from falling.

Wide brown eyes were staring right at her, so close she could see herself reflected in them.

By habit, her hands curled into fists.

"Sorry," the boy whispered.

"Tanner Hartson, you can't go knocking girls over on your first day." His mom ruffled his hair affectionately. "Are you okay, Savannah?" she asked. Her smile immediately made Van feel better.

Van nodded, her fingers slowly unfurling. "I'm okay," she said, as the other children pushed past them, heading into the classroom.

And she was. For then. But that was only the first time Tanner Hartson would knock her off her feet.

CHAPTER ONE

*T*he first thing Van Butler noticed was the silence. She'd forgotten about that, and it took her ears a moment to get accustomed to it as she climbed out of the car and looked at the neglected bungalow in front of her. *Home*. That's what this place had been for the first twenty years of her life, though for the past eight it had been Mom and Craig's, and somehow that had been easier. It hadn't been Van's job anymore to keep the grass mowed or the stoop swept or any of the other things that Craig had taken on. For the first time in her life her only responsibility had been to herself, and it had been glorious.

She smoothed out the creases on her cream skirt, the humidity already making her feel a little less pristine. Her pale blonde hair was neatly tied back in a low-pony tail, her white sleeveless blouse holding its shape in spite of the early summer heat. She took care of her appearance, it was the first thing people saw, after all. From an early age, she'd learned that people judged from appearances.

"Savannah Butler? Is that you?"

Van turned her head to the right. She hadn't noticed her

mom's neighbor there. Mrs. DeBoone was kneeling on a bright red gardening pad, a scarf covering her hair and canvas gloves covering her hands as she planted brightly colored flowers into earthy beds.

"Hello, Mrs. Deboone." Van formed an appropriate smile on her face.

"You here to see your momma?"

Van nodded. "That's right."

"Did you hear Craig's gone? Went off with the girl who works in the gas station." She dropped her voice. "Your mom and him were fighting like cats and dogs a couple of weeks ago."

Yeah, Van knew. She also knew that Craig was already living with the woman, some twenty miles from here. Her little sister, Zoe, had told her during a quiet, tear-filled phone call last week. That's why she was here. Because she was needed.

Thank god she'd saved up enough from her freelance work to take a break for a while.

"Sorry if they disturbed you," Van said, shooting the old lady a quick smile. She walked up the path, her heels catching in the cracks. Craig had only been gone two weeks yet the bungalow already looked like it was missing him. The grass that lined the pathway was up to her calves.

Mrs. DeBoone picked up the empty plant pots, slotting them one into the other, before she slowly pushed herself up to standing. "I should go in, before my knees give up." She gave Van a smile. "Give my regards to your mother." She glanced at Van's mom's bungalow and back to Van. "And I'm glad you're back. For Zoe's sake."

She shuffled up the pathway. Van knew without a doubt that she was planning to call her friends to tell them Savannah Butler was back in town. That's what happened in places like Hartson's Creek. People filled the silence with gossip, because it was better than sitting alone.

Maybe that's why she'd moved to Richmond as soon as her mom and Craig got married, back when Van was twenty-years-old. Zoe had been two then, pretty as a picture, with her chubby face and golden hair that matched Van's.

In so many ways, Craig had been her savior. Taking care of her mom and loving Zoe as his own so that Van didn't have to worry about them. For the first time in years she'd been able to breathe. To not have to anticipate her mom's dizzying mood swings, or wonder whether the empty whiskey bottle in the sink was the second or third one of the week.

Life had been good, for the most part, since then. Yeah, there had been sad times. Particularly whenever she thought of the things she'd lost. But there were good times, as well. She was good at her job – working as a freelance event planner in the state capital. And she earned enough to not only live in a pretty apartment, but to live a good life and save money, too.

She'd always been obsessive about saving. Maybe somewhere deep inside she'd known her mom was a ticking time bomb. It was a matter of when, not *if*, she'd detonate.

Van rapped her knuckles twice on the door, but nobody answered. Without bothering a third time, Van knelt down on the dusty top step and reached into the planter whose contents were long dead. Crisp brown leaves covered the parched soil as she dug her hand around, a smile curling at her lips as her fingers found the key she was looking for. She slid it into the lock, and pushed the creaky door open.

"Mom?" she called out. "Are you home?" She caught her toe on a stack of mail. Leaning down to pick them up, she noticed how many of them were bills. *Red ones.* "Mom?" she called again, setting the envelopes on the hall table and walking toward the kitchen.

The counters were covered with dirty plates and wrappers. Half-drunk coffee cups had white and green mold floating in the dusty liquid. The room stank of stale food and alcohol, emanating from the empty liquor bottles flung in the sink.

She gagged at the aroma. Swallowing hard against the impending nausea, Van walked back into the hall. Gently, she rapped her knuckles on her mom's bedroom door. "Are you in there?"

A groan echoed from inside and Van's stomach curdled again. Maybe she was hungry. She'd driven straight here from Richmond, not bothering to stop to eat. Sighing, she pressed down the handle and opened the door, wincing at the mess of clothes covering the brown carpeting.

Her mom was curled up on the bed, her soft blonde hair stuck to her face. Her eyes were closed, her mouth gaping wide.

The closet doors were open. One side held her mom's clothes, a clash of bright colors all pushed together. The other side was empty.

So Craig really had gone. Van looked around to see if he'd left anything behind. A razor, a tie, maybe a photograph or two. But there was nothing except the mess her mom had let build up. Typical Kim, she always did hate housework.

"Close the door," Kim rasped, turning on her side and covering her eyes. "Don't let the light in."

Van pulled the door until it clicked shut behind her. Her mom groaned again as Van started to pick up the scattered clothes. "Where's Zoe?" Van asked her.

"At school."

"It's six o'clock in the evening. School finished hours ago."

Kim let out a sigh. "Then she's probably with a friend. Or

at the library. She goes there almost as much as you did." Her mom reached out for the glass beside her bed, sighing when she saw it was empty. Finally, she opened her eyes and moved her gaze to Van. "What are you doing here?"

"Zoe told me you weren't well."

Kim rolled over and pressed her face into the pillow. "Did she tell you Craig's gone?" she asked, her voice muffled.

"Yeah. I was sorry to hear it." Van stuffed the final piece of clothing into the laundry basket. It was overflowing. She'd put a load of laundry in tonight, then another in the morning. If she was staying here, she'd have to tidy up.

She hated mess. Her pristine apartment in Richmond was testament to that.

"Everybody's talking about it." Kim sat up in the bed and attempted to smooth her hair down. "How he's gone off with a girl half his age. I bet they're all laughing at me." Her face crumpled. "I hate him," she hissed.

Van sighed and sat on the bed next to her mom. "No you don't. You're just sad." Kim looked up at her, her eyes pleading as though Van was some kind of savior. "Why don't you go take a shower?" Van suggested. "It might make you feel better."

Her mom flopped back onto the bed. "I don't want to get up. There's no point anyway. I can't go anywhere. Not when everybody is talking about me."

The front door slammed. "I'm back!" Zoe called out, her voice echoing in the hallway. Van jumped up from the bed and flung her mom's door open, grinning when she saw her sister. Zoe's pink sparkly backpack completely dwarfed her ten-year-old frame.

Slowly, Zoe looked up, her mouth dropping when she saw Van standing in the hallway.

"You're here!" she shouted, her lips erupting into a grin. "Oh god, you're here." She dropped her backpack and threw herself at Van, her arms wrapping around her sister's waist. "I didn't think you'd come."

Van kissed the top of her sister's head. "Of course I came. I told you I would."

Zoe looked up, her face shining brightly. "How long can you stay? Has Mom seen you?" She hugged Van tighter, pressing her face against Van's shoulder. "I'm so happy right now."

It was impossible not to feel warmed by Zoe's excited reception. "I'm here for as long as you need me," she murmured into Zoe's blonde hair.

"Really?" The expression of hope on Zoe's face nearly killed her.

A loud sniff came from their mom's bedroom. Van turned her head, to see Kim laying on her side, tears streaming down her face.

"Of course she's staying," their mom said, giving Van a watery smile. "She's a good girl. She'll take care of us, Zoe."

Van took in a deep breath, and smoothed Zoe's hair with the palm of her hand. She'd stay for as long as they needed her. Even if a part of her wanted to run as fast and as far as she could from here.

Her mom had always relied on the kindness of strangers and friends. But most of all she'd relied on Van. For a few years, Craig had taken on that role and Van had felt free. Enough to move away and begin a career of her own.

But now he was gone and the burden was hers to carry again.

Funny how it felt heavier than ever.

CHAPTER TWO

"Another beer?" Tanner Hartson called out to his brothers, carrying four bottles of *Sierra Nevada* in his large hands as he made his way across his eldest brother's backyard. Not that you could really call it a backyard. It was more of an estate. Gray's sprawling mansion sat on twenty acres of land, along with a purpose-built recording studio, a mother-in-law apartment for Gray's girlfriend's mom, plus a swimming pool, hot tub, and pool house. It was like he'd picked up a little piece of L.A. and moved it to their sleepy home town of Hartson's Creek.

Tanner passed the bottles to his brothers, then sat in the spare adirondack chair and lifted the beer to his mouth, closing his eyes for a second as he swallowed, the liquid cooling his belly. He leaned his head against the chair, and raked his fingers through his thick, dark hair. He sat low in the chair, his denim-clad legs stretched out, the fabric pulled tightly over his thigh muscles. His white shirt, unbuttoned at the neck showed a smattering of dark hair, was crumpled thanks to the afternoon heat. Like his brothers, he was tall, strong, and had a jaw most models would die for. As teenagers, the town had coined the term 'Heartbreak Brothers' to describe them. Something all four of them had come to loathe.

"I hear congratulations are in order," Gray said, lifting his bottle to Tanner. "Logan told me you sold your business. Way to go, man."

"Thanks." Tanner clinked his bottle against Gray's, then took another large mouthful. It had only been five days since he and his two co-owners had signed on the dotted line, selling their company for an unimaginable profit. He, Austin, and Jared had created their own software company from nothing when they'd graduated from Duke, the three of them working together on coding to improve the security of banking systems and apps throughout the USA.

Two months ago, they'd been made an offer that was impossible to refuse. Jared and Austin had wanted to accept it immediately. Jared had a family now, and the business was taking him away from his wife and baby seven days of the week. Austin's dad was sick with cancer, and living in California. It was only Tanner who had no other responsibilities, and there was no way he could hold out on the two people who needed his signature on the dotted line.

So here he was, richer than he'd ever imagined, but with no idea what to do next. He rubbed the back of his neck with his palm. He should be happy, he knew that. Yet the thought of all this free time on his hands made him uncomfortable as heck.

"So what happens now?" Gray asked him.

"We hand over all the intellectual property and make sure the transfer goes smoothly." Tanner shrugged. "Then I'm a free man."

"You gonna set up another company? Keep coding?"

Tanner lifted his beer to his lips. "Can't. Part of the deal is that we won't do any coding that might compete with the business for a year." He took a sip, swallowing it down. "So unless I want to go serve pancakes at the diner, I'm a man of leisure."

"That's rough." Gray nodded at him.

"Hey, don't worry about him," Logan said, grinning. "Has he told you how much they're paying him for this? The guy never has to work again if he doesn't want to."

"How much?" Gray asked, tipping his head to the side.

Tanner told him, and Gray's brows lifted up. "Whew."

Not that Gray should be *that* impressed. As a successful singer, he'd earned more than enough money over the past few years to not worry about cash ever again. He'd spent years touring the world, and not visiting home, thanks to the animosity between him and their father. Then last year he'd returned and fallen in love with Maddie Clark, and the two of them had built this house together.

"You might not be the richest brother any more," Logan said, grinning at Gray. "Now we'll all be begging Tanner for a loan."

"I'm pretty sure Cam's the richest," Tanner pointed out. "He just got signed for another season."

"I can categorically state I'm the poorest," Logan said, shrugging as if he didn't care in the slightest. "In cash at least. I just bought another restaurant."

"Are you guys waving your cash around again?" their little sister, Becca, asked, as she bumped Tanner along the chair, somehow squeezing into the tiny space beside him. "You're all disgustingly rich. And you need to stop making me look bad. I'm sick of going on dates and having to tell guys who my brothers are. All they want to know is if I can get them tickets to Cam's football games or Gray's concerts." She shook her head. "I wish we had a normal family." Her voice was wistful.

"You shouldn't be dating anyway," Tanner said with a grin, pressing his elbow into her side. "You're only a kid."

She rolled her eyes. "I'm twenty-four."

Gray caught her gaze. "Tanner's right. No dating."

She raised an eyebrow. "You want me to grow up old and lonely like Tanner? No thanks."

Tanner rested the base of his bottle on the grass beside the chair. "I'm not old and lonely."

"Okay then. Young-ish and lonely. Same difference." Becca grinned, her upturned nose wrinkling. "Speaking of which, are you going to say hi to Savannah Butler when you see her in town?"

"Who says I'm going to see her in town?" His stomach dipped at the thought of it. It had only been a few hours since he'd learned Savannah Butler had come back to Hartson's Creek. He had no idea why she was here, either. The days when they told each other everything were long gone.

Had been for years.

Becca shrugged. "It's a small town."

"Sure is." Gray's girlfriend, Maddie, walked over, carrying two glasses and a half-full bottle of champagne. She poured a glass for Becca and herself, passing one to Tanner's sister. Gray opened his arms up, and Maddie snuggled into his chair with him, whispering something in his ear.

Becca took a sip of champagne and turned to Tanner. "I wish you and Van were still friends. I miss her. She was like a sister to me growing up."

There was a time when Van Butler spent more time at the Hartson house than her own. Tanner's Aunt Gina, who'd taken care of the five Hartson siblings after their mom died, had grown used to making an extra portion for the girl who lived a few streets away.

And every evening, when Aunt Gina told her it was time to go home, Tanner would walk her to her tiny, ramshackle bungalow and watch silently as she stepped inside, grinning when she'd turn back and stick her tongue out at him before closing the door.

"You have Maddie now," Tanner pointed out, nodding his head at Maddie and Gray. They were laughing at something she'd just said. "She's like a sister to you as well."

"Yeah I know. But we're still outnumbered." Becca took a sip of wine.

"Maybe Cam or Logan will bring a girl home," Tanner said in an attempt to appease her. Becca was his little sister, after all. Like she was with all of his brothers, Becca was his soft spot. The one they made sure was happy. Anybody else would probably have been spoiled by it, but not Becca. She was too good for that.

She choked on her wine and he swallowed down a laugh. Logan gave her a half smile.

"I'll believe that when I see it." She put her glass back down and turned back to Tanner. "What happened with you and Van anyway? One minute you guys were best friends, the next it was like you didn't even know each other. I kept asking, but nobody told me why."

Tanner lifted Becca off him, then stood and stretched his arms. "This beer isn't cutting it," he said, ignoring her question. "Anybody ready for whiskey?"

"Not for me." Gray shook his head. "But you guys go ahead. Becca brought some bourbon home from the distillery."

She nodded, her questions about Savannah Butler forgotten. "We haven't released it to the public yet." She turned to Logan, her eyes sparkling. "I can probably get you some for your restaurants if you like it."

Becca had worked at the *G. Scott Carter* distillery since she'd left college three years earlier, first as a trainee, now as a distiller.

"Sounds good." Logan nodded and looked at Tanner. "I'll take a glass, please."

"Me too." Cam nodded. "And then I need to hit the sack. I'm back to training next week." He stretched his arms.

"When are you guys going back to Boston?" Becca asked the twins. Cam and Logan had settled there after college, when Cam had been one of the top draft picks and Logan was looking at starting his restaurant career.

"Monday," Logan told her. "I need to be back at work by then." He flashed her a smile. "The fun of being in the hospitality industry."

"But you're staying for a while though, right?" Becca asked Tanner.

There was something about the way she was looking at him that tugged at Tanner's heartstrings. Where there was only three years between him and Gray, with Cam and Logan slap bang in the middle, Becca was the youngest by four years. Growing up, she'd always chased them around on her tiny legs, panting loudly when she couldn't keep up.

Then as they'd left home one by one, she'd been forlorn without them. If you took his arm and twisted it behind his back he might just admit he missed her, too.

He'd never tell her that.

"I might hang around for a bit," he conceded. "It's not as though I've got anything better to do." Counting the dollars in his account had already bored him to death. He needed to get a hobby and fast.

What was it that Aunt Gina always said? *The devil makes work for idle hands.* Right now his whole body was idle. Who knew what the devil had planned for him next.

CHAPTER THREE

T anner, age 6

TANNER GLANCED at the girl out of the corner of his eye, willing her to stop rocking back and forth on her chair. Any minute now Mrs. Mason was going to notice, and he knew she was going to tell her off.

He hated getting told off. It made his stomach feel all twisty and sick.

The girl tipped back again, and he automatically reached out to the back of her chair, stopping her mid rock.

"Hey. What'ya doing?" she asked, shocked at the abrupt halt to her fun.

"You're gonna get in trouble," he told her, his eyes wide.

She shrugged. "So what?"

"Tanner Hartson, is that you talking?" Mrs. Mason asked, turning around from the chalkboard at the front of the room. "I swear you Hartson boys will be the death of me."

He narrowed his eyes and glared at the girl. She stuck her tongue out and winked.

She could wink? That was cool.

The sun was beating through the window to her left, turning her hair as golden as the cornfields at harvest time. Without even thinking, he reached out to touch it, surprised at how silky it felt between his fingers. His own hair – and his brothers' was thick and coarse like wool. Baby Becca's hair was soft and downy, but not silky like that. He liked the way it felt.

The girl gave him a strange look.

"Your hair is pretty," he whispered.

"Thanks." She grinned the biggest, widest smile he'd ever seen. It was like being blinded by the sun.

"Okay, who in here knows how to write their name?" Mrs. Mason asked, her eyes scanning the six-year-olds sitting in front of her.

Tanner shot his hand up. His mom had painstakingly taught him that a year ago. He noticed the rest of the class do the same.

All except the girl next to him. The smile on her face dissolved as she looked around and realized she was the only one in the class with her hand down. Slowly she pushed hers up, her jaw jutting out like she was gritting her teeth.

"Okay, children. I'd like you to show me how you do it. Use the paper and crayons on your desk, please." She smiled at them. "Make me proud."

Tanner pulled a piece of the drawing paper toward him, and took a green crayon from the plastic pot in the middle of their wooden desk. Curling his fingers around it, he slowly moved the crayon across the white expanse, drawing his 'T' as straight as he could, before slowly forming the rest of the letters.

When he stopped, he wrinkled his nose at his efforts. His

letters were too slopey. Gray had told him to write in a straight line. He sighed and went for another piece of paper when he realized the girl hadn't begun to write her name.

"You need to write your name," he whispered. "Before Mrs. Mason comes to look."

The girl's gaze slid to their teacher then back to Tanner. "I don't know how."

"Didn't your mom show you?"

She shook her head.

"What's your name?"

"It's Savannah." He must have grimaced at the long name because she quickly added, "But everybody calls me Van."

"Van. That's not so bad. Just a *vee* then an *ay* and an *en*. It's kinda like my name. I'm Tanner." He pointed at the paper in front of him. "See?"

"Not really."

"What color do you want to do your name in?"

"Red." She nodded, as though it was a given.

He grabbed the red crayon from the pot, along with a fresh piece of paper, and painstakingly traced out the three letters, this time making them as straight as he could. "There," he said. "Van."

She took the paper and held it up, admiring it like she would a piece of art. "Van," she said. "That's my name." She grinned again, and he felt the warmth of it. "Thank you," she whispered.

"You're welcome." He nodded, his expression serious.

Mrs. Mason was walking around the room, looking at her students' attempts at their name. When she reached Tanner's table, she looked down at his paper and smiled. "That's lovely, Tanner. And how about you, Savannah. Let's see your name."

Van pushed her paper forward, still beaming.

"That's not your full name," Mrs. Mason said. "Can you write Savannah for me?"

Van shook her head. "Everybody calls me Van," she said, nodding to emphasize her words.

"But Savannah is such a pretty name," Mrs. Mason said. "And you're such a pretty girl."

"It's Van," the girl said again, rolling her eyes. "I don't need a pretty name." Tanner had to curl his nails into his palms to stop himself from laughing out loud. Watching the two of them was like a battle of wills. He wasn't sure who'd win.

"Well, I shall call you Savannah." Mrs. Mason said, as though she was trying to have the last word the same way Tanner's dad always did. "Okay, Kindergarteners, well done. Now let's try our numbers." She clapped her hands and walked away, shaking her head like his mom did when she was annoyed.

When the teacher had turned her back on them once more, Van elbowed Tanner to get his attention. "Hey, Tanner," she whispered loudly.

"Yeah?"

"Thanks."

He smiled. "That's okay."

"You wanna play with me at recess?" she asked him. "I know all the good games." She gave a slow nod, like she was weighing something up. "I'll even be your best friend if you want me to be," she told him. He felt warm inside, like she'd just given him a birthday present.

The sun hit her hair again, making her look like the angels in his mom's illustrated bible, and Tanner found himself nodding at her suggestion.

"Yeah," he agreed solemnly. "I'd like that a lot."

CHAPTER FOUR

*I*t had taken three days, but her mom's bungalow was finally clean from top to bottom. Van stepped back, admiring the way the kitchen surfaces shone. Her hair was tied back from her face, her skin glowing from exertion, but she couldn't help but grin as she took it all in.

"Hey, Zoe!" she called out, turning as her sister walked through the kitchen door. "Take a look at the stove. You ever seen it look that clean?"

Zoe pressed her lips together, staring at Van as though she was crazy. "Um, no."

Okay, so maybe she *was* crazy. But since her mom had spent the past few days either laying in bed or moping on the living room sofa, it had given Van something to do.

"I cleaned the windows, too," Van told her sister.

"Nice." Zoe looked around, her brows lifting. "But isn't it all gonna get dirty again?"

"What do you mean?"

Zoe glanced at the chrome clock hanging over the back door. Van had put a battery in it earlier when she'd taken it down to polish it. "It's almost dinner time," Zoe pointed out.

"And we'll have to use the stove to cook it. Then it's gonna get dirty."

Over Van's dead body. "We'll go out to eat tonight," Van said quickly. At least that'd give her a few more hours of a clean house. "Where do you want to go?"

"The diner?" Zoe suggested. "They have good milkshakes there."

Van grinned. "I haven't been to Murphy's in ages. Are the eggs still bad?"

"The worst."

"Okay then. The diner it is." Van put away the last of the cleaning supplies, then washed her hands. At least she didn't need to tidy herself up much for the diner. Just a quick shower and a change of clothes. "Mom?" she called out. "You want to come out for dinner?"

It took a moment for her mom to reply, "No. Just get me a burger or something. I'm too sleepy to go out."

Van sighed. Compared to sorting out her mom, getting the house clean was easy. "Give me twenty," she told Zoe. "Then we'll head out."

"Sounds good to me." Zoe grinned. "I'll be ready."

"Are you sure you want to eat here?" Tanner asked his sister, holding the door open for her. The aroma of coffee and fried food hit him instantly.

"Of course. Murphy's is a Hartson's Creek institution. If you're staying here for a while, you need to reacclimatize yourself." Becca grinned at him, ducking under his arm and heading straight for her favorite booth. "And I won at cards last night fair and square. Winner picks the food, loser pays. It's our rule, remember?"

Tanner slid into the tattered bench seat opposite Becca,

his legs barely fitting beneath the peeling table. He was wearing a thin grey sweater, his hair freshly washed after his evening run, though he hadn't bothered to shave.

This had been his favorite booth as a kid. His and Van's. Murphy's had been one of their favorite places to hide out, accompanied by a milkshake and fries, as they laughed like crazy at each others' jokes.

Murphy's Diner had been a local institution for as long as he could remember. With its shiny chrome décor and red faux leather seats, it was the center of Hartson Creek life. It overlooked the town square, complete with a painted white bandstand and colorful flower beds, the verdant grass dotted with benches where the townfolk loved to sit and talk.

Along with the bakery, Laura's Dress shop, and Fairfax Realty, it faced the large white building opposite – The First Baptist Church of Hartson's Creek, the other focal point of small town life.

He and Van had introduced Becca to the diner and their favorite booth when she was old enough to appreciate it. She'd been maybe nine or ten years old. He'd regretted it later, when she'd beg him every day to let her come with him to meet Van. But it was still her favorite place to sit. For some reason, that warmed him.

He looked down at the tattered bench seat. The stuffing was coming out at the corner, looking like fluffy white clouds against the scarlet seat. "I don't think they've updated this place since I lived here." To be fair, it wasn't a big surprise. He would have been more shocked if they *had* updated.

Becca widened her hazel eyes, pretending to be affronted. "Stop your moaning, Tanner Hartson. I hope all that money and living in New York hasn't changed you. There was a time when this was your favorite place."

He arched an eyebrow. "Wasn't bitching. Just observing."

She leaned forward, grinning. "You think you're too good for this place now that you're rich?" she asked him. "Maybe I should tell Murphy you don't like the décor."

"You do that."

"Ha. Look at you pretending you're not scared of Murphy." Becca shook her head. "Everybody's scared of Murphy. Even Murphy."

"I'm not scared of him," a sweet voice said. Tanner turned to see Cora Jean Masters standing there, a pad in her hand. Like the décor, she'd been part of the diner for as long as he could remember.

"Hey, Cora," he said, standing up to kiss her cheek. "I swear you keep getting better looking."

"Now stop that." She swatted his arm and bit down a smile. "What can I get you?"

Becca looked up from her menu. "I'll start with a chocolate shake please. With extra whipped cream."

"And I'll take a coffee," Tanner said, then under his breath he added, "Because I'm not five."

Becca kicked his shin. "I heard that."

"So another Hartson boy is back in town," Cora Jean said. "You here for a while?"

"I'm not sure how long I'm home for," Tanner told her. "It depends how much Becca annoys me."

This time her kick hurt. He winced, the pain shooting through his leg.

"Serves you right," Becca told him, sticking her tongue out. "Now be nice."

Cora Jean shook her head at their antics. "No wonder your aunt had her hair cut short. Stopped her from pulling it out."

Tanner laughed. "She's crazy about us."

"You have no idea how true that statement is," Becca told him. "You drive her crazy."

"You want to order your food now, or shall I come back?" Cora Jean asked them.

"I know what I want." Becca looked at Tanner. "How about you."

"Go ahead." He gestured at her.

Becca smiled up at Cora Jean. "I'd like a half pound hamburger with the works. And extra onions. Large fries and onion rings, too. Please."

"Have you considered eating vegetables?" Tanner teased.

Becca shrugged. "I'm hungry. I've been working all day. Unlike some."

"I'll take the BLT and a green salad," Tanner said, handing the menu to Cora Jean.

"You want fries with that?"

"Yeah he does," Becca answered for him. When he gave her a questioning look she shook her head. "You can't eat in here without having fries. Murphy would kill you."

The bell above the diner door dinged, though from where they were sitting neither Becca nor Tanner could see who it was.

"You folks want anything else?" Cora asked.

"Nope. We're good. Thanks, Cora." Becca handed her own menu over. As she walked away, Tanner leaned down to rub his shin, wincing at the bruise Becca's pointed shoes had caused.

"You're a baby," she told him.

"You want me to kick you back?" he asked, raising an eyebrow. It was impossible not to smile at her. Every time he went back to New York he missed this. Bickering with Becca cheered him up, the same way roasting Gray and his brothers made him grin. It was the one time he felt alive, part of something.

Part of a family.

Maybe the diner wasn't so bad after all.

∾

"THE DINER WAS ALWAYS Craig's favorite," Zoe told Van as she pushed open the glass door and they walked onto the white tiled floor. The smell of fried food wafted around them, making Van's stomach growl. "He used to bring me here sometimes. Not for a while though."

"How are you feeling about him leaving?" Van asked her.

"I dunno." Zoe's face was impassive. "Where do you want to sit?"

Van bit down a smile at her unwillingness to talk about her emotions. She was like Van's miniature in that respect. "How about we go to the booth in the corner. It used to be my favorite when I was a kid. Nobody can see you there, or judge what you're eating." She winked. "Or how much."

"You used to eat here?" Zoe asked, looking at Van with interest. "That's cool."

"It was my second home as a teenager," Van told her. "Along with…" She swallowed hard. Zoe wouldn't even know who Tanner was. She wasn't even born when her and Tanner's friendship ended spectacularly. "Anyway, it was a nice place to spend time when I didn't want to be at home."

Zoe caught her eye, as though she knew exactly what Van meant. "I've been spending a lot of time at the library since Craig left."

"The library's cool, too." God, Craig had a lot to answer for. "Here's the boo—" Her words stopped abruptly as she stopped in front of her favorite seat, her tongue sticking to the roof of her mouth. For a moment, all she could do was stare at the two people already sitting on the familiar red-and-white benches, her heart flailing wildly against her ribcage.

Tanner Hartson. When was the last time she'd seen him this close up? A decade ago? On the rare occasion she'd caught sight of him since, on those unlucky days when they were both visiting home, she'd managed to cross the road and keep her distance.

What the hell should she do? Say hello? She swallowed hard, taking in his dark, thick hair, raked back from his face like it always was, tapering down to the nape of his neck. His shoulders were wide, his broad chest stretching the thin knit of his sweater. And then there was the dark shadow on his strong jaw which made him look older. Sexier. No longer the boy she remembered, but a man now. One that could take her breath away if she let him.

Becca was the first one to recover. She looked up at Van with a smile. "Hey, I heard you were back in town. How are you doing? That can't be Zoe. She's so grown up."

Somehow Van managed to form a smile on her lips. She always had time for Becca. She'd been like a little sister to her growing up. "I'm good," she said, keeping her gaze away from Tanner. "And yeah, this is my sister, Zoe."

"Hey, Zoe. You probably don't remember me. I'm Becca Hartson."

"Are you Gray Hartson's sister?" Zoe asked.

Becca nodded. "That's right."

Zoe's eyes lit up. "That's really cool. Me and my friends *love* his music."

"And this is Tanner, one of my other brothers." Becca nodded her head at him. "I promise you he talks sometimes."

Tanner swallowed hard, his prominent Adam's apple undulating against his throat. "Hi, Zoe." His smooth, dark voice made the hairs on the back of Van's neck stand up. Awareness washed through her like the ocean across the shore.

Zoe nodded at him.

Then he was looking right at Van with those piercing eyes, and she felt a shot of electricity pulse down her spine.

"Hi, Van. You doing okay?" he asked softly.

She nodded quickly. "I'm great. How are you?"

"I'm good." He gave her the ghost of a smile and it jolted a memory in her mind. Of the day everything changed. She swallowed down the bitter taste of it.

"Do you guys want to join us?" Becca asked them, gesturing at the booth. "There's enough room for all of us."

Tanner's dark, assessing eyes met Van's. She felt a jolt of alarm shoot through her.

"Thank you, but not this time." As though there'd be a next time. "I haven't been in town for long. Zoe and I have a lot to catch up on."

"That's a shame." Becca was still smiling, as though she had no notion of the atmosphere dancing around the booth. "Maybe I'll see you soon. Are you going to *chairs* this Friday?"

"*Chairs?*" Van wanted to laugh. "You guys still do that?"

Chairs was the name the folk of Hartson's Creek gave to their weekly gatherings by the creek. Every Friday night they'd congregate in their front yards and on the grassy field along the water, bringing food and drinks to share. The old folk would sit in the chairs and gossip, while the younger ones played flag football or dangled their hot feet in the cool creek.

"Every Friday between April and October." Becca grinned. "You should both come. It'll be good to see you."

"Mom doesn't like *Chairs*," Zoe said softly. "She says there are too many gossips."

Becca laughed out loud. "Your mom's right about that."

"We'll see," Van said, putting her hand on Zoe's shoulder, ready to steer her to another booth. One far away from this one. "We should go and put our order in," she told them, flashing the briefest of smiles. "I'll see you both around."

"I hope so." Becca beamed brightly. Tanner, she noticed, said nothing.

It didn't stop her from feeling his eyes burning into her back as she and Zoe walked to the other end of the diner and sat down in an empty booth.

"They're nice," Zoe said, smiling for the first time since Van had gotten home. "Maybe we *should* go to *Chairs* on Friday."

Van could still feel her skin tingling from seeing Tanner. "Maybe," she said, squeezing Zoe's shoulder. "We'll see."

∼

"ARE you eating those fries or just playing with them?" Becca asked.

Tanner looked up from his plate, blinking as Becca's voice brought him out of his thoughts. Since he'd seen Van Butler he'd been stuck in them. Maybe it was the way she'd felt so familiar yet distant. Like a wisp of dust in the air that he couldn't grasp ahold of. Or the way she looked even better than he'd remembered, with her wide blue eyes and full lips, and that golden hair that seemed to light up the room.

"Tanner?"

He shook his head. "I'm not hungry." His eyes slid over to where Van and her sister were sitting by the window. The evening light was shining in, making her skin look warm and soft. Zoe was saying something to her, gesticulating wildly, then her spoon flew out of her hand, banging onto the tile floor.

Van chuckled, and it did something to him. What the heck was wrong with him? She was history. He'd made sure of that. Yet his body responded every time he looked over at her.

"You might want to take a picture," Becca said. "That way you wouldn't be so obvious."

"Shut up." He pushed his plate over. "Here, have my fries."

Becca grinned and forked them up. "I thought you'd never ask."

Cora Jean walked over to Van's table, carrying a white plastic box. Van smiled at her, then said something that looked like she was asking for the check.

She was going to leave in a few minutes. Maybe that was for the best. Because right now his damn heart was clattering against his ribcage.

A minute later, Cora Jean brought over a silver tray with a printed receipt on it. Van laid some bills on top and nodded over at Zoe, who was grabbing her jacket to leave.

Before he could even think it through, Tanner was on his feet, walking over to the table by the window. Van looked up at him, her brows creasing as if in surprise.

"Can I have a quick word?" he asked.

She ran her tongue over her bottom lip, sliding her eyes to Zoe. "Um yeah." She smiled at her sister. "Zoe, can you wait for me in the car?" She threw her keys, and Zoe caught them easily, looking at Tanner with interest before leaving the table.

Then it was the two of them, and he was already regretting coming over here, because he had no idea what to say to her.

Sorry I broke your heart didn't really cut it.

"What can I do for you?" she asked, smiling in that old familiar way. Up close, he could see the lines that crinkled next to her eyes. They did nothing but add to her attractiveness.

"I was just wondering if you're planning on staying in town for a while," he said, his voice low.

"Um, yeah. For a bit. Why?" She was still smiling. God, he wanted to smile. Wanted to grab her hand and pull her out of there. Run around town with her the way they used to.

"Because I don't want things to be awkward between us if we bump into each other in the street."

The smile on her lips slowly faded. "Why would it be awkward?"

Because I broke you. Us. He stuffed his hands in his pockets, looking down at her. "No reason. I just wanted to check if we're okay."

Her eyes caught his. "We're okay."

His smile took him by surprise. "That's good," he said, his voice gruff. "I'm glad."

She stood, grabbing her purse in one hand, the plastic box in the other. "I guess I'll see you around."

"Yeah, you will." He caught her eye again. "You're looking good, Butler."

She blinked. For just a moment, her poise seemed to disappear. She was Van again, the kid who used to run around town with him, driving people crazy.

"Thanks," she told him, her lips curling up. "You're not looking so bad yourself." With that, she turned and walked out the door, her hips swaying from side to side. And if he appreciated the way her jeans clung tightly to the curve of her ass? Well, at least that proved Aunt Gina right.

The devil really did make work for idle hands.

CHAPTER FIVE

*I*t had been a long night, full of tossing and turning. Her head had been too full of thoughts to sleep. Van sighed and sat up in bed, checking her phone to see it was only six-thirty a.m. It was pointless to try and sleep anymore. She felt more restless than ever.

She'd done her best to keep her poise in front of him yesterday. Something she'd learned from an early age. Put on a mask, don't let people know they're affecting you. That way they couldn't hurt you.

For a long time, he'd been the only one who'd seen beneath the armor she wore. And now he was a stranger.

A really hot, built, handsome stranger who made her heart race like crazy, damn him. With his slow grin and muscled arms he knew exactly how he affected people. And it worked. She was affected. *Ugh.*

Rubbing her eyes with the heels of her hands, she padded barefoot to the kitchen and switched on the coffee pot. It hissed and spat as she grabbed a pen and paper, determined to focus on the present, and all the things she had to do.

Go through her mom's bills, make sure she had enough

money, and somehow persuade her to get out of bed today. Who knew, maybe Kim would even leave the house. Van had saved enough to see her through the next few months, but that money would be gone soon enough, and then she'd either have to go back to Richmond to work, or find something locally. It would help a lot if her mom was bringing in some income, too.

By the time Zoe got up, Van was dressed in a pair of tight running shorts and a sturdy sports bra, her hair pulled back into a tight ponytail, waiting for her sister to go to school before she took a run.

"Hey." Zoe grinned at her, pulling a bowl from the cupboard and filling it with cereal. She grabbed the milk, shaking it. "We're nearly out."

"I know." Van looked up from her list. "I need to go to the grocery store. You wanna come? I can wait until you're home from school."

"Can I buy some treats?" Zoe asked, shoveling the cereal into her mouth. She sure was a fast eater.

For a moment, Van watched her load up one spoonful after another, impressed by her speed. "Sure," she said. "You got everything you need for school?"

Zoe spooned the last mouthful in, and swallowed it down. "Yup. I'll see you later." She kissed Van on the cheek and put her bowl into the dishwasher, then grabbed her sparkly pink backpack from it's new home in the hall closet.

"Have a good day," Van called out as her sister pulled the door closed behind her.

A moment later, her mom walked out of the bedroom. "What time is it?" she asked, her pink satin robe knotted around her slim waist.

"Seven-thirty. Zoe just left." Van stood and stretched her arms. Still so early, yet she felt like she'd done a day's planning already.

"That's what woke me up." Her mom pulled a mug from the cupboard and poured herself some coffee. "She always slams that damn door." She turned to look at Van. "What are you wearing?" she asked, looking her up and down.

"I'm going for a run." Van glanced down at the tight running shorts and sports bra she'd pulled on this morning. "When I get back we can work on this list I've been making. Starting with going through all the bills."

"I'm sick." Her mom touched her brow, wincing as though in pain. "Can't the bills wait until tomorrow?"

"Maybe if you drank a little less, you wouldn't be so sick," Van pointed out.

"I don't drink a lot."

Van lifted a brow. "Sure you don't." The empty vodka bottle in the trashcan said differently.

Kim slumped at the table, lifting her mug to her lips. "I can't believe you're into running. It sounds like torture."

Van shrugged. "I like it. It's a good way to start the day." She grabbed her earbuds and pressed her smartwatch to sync up. "I'll be back in an hour or so. Maybe you could take a shower while I'm gone?"

"Maybe."

Van took a deep breath and headed for the door, cueing up the playlist on her watch as she ran down the steps toward the sidewalk.

She'd started running years ago. It had felt weird at first, because she'd never been into sports at school, not like Tanner and the rest of his brothers. They'd teased her about her lack of athletic prowess. Not in a mean way – they were never mean. Well, not until the day Tanner had hurt her like nothing else. No, they'd asked her where the hell she put all the food she ate when she was constantly inventing excuses for getting out of gym class.

She couldn't remember who'd first suggested she try

running as a way to work through her anger. Maybe it was Craig. He always loved sports. Whoever it was, she'd tried it because she needed something to get her head straight, and nobody had been more surprised than Van when it actually worked.

Starting off easy, she jogged down the sidewalk toward the town square, doing a full circle before heading west on Main Road, out of town. As the space between houses increased, and the verdant green of the cornfields appeared in the distance, she felt her breath begin to shallow as her lungs worked overtime.

It always took a good two or three miles for her to get into her stride. Only when she'd reached an unconscious rhythm could her brain push out all the worries and anxieties and leave pure, blissful nothingness in their wake. She panted as the sidewalk ended and dusty country roads began, her skin heating up beneath the early morning sun.

This was where the road bent to the left. On one side the corn fields continued – green now, but in a month or two they'd begin to turn golden. On the other was a field, full of overgrown grass and a huge wooden screen whose white paint had long since peeled away. The box office was still there – a wooden cabin where she'd sat as a teenager and sold tickets to cars as they lined up for whatever movie the drive-in was showing that week. That job had been her ticket out of town.

Or so she'd thought at the time.

The Chaplin Drive-In Movie Theater had closed eight years ago, right after her mom and Craig got married. It had felt like the end of an era, even though Van wasn't working there any more. Her heart clenched to see it so neglected.

For years it had been a huge part of Hartson's Creek life. It had never shown the latest and best movies – in fact the owner, Mr. Chaplin, had a preference for showing movies that were at least ten years old. They kept costs down that way, and nobody really seemed to mind. Back in those days, before Netflix and other services were king and everybody could stream, it was somewhere to go and watch an old favorite.

One of her best memories were the meetings they'd have where they would talk through the showings for the next few weeks. He'd let the kids who worked there make suggestions. The whackier the better.

They were good times. There had been a lot of those, growing up. A lot of them in this very field.

Leaning on the old sign that used to proclaim the show times, she gulped in a breath, ignoring the burning of her calf muscles. To her right, she sensed some movement. Another runner? It was a strange enough occurence to make her turn her head to look.

It only took a moment for her to recognize that gait. She'd seen it enough growing up. First when they played games here and there all over town. Then when he'd been part of the football team at school, throwing his body into winning games the way he always threw himself into everything.

She froze for a moment. If she recognized him, there was every chance he recognized her, too. There was no opportunity to leave and outrun him, either. Tanner Hartson could always catch her. It had been the source of much irritation when they were younger.

There was nothing to it but to get it over with. He was right. This was a small town and the likelihood was that she'd see him a lot more the longer she stayed in Hartson's Creek.

"Hey." He slowed down, his breath barely labored. "I didn't know you ran."

She shrugged. "I took it up a few years ago. When the chocolate started to make itself known on my hips."

His gaze automatically dropped to her legs. She felt her cheeks warm at his scrutiny.

"I don't believe that for a second," he said, his jaw twitching as he resolutely pulled his eyes up to hers. "You could eat any guy under the table when we were kids, and never put on a damn ounce."

The corner of her lip curled. "I guess things have changed since then."

"I guess so." He inclined his head toward town. "You going back?"

"As soon as I catch my breath."

He ran his tongue along his bottom lip. "I'll wait for you."

Anxiety shot through her. "You don't have to."

"I want to," he told her, his eyes still holding hers.

Okay then. So this was how it was going to be. Maybe it was time to take control of the situation.

She pushed herself off the peeling sign, and took a deep breath. "Race you back!" Launching herself forward, she felt the air rush past her as her gait sped up. She heard a chuckle, then the pounding of feet against the dusty country road as he easily caught her.

"So you still play dirty." Unlike Van, he wasn't breathless at all as he slowed his speed to run beside her.

"Gotta use whatever advantage I have."

It was only when he was this close that she could see the difference in him. Sense it, too. His body was stronger than ever, his running shirt tight across his chest, revealing muscles that rippled a little too much for her liking. His legs were tan and defined as they moved in a laid back rhythm.

She'd never noticed the height difference between them so starkly before. Not even during junior year when he'd shot up almost a foot over the summer and all his jeans had ended above his ankles.

It was so strange running next to him. Familiar, yet

completely alien, too. Ten years ago being together would have been their normal, but now there was so much history that it hurt like a knife.

He hadn't said a word for the last five minutes, and neither had she. The air was silent, save for their soft breathing and the chirp of the birds in the fields. She found herself glancing at his legs *again*, then quickly pulling her gaze up. He was looking right at her. Had he noticed her scrutiny? Thank god her face was hot already and he couldn't notice her blush.

When they reached the town square, she expected him to turn off and take the direct road home, but instead he ran next to her, taking the parallel street that led to her house. She gave him a questioning look and he shrugged. His thick, dark hair was ruffled by the breeze, lifting it from his chiseled face.

When they reached her street, Van slowed down to a walk, her breath shallow as it tried to catch up with the oxygen her body needed. Tanner slowed, too, and she turned her head to look up at him.

"You can carry on running," she said between pants. "You've barely broken a sweat." From the look of him he could probably handle at least another ten miles.

Van, on the other hand, was beat.

He shrugged. "I'll walk you to your house."

She blinked. "Why?"

"Because I want to."

How many times had he walked her home in their lifetimes? First from grade school, then as she grew older and her mom was more neglectful, from his house after dinner, when his Aunt Gina insisted on feeding her. And after she started working at the drive-in, he'd arrive every evening when her shift ended and insisted on making sure she got home safely.

But that was *then*. When they were kids. Best friends. *More.*

Something they hadn't been for the longest of times.

They reached the edge of her mom's front yard, and the messy, overgrown lawn made her feel exposed. Another thing to add to her list of things to do. Did her mom even have a lawn mower that worked?

She noticed he was staring, too. Heat stung at her cheeks.

"I'm going to cut it later," she told him. "Craig's left and Mom's not well."

He frowned. "You need any help?"

"We're good. She'll be okay. Zoe and I have it covered." She inclined her head at the tiny house. "I should go inside."

"Sure. But if you need anything, I'm around." The ghost of a smile passed over his lips. "Same place as always."

"Okay then…" she trailed off, knowing she wouldn't take him up on his offer. "I guess I'll see you sometime."

"I guess you will." He sounded certain of it. And damn if that deep, warm voice didn't send a shot of pleasure right through her. Stupid, betraying body. It was so easily pleased.

She walked along the cracked path to the dirty front steps of her house, ignoring the way her heart was clamoring against her ribcage. It was the exercise, that was all. A simple physiological reaction to a five mile run.

Nothing to do with the six-foot-three muscled guy who was watching her from the end of her front yard.

What the hell was he still doing there anyway?

"So, bye," she said, lifting her hand up. She crouched down to find the key she'd stashed back in the dry plant pot, then stood and slid it into the lock.

When the door creaked open, she allowed herself one last glance over her shoulder.

Luckily for her heart, he'd gone.

CHAPTER SIX

"These are all overdue," Van said, passing the stack of bills to her mom. "They need paying or everything gets shut off."

"They won't shut us off," Kim said, sounding certain of herself. "I'll call and tell them Craig's left. That should give us some time."

Van blew out a mouthful of air, trying hard not to get frustrated. Her mom still didn't have a clue how the real world worked. She never had. As long as Van could remember, she pushed responsibility onto other people.

Van. Craig. Maybe Zoe one day.

"Have you paid the rent this month at least?" Van asked, trying to keep her voice even.

Kim shrugged. "No. But it doesn't matter. They don't mind when I don't pay."

"Mr. Klein doesn't mind?" Van still had the vivid memories of hiding behind the sofa with her mom when he'd come over and hammer on the door, demanding payment. Her mom would hold her palm over Van's mouth as he walked around the house, peering through windows to see if they were there.

She could remember the times he'd come at night, too. Those were when her mom would let him in wearing only a shiny silk wrap and and shoo Van to her room, telling her to go to bed and not come out.

The memory sent an unwelcome shiver down her spine.

"Mr. Klein sold this place years ago. No idea who the landlord is now. I pay through Fairfax Realty." She screwed her face up, and no wonder. Before Van was born, her mom worked for Johnny Fairfax as his assistant. According to the town gossip, she was fired under a black cloud, accused of stealing a large amount of money. Whether that was true or not, Van had no idea. Her mom refused to talk about it, and Van really didn't want to know.

Didn't stop Johnny and his wife, Nora from looking down on her when she was growing up, though. Or their daughter, Chrissie, treating Van like trash at school.

"They don't mind when you pay the rent late?" Van asked, frowning.

"They don't have a choice. I'll pay when I can." She shrugged and walked to the refrigerator, scowling when she pulled it open. "Ugh, Zoe must have finished the juice."

"I'm going grocery shopping later. You'll have to drink water until then." Van took the bills and piled them up. The need to get out of this house pulled at her. "I think I'll head into town for a while. Do some work at the diner." She gave her mom a pointed look. "Tomorrow we need to make a budget. And talk about you getting a job."

"Do we have to?" her mom's voice sounded pained.

"Yes. Has Craig been in touch? Offered to send you any money?"

"Nope." Kim's lip wobbled. "Too busy in bed with his new woman, I'm guessing. The asshole."

At least they could agree on *one* thing. Van placed the bills into her laptop bag and slid it over her shoulder. "I'm sorry," she said softly. "I know how much it hurts."

Her mom gave her an interested look. "You've been hurt?"

"A long time ago," Van said softly.

"But you don't have anybody now, right? Not since that Damon guy a couple of years ago?"

"Nope." Van smiled. "I'm single and happy about it. And maybe you can be, too."

"Maybe." Her mom didn't sound too certain. To be honest, Van wasn't certain either. Her mom had always based her self-worth on the way she was viewed by men. For as long as Van could remember, her mom had either been in a relationship or had some sort of arrangement with a man. These past two weeks since Craig had left was probably her driest spell in decades.

Maybe it was a good thing she wasn't leaving the house right now. Because where Van's mom was concerned, men were almost always trouble.

THE EARLY AFTERNOON sun was hazy as Van pushed the door to Murphy's Diner open, the smell of bacon and coffee assaulting her senses as she grabbed a table next to the window, overlooking the town square.

She wasn't going to try her favorite booth. Not after yesterday. Better to sit in the open and be able to see anybody who approached. That way she wouldn't be blindsided.

"Savannah Butler? Is that you?"

Van looked up from the table, her eyeline filled with a swollen, pregnant stomach. She lifted her gaze to see its owner, a petite dark haired woman who she didn't recognize at all.

Van immediately plastered a smile on her face. "Yeah, that's me," she said, still trying to work out who this was. "I'm sorry, I don't know your name."

"I'm Regan Laverty. Used to be Regan Nash. We went to high school together, you remember?"

"Oh. Hi." Van took another look at her. Maybe she did look familiar. She stood and shook Regan's hand. "And congratulations," she said, glancing down at Regan's stomach.

Regan laughed. "Thanks. This is our fourth so I don't get a lot of that." She lowered her voice. "It's more commiserations than anything. Yesterday, my boss's wife took me aside for a talk and asked if I needed her help with birth control."

Van swallowed down a laugh. "Sounds like folks around here."

"Mrs. Fairfax means well," Regan said, shrugging. "But I like having babies. It's kind of who I am."

"You work for Johnny Fairfax?" Van asked.

"Yeah, next door at Fairfax Realty. I'm on my break right now." Regan glanced at her watch. "I only have ten minutes until I have to get back to the office. Can I join you?"

"Sure." Van watched as Regan wedged herself into the bench seat, her stomach pressed up against the table. "You want a coffee?"

"Better make it decaf. Otherwise people will talk." She lowered her voice as though it was a secret.

Five minutes later, Van was all up to date with Hartson's Creek gossip. She knew that Tanner's brother, Gray, had built a huge mansion on the edge of town and somehow ended up living with his ex-girlfriend's sister, which according to Regan had caused a hell of a hullabaloo in town. She also knew that Reverend Maitland had broken his leg, but was still running Sunday services on crutches, and that Della Thorsen's dog had bitten her arm so bad it had bled for hours, yet she was still refusing to have him put to sleep.

Van took a sip of her coffee, amused at how fast Regan could talk. "Poor Mrs. Thorsen."

"Ah, she had it coming. She's awful. She made my mom cry at *Chairs* last week."

Another mention of *Chairs*. Van was pretty sure her own mom had been the main topic of conversation these past two weeks at the weekly gathering.

"Have you worked at Fairfax Realty long?" Van asked her when she finally got a word in.

"Five years. I started working right before I got pregnant with my second." Regan shrugged. "Mr. Fairfax nearly blew a gasket when I told him."

Van bet he did. "So you must know who owns my mom's house. One seven five Second Street?"

Regan pulled her lip between her teeth. "One seven five?" she mused. "The one with the oak in the front?"

"That's the one. Used to be owned by Simon Klein."

Regan's face lit up. "Oh, Mr. Klein sold that four years ago. He's moved to Florida. Last I heard he'd found a girlfriend who was twenty years older than him. I have no idea where they get the energy. As soon as I feed the kids all I want to do is climb into bed and sleep."

"But do you know who he sold it to?" Van prompted.

"Oh yeah. Tanner Hartson owns it. I'd have thought you'd known that. Aren't you two best friends?" Regan glanced at her watch. "Oh sugar, I have to go." She shuffled her behind along the red bench seat, sliding her stomach along the rim of the table. "It was real good to see you, Van. Maybe I'll see you at *Chairs*."

Van nodded. "Sure. It was great to see you, too."

Regan finally got to the edge of the seat. Feeling sorry for her, Van stood and helped her up, curling her fingers around the pregnant woman's palm.

"Thank you," Regan said, leaning forward to give her a hug. "You're very kind." She hobbled to the door, and Van found herself running past her to pull it open.

"There you go."

Van watched her slowly walk toward Fairfax Realty, as her stomach dropped at the news Regan had let slip.

Tanner Hartson owned her mom's house, and by the sound of it he had for a few years now. But why would he do that when they weren't even talking to each other?

Blowing out a mouthful of air, Van watched as Regan waddled back into her office, the door closing quickly behind her. Van walked back to the table, the thought of Tanner, her mom's bungalow, and Johnny Fairfax rushing through her mind.

A few days ago she'd thought she'd come back and not let this town affect her.

So much for that.

TANNER STRETCHED his long legs out beneath the kitchen table the next morning, scrolling through the laptop he'd had couriered over yesterday. His work laptop had been surrendered as part of the company sale, along with his work phone and his sense of purpose. He raised an eyebrow, remembering how he used to be cash rich and time poor. All those things he'd said he'd do when he had the time to do them, and now he couldn't remember any of them.

So instead he was spending way too much of his free time remembering how Van Butler's ass looked in her tight shorts when she was running. Which really didn't feel like a bad way to waste away the minutes.

He shifted in the chair, scanning the screen in front of him, shaking his head as he scrolled down again.

"What are you doing?" Becca asked, walking into the room. She leaned over the table to look at his laptop.

"I'm looking at houses."

"In Hartson's Creek?"

He scrolled down again. "Yep."

"For an investment?" She poured some coffee into an insulated mug, then grabbed an apple and a candy bar from the cupboard. "What?" she asked, noticing Tanner's amused stare. "I'm late for work. And I need the energy."

"If there's one thing you don't need, it's more energy," Tanner said dryly. "And no, it's not for an investment. It's for me."

"Good morning," Aunt Gina said, walking into the kitchen with the newspaper in her hand. She pulled it from the plastic wrap and placed it to the side, the way she always did for his dad. It was hard to remember his life without Aunt Gina in it. She'd arrived the day after Tanner's mom – her sister – died, and hadn't left since. They'd been lucky to have her, especially with their dad being as taciturn as he was.

Aunt Gina was the balm to his father's sting. More than once she'd stepped between his dad and Gray as they faced up to each other, before Gray left town in search of stardom. And though he'd mellowed a little over the past year, their father still made them all feel uncomfortable. Maybe it was a good thing he spent most of his time in his office.

Aunt Gina pulled a pan from beneath the stove, lighting up the heat and pouring oil into the center. "How many eggs do you want with your breakfast?" she asked Tanner.

"None." Tanner winked at her. "I'm going running in a minute. I don't want any breakfast, thank you."

Their father walked into the kitchen and sat in the chair

opposite Tanner's. The light atmosphere almost immediately dissipated, the way it always did when he was around. Aunt Gina gave him the paper and he folded it over, unfolding his reading glasses and perching them on the tip of his nose.

"Oh shoot, I'm late. But I want to hear more about this house." Becca gave Tanner a meaningful look. "And by the way, I heard you weren't running alone yesterday. Is that why you're so keen to go out again this morning?"

"I run every day," Tanner said mildly. Becca had no chance of making him uncomfortable. He'd lived most of his life with Gray, Cam, and Logan. All masters at making others squirm. She was a mere pretender.

She glanced at her watch again, her expression torn. "But not in the mornings. You usually run in the evenings. You always have."

He shrugged. "I've got more time on my hands. I'm switching things up."

Letting out a grunt of annoyance, Becca stomped out of the kitchen, waving her hand in goodbye and spilling coffee everywhere. Tanner smirked but said nothing.

"Who have you been running with?" Aunt Gina asked, sliding the eggs onto the crisp bread she'd toasted. She put the plate in front of his dad.

"Nobody you know." He finished his coffee, putting his mug in the new dishwasher Gray had bought last Christmas. "I'm off, I'll see you later."

"Will you be back for lunch?" Aunt Gina called at him as he grabbed the backdoor handle.

"Probably not. Don't make anything for me." When he turned to shoot her his usual grin she was staring at him, her brows dipped. "You okay?"

"Yes…" She trailed off, but he could still feel her scrutiny. "Are you?"

"Yeah. I'm good."

"Everybody's good," his dad mumbled into his coffee. "Now can I get on with eating my breakfast in silence?"

And that was why Tanner needed to find a house. If he was going to stay around here for a while, he'd need to get his own place before he ended up strangling his father.

Everybody knew he was too pretty to wear prison stripes.

VAN ROLLED her neck around in a circle, trying to loosen her tight muscles. Walking onto the porch, she lifted her right foot onto the railing, leaning forward to feel the stretch through the back of her thigh as her hamstring protested the movement.

Her eyes lifted, and she saw Tanner leaning on the oak tree, his arms folded across his chest, making his biceps bulge beneath the sleeves of his tight running top. He was wearing shorts again, but this time she refused to look at his tan, defined legs. She didn't need to anyway. They were etched into her memory.

Ignoring him, she stretched her left hamstring, counting to twenty before she turned and put her right foot on the rail, gracefully leaning forward until the fronts of her thighs began to loosen.

From the corner of her eye she could see he hadn't moved an inch. Hadn't said anything either. He was just staring at her with those dark eyes. She wasn't going to blush – she wouldn't give him the satisfaction. Instead, she stood and stretched to the right and the left, then jogged down the steps to the path.

As soon as she passed him, she heard his running shoes pound against the concrete flagstones, matching her stride for stride as she made her way down the street. When the sidewalk widened, he sped up just enough to run beside her, then slowed to match her gait once more.

She took the same route as yesterday, first into the town square, past the bandstand and benches that overlooked the flower beds that were overflowing with color. Then through the gate at the other side, past First Baptist Church and continuing on Main Road out of Hartson's Creek.

"Remember when we let those mice loose during Sunday Service?" Tanner asked, glancing back at the church before they turned the corner.

Van lifted an eyebrow. "So we're reminiscing about the old days now?" God, it had been funny watching everybody scream and lift their feet up. It had taken them all week to find enough mice to make it a good prank.

He shrugged, still matching her gait. "We can talk about whatever you want."

She licked her lips and sped up just a little. She could already feel her lungs starting to ache. "How about you tell me why you're back in Hartson's Creek. Last I heard you were something big in New York."

"You've been asking people about me?"

She could see his grin from the corner of her eyes. "It's amazing how much people want to share whenever they see me in town. Maybe I have a sign on my front saying 'tell me about Tanner Hartson.' They think they're providing an update service."

He chuckled. "Yeah. I get the same thing but with you."

"You do?"

"Oh yeah. I can tell you the exact day you moved to Rich-mond. How many bathrooms and half bathrooms your apartment has. And every time one of the events you plan is on TV, my phone pretty much blows up."

"People are assholes."

"They are," he agreed.

49

"I'm glad we scared them with the mice. They deserved it." She felt her lips curl into a smile.

He laughed. "Maybe we should do it again."

"I'm pretty sure I'm banned from church. I'd give Reverend Maitland a heart attack if I walked in on Sunday." Van shook her head. "We were terrible kids, weren't we?"

"We were bored. And got a kick out of other peoples' shock." Tanner shrugged. "Anyway, the mice were nothing compared to the time when we put laundry soap in the school toilet tanks. Every time somebody flushed there were bubbles spilling over the floor." He chuckled. "It was worth the punishment just to see everybody's faces."

She grinned at the memory. The janitorial staff hadn't found it so funny, though. God, they'd been brats.

They were on the open road now, fields stretching out in front of them. She both hated and loved how easy it was to talk with Tanner. Hated, because she'd missed it so damn much.

And loved, because he'd always been her best friend. Until he wasn't.

"Why did you buy my mom's house?" The question came out of nowhere, spilling from her lips in a mash of words.

"You know about that?" He tipped his head to look at her. Her legs were slowing, her breath catching as she tried to maintain a rhythm.

"Yeah, I know. But I don't know why you did it. She's not exactly the best tenant in the world."

"I had a lot of money and needed to make some investments. It came on the market at the right time."

"So it's just a coincidence?" She lifted an eyebrow. "Of all the places you could buy, you just happened to choose my mom's?"

"What else? You think I deliberately bought the house

because of its connections with you?" His lips twitched as their eyes met. She quickly turned her head away.

Yeah, she did think that. But then she realized how egotistical that made her sound. "I know she owes you rent. I'll write you a check when I get back home."

"It's okay. I don't need your money."

She glanced at him from the corner of her eye. "All the same, I pay my way. I don't like owing anybody anything."

"I know that," he said softly. "Look, can we stop running for a minute?"

"Are you getting worn out?" She slowed down, stopping at almost the exact place she'd caught her breath yesterday. He'd been on his way back then, from wherever he'd run to. There was no way he could be breathless yet.

"I just want to look at you when I'm talking to you." He leaned on the half-rotten wooden fence that bordered the overgrown drive-in. She could remember being part of the team that painted it all those years ago.

Tanner had been there, too, though he'd managed to get more paint on her than the wood.

"What are you smiling at?" he asked her.

"Just remembering what a goof you were as a kid."

He chuckled. "You were pretty goofy yourself."

"I was the Brain to your Pinky," she said, grabbing her water bottle from the belt around her waist. Flipping the lid, she took a long, deep swallow. The water was still cool from being refrigerated overnight.

"Funny how everybody always blamed me for our tricks, when they were all your idea," he said pointedly.

She could feel his gaze on her face, warming her skin like the sun. Pulling the water bottle from her lips she offered it to him. "Want some?"

He shook his head. "I'll drink when I get home."

"You should drink while you run. Otherwise you'll get dehydrated."

"I only drink when running marathons. I don't bother with water for short runs."

Oh, *burn*. "You run marathons?"

"I have a few. I like running long distances. They clear your mind."

Van glanced at his legs again. "You don't look like a long distance runner," she pointed out, managing to drag her gaze back up to his.

"Are you calling me fat, Butler?" he asked, his eyes crinkling with amusement. "Because that's just rude." He lifted his arm, curling his bicep up. "I'll have you know I'm all brawn and muscle. Come on, feel this."

She shook her head, trying not to laugh at his mock-horrified expression. "It's okay, I'll take your word for it."

"Come on," he said, reaching for her hand and curling it around his bicep. "Guns of steel, babe."

Her fingers dug into his hot, taut skin, feeling the iron of his muscles underneath. He was standing close enough that she could smell him, the warm, woodsy essence of his soap made more potent by the heat of his skin.

It was so familiar. A reminder of everything... and how easily they'd thrown it aside. It set her alight and cut through her all at the same time.

"I need to go," she said, releasing her hold on him and stepping back. Her stomach was swirling with nausea and she gasped for fresh air. "I'm late for something."

Tanner blinked at her sudden change of mood. "Is everything okay?"

"I just remembered I promised to pick something up for Zoe." She was flailing around for excuses. This was what they'd ended up as, two people who were completely polite to each other. Because anything else hurt too much. "You carry on running, I'm heading back."

"I'll come with you."

"No, it's okay," she replied quickly. "You said yourself that you like running distances. My runs are five miles at the most." She managed to smile at him. "Thanks for the company. I'll see you around."

She turned on the ball of her foot and launched herself down the road, pushing her legs to speed despite the protest of her muscles. It didn't stop her hearing his sad goodbye, or from remembering the hurt look on his face when he realized she really didn't want him running with her.

And if she ran home so fast that her lungs were screaming by the time she arrived at the end of her overgrown yard? Well that was okay. Maybe she deserved it. God knew the hurt felt pretty good right now.

CHAPTER SEVEN

"So that's two months' rent," Regan said, writing a receipt out for Van as she sat in a guest chair at Regan's desk. "Next month's is due on the twenty-second."

"Do you have a way my mom can pay it automatically?" Van asked. "I'm trying to get her into online payments so she doesn't forget."

"We do." Regan smiled brightly, pulling open her drawer and taking out a leaflet. "Your mom always insists on checks. I figured she was old fashioned that way. A lot of our clients are."

Van took the leaflet and slid it into her bag. "It's time she came into the twenty-first century."

"I kind of miss the old days," Regan told her. "My eldest is already asking for a phone and he's barely finished Kindergarten. Remember when we were all happy with a crayon and a piece of paper?"

"I remember," Van said dryly.

"Speaking of my babies," Regan said, glancing down at her swollen stomach. "I have a sprinkle next weekend. Would you like to come?"

"A sprinkle?" Van asked, biting down a smile. It sounded like some kind of incontinence problem. "What's that?"

"It's like a baby shower, but without all the gifts." Regan shrugged. "After three kids I have almost everything I need. And anyway, Mrs. Fairfax said it would be bad form to ask for gifts for the fourth time around." She blinked, then forced a smile on her face.

"What does Mrs. Fairfax have to do with it?" Van asked.

"She's hosting for me. The Fairfaxes are very generous like that. You know where they live, right?"

"Yeah. I don't know if I'm free though…" The thought of subjecting herself to Nora and Johnny Fairfax for an afternoon was almost at the bottom of her list. Only above pulling her toenails out one by one and then baking them into a nice pie.

Regan grabbed her hands. "Please come. I don't have that many friends. Don't have time, what with the rugrats and my hubby."

Letting out a mouthful of air, Van nodded. "Sure. Okay. I'll be there."

"Yay!" Regan clapped her hands together. "I'll tell you what, I'll pop an invitation through your door on my way home from work. That way you'll know exactly when and where it is." Her grin was so wide it made Van feel bad about not wanting to go. "And remember," Regan said, waggling her finger. "No presents, just your presence."

Van was almost certain that exact phrase was written on the invitation, right below a command to RSVP to Nora Fairfax by a date that had long since passed.

And now she had some shopping to do to. Because little baby Laverty number four deserved at least one gift.

"Thanks," Van said, smiling as she stood and waved goodbye to Regan. "I'm looking forward to it."

∾

"Do you have anything else?" Tanner asked, looking up from the glossy realty brochures Johnny Fairfax had spread over his desk.

"That's all the houses we have for sale at the moment. Hartson's Creek is a sought after place to live, especially since your brother put it on the map." Johnny gave him a pointed look. "Houses are being snapped up as soon as they are listed." He ran a tongue over his dry lips. "Have you thought about building a home instead?"

Tanner shook his head. "Nope." It would take too long and he'd end up strangling his father, and possibly Aunt Gina and Becca, too. He was used to his own space in New York, and as much as he loved his family, he preferred them alive and at arm's length.

"You should think about it. That way you'll get the right location with the exact specification of house you're looking for. I'll get Regan to find some details of land we have for sale." Johnny began to fold up the glossy brochures, piling them one on top of the other. "Regan!" he called out, his booming voice bouncing off the walls. "Can you come in here?"

Who needed intercoms when you could shout loud enough to burst eardrums? Tanner winced at the way the sound reverberated around the room. It seemed to work, though, because the next moment Regan Laverty was pushing the door open and nervously stepping in, her bump so big it entered about a minute before she did.

"Oh hey, Tanner. How are you?" she asked, smiling. "I have a check for you actually. Savannah Butler just brought it in. She's paid the arrears and is setting up online payment for the future. Isn't that great?"

"That's wonderful news." Johnny clapped his hands together. "Well done, Regan."

She glowed at his praise. "I told you we'd get it," she said, nodding.

Tanner glanced at the open door. The main office was empty. Had Van been here when he was going through houses with Johnny? He was disappointed he hadn't bumped into her again. After her abrupt departure from their run, he'd been feeling restless. As though his muscles didn't want to slow down long enough for him to think. He'd run almost sixteen miles that day, and he'd been aching ever since. And trying not to think about the way she'd touched him. Her fingers had been soft and gentle, yet they'd sent a shot of pleasure through his body. He wanted her, the same way he always had. He just needed to find a way for her to reciprocate that feeling.

Maybe he'd join her on her run again sometime. The thought of it made him grin. Bumping into her was his favorite way to pass the time. It was pretty much what got him up in the morning.

"Well now, Regan, can you rummage through the land files and see what we've got that might suit Mr. Hartson?" He turned to Tanner. "What are we talking about, six bedrooms? Or maybe eight. I know your brother built eight. How much acreage are you looking for? You'll want it set back from the road, right?"

"Oh you should definitely have it set back." Regan nodded. "Maybe have some gates. I love those iron ones that Gray and Maddie have."

"In that case, Regan, let's look at land of two acres or more. What have we got?"

Tanner watched as Regan waddled over to the gunmetal filing cabinet in the corner of Johnny's room. She braced her hands on the top before slowly lowering herself to her knees.

Tanner stood. "Don't you have the details online?" he asked, walking over to where Regan was inhaling sharply. Gently, he touched her arm. "Let me help you up, you can't stay down there."

"Our land files aren't online yet," she huffed out. "Most of our clients want the paper copies. Plus the owners don't always like people knowing their business, if you know what I mean." She let Tanner carefully help her stand, then blew out another mouthful of air. "You'd think it would get easier by the fourth time," she joked. "But I swear this one's as heavy as a bowling ball."

Shooting Johnny a glance, Tanner knelt in front of the cabinet and pulled out the files that Regan pointed at. "You should sit down," he told her, inclining his head at the chair he'd vacated. "Take the weight off your feet."

"Ah, Regan's okay. Aren't you, honey?" Johnny said, pressing his lips together. "If she didn't want more kids she would have kept her legs closed, right Regan?" He winked at her. "Nothing will knock her down. Can you find the one off Main Road?"

What. The. Hell? Tanner glanced at Regan to see if she was as insulted as he was, yet she looked as serene as ever. "Here it is," she said, pulling a brochure from the bottom file he was holding. "This is a good one. Plenty of space to build on if you get the right zoning permission."

He glanced down at the particulars, opening his mouth to remind them that he wasn't interested in building his own place. But then he saw the overgrown grass and the falling-down white wooden fence surrounding the lot.

"They're selling the drive-in?" he asked. Just looking at the overgrown field on the paper in front of him was enough to bring back all the memories. Van sitting in the payment booth while he hung around with her until the movie started. The two of them climbing to the roof and watching whatever was playing that week, making jokes with each other and laughing like crazy.

His stomach pulled tightly.

"It's been empty for years. I finally managed to persuade Arthur Chaplin to put it on the market. I've no idea why he's sat on it for so long. It's not as though he was ever going to reopen it." Johnny shrugged. "He doesn't even live in town anymore. Moved to Charlston to live with his daughter. Damn place is an eyesore." He looked up at Tanner. "Of course, it wouldn't take a lot to make it beautiful," he added, his smooth salesman pitch taking over from his distaste at the state of the lot. "It'll get snapped up once I send it out to my list of interested developers. If you're interested, I can give you the first refusal, though."

Tanner looked at the thumbed piece of paper. Though it wasn't dated, he really doubted the land was fresh on the market. "Why developers?" he asked. "Wouldn't somebody want to reopen the drive-in? It was always busy when I was a kid."

Johnny shrugged. "Times change. Kids are too busy watching Youtube and Netflix now. And then there's all those damn environmental campaigners. They'd probably shit a brick at all the exhaust fumes coming out of those cars."

"Oh, I used to love the drive-in," Regan said, her eyes crinkling as she smiled. "So many good times there. I wish somebody would buy it to open it again."

"Thank you, Regan," Johnny said sharply. "That will be all."

She blinked. "Oh, of course."

"And can you bring coffee in for me and Mr. Hartson, please?"

"Not for me." Tanner shook his head. "I need to go. I have another appointment."

"But what about the drive-in?" Johnny asked him. "Are you interested?"

Tanner glanced at the brochure again, idly flicking to the second page. It showed a longer-distance view of the field, with the pay booth next to the barred entrance. How many times had he sat with Van in that booth, the two of them talking shit about every car that drove beneath the sparkling sign? While Van counted the takings, he'd amble to the refreshments booth and buy them buttered popcorn. Then they'd climb onto the roof and watch whatever movie was being projected onto the screen that week.

The memories were like tiny flashes of electricity in his brain. He slowly ran his tongue over his lip, blinking hard. All that money he had. And all that time. Could this be what he was looking for?

"Yeah," he said, slowly lifting his gaze to Johnny's. "I'm interested."

"Great." Johnny beamed. "Make an appointment with Regan and we can talk specifics. I've got a feeling we're going to do beautiful business together."

CHAPTER EIGHT

*C*hairs took place every Friday night in Hartson's Creek while the weather was nice. In practice that usually meant from April, when the risk of snow had gone and the sun was finally winning her battle against the clouds, until October, when sweaters were no longer enough to shield the older folk from the bitter chill as fall turned into winter. It was a simple enough concept. Everybody was invited, all you had to do was bring a chair and some refreshments to put on the communal tables. In reality, since it took place on the wealthy side of town, where proud brownstone Victorian houses gave way to lawns that bordered the water's edge, it was dominated by the richer townfolk.

Zoe was buzzing like a firefly next to Van as they unloaded the trunk of Van's car. Two fold up chairs she'd bought from the local hardware store, a pitcher of lemonade that definitely wasn't made at home, and an assortment of cakes from the bakery, because Van was no culinary expert. She could probably burn water if she tried hard enough.

"There are my friends," Zoe said, her face lighting up as

61

she pointed at the group of kids playing on the far side of the lawns. "Can I go join them?"

"Sure. Put the pitcher on the table." Van nodded, watching as Zoe skipped happily over to the large group of tables nestled together in the middle of everything. They were overflowing with food and drink. Van followed behind, and busied herself arranging the cakes she'd bought, because it was so much easier than walking over to a group and asking if she could sit with them.

"You came. I didn't think you would." Becca Hartson smiled shyly at Van from the other side of the heaving tables. "I'm so pleased you did, though. Not least because Tanner owes me ten dollars."

"He bet that I wouldn't come?" Van asked, ignoring the stupid way her heart sped up at his name.

Becca smiled. "He said you refused to show your face at *Chairs* again after the time you sprinkled laxatives on Mrs. Olsen's brownies, and Tanner forced one into your mouth."

Van grimaced. "I'd completely forgotten about that." She looked at the cakes she'd beautifully arranged and grinned at Becca. "I promise I haven't spiked these ones."

"That's a shame." Becca's eyes twinkled. "It would have livened things up." She glanced over her shoulder. "You want to come and sit with us?"

"I'd love to." Van followed Becca to a group of ten chairs clustered beside the creek. As she sat down, she could hear a loud voice from a group of old ladies call out.

"Is that the Butler girl?"

"I think so."

"I didn't know she was back. She sure looks like her mom."

Van straightened her spine, and made sure she smiled over in their direction.

"Yeah, I hear her husband left her for another woman."

"The Butler girl?"

"No, her mom, silly. Anyway, probably want to avoid the brownies tonight. Just in case she's up to her old tricks."

A few of them laughed. Van sighed and turned her back on them.

"So this is Maddie. You might remember her?" Becca said, pointing at a pretty brunette sitting in the chair next to hers.

Van didn't, but she remembered what Regan had told her in the café. Maddie was Ashleigh Clark's sister. She remembered Ashleigh from when she was dating Gray, back when he was in high school. Van had never really liked her. Tanner hadn't either. The girl had had a mean streak that could cut like a knife.

"Hi, Maddie," Van said, reaching forward to shake her hand.

Maddie grinned happily at her. "You probably don't remember me. But I remember you. I loved hearing about your and Tanner's escapades when I was little."

Van felt herself relax. "I guess my reputation precedes me."

Maddie laughed. "Ah, I wanted to be just like you when I grew up. Except I was too scared of getting in trouble."

"You wouldn't believe how freeing it is to not give a damn," Van told her. "You should try it."

"I can't wait to tell Gray I met you," Maddie told her. "He told me about the time you restrung his guitar right before his first concert at Murphy's."

"Oh no." Van covered her face with her hands. "That one was all Tanner's idea."

"Oh, he knows that. He'll still be happy to hear I've met you. I think he has a soft spot for you."

"All my brothers loved Van," Becca said, grinning. "She took the heat off them, and that's saying something."

Van smiled at the memories of the Hartson brothers, all

around the kitchen table, bickering as they shoveled food into their mouths. Gray who was either humming a song or arguing with his dad. Cam who would run home from football practice and eat everything in sight. Logan who had the best way of talking to you, so you ended up spilling your guts to him without even noticing.

And then there was Tanner. Her best friend. He'd start a sentence and she'd end it, then they'd both collapse into laughter.

"Don't believe her," Van told Maddie. "They were all much worse than me."

"Savannah," a voice called out, making Van turn in her seat. "Johnny told me you were back in town."

Van looked up to see Nora Fairfax standing over her, a strange smile on her lips.

"Hello, Mrs. Fairfax." Van smiled back, determined to be civil. "How are you?"

"I'm very well. More importantly, how's your mother? I heard her husband left her."

"She's doing just fine, thank you." Van would have said that no matter what. Nora and Johnny had always looked down on them, ever since her mom had been fired from her job at Fairfax Realty. Pointed remarks, insincere words, all aimed at making Van and her mom look small in front of other people. They had a longer memory than an elephant.

Nora's smile didn't waver. "It must be hard for her. Getting older and losing her looks. I know how much she depended on them." She gave a little laugh. "I guess that's a warning to us all. To make sure we are all more than a pretty face." She looked Van up and down. "You look very much like her."

"Thank you." Van was determined not to let Nora get to her. "I'll take that as a compliment."

"I'll have to let Chrissie know you're back," Nora said, her eyes still staring right at Van's. "Just in case you're thinking of hitting her again."

And there it was. Nora Fairfax's final jab. Van took it like a pro. During their junior year, Chrissie had said something about Van's mom. She could barely remember what it was now. But Van had been furious, enough to punch Chrissie in the jaw. Nora had stalked to the school and made sure Van had been suspended as a result.

"My boxing days are over," Van said, keeping her voice light. "Unless I'm really riled up. And how is Chrissie? Is she married now?"

Nora's smile faltered a little. "No. She's choosy. It'll take a strong man to make her give up her independence."

"That's a shame. I'm sure you're desperate for grandkids."

Nora blinked. "Well, yes. It would be nice one day."

"Well, I hope she settles down before she gets too old and loses her looks." Van smiled at her. "For *your* sake."

Becca coughed out a laugh. Nora blinked, as though she couldn't quite work out whether that was a compliment or an insult.

"Oh, and Regan invited me to her splash next Saturday. I'm looking forward to it." Van smiled.

"It's a sprinkle," Nora said quickly, a frown pulling at her painted lips.

"Of course it is." Van nodded. "Though I don't know what's wrong with a good old fashioned baby shower. These young people, they keep changing the rules." She winked at Nora, who was still blinking. "So I guess I'll see you there."

Nora's smile dissolved. "Yes, I expect you will." She looked over Van's shoulder, her eyes moving like they were seeking something. "Well, I must go. Please give your mom my condolences. Maybe one day she'll keep hold of a man."

With that she was gone, leaving her insult behind her. Van wrinkled her nose, and turned back to her friends, smiling as they exchanged stories from their week. She was determined not to let people like Nora Fairfax spoil her evening.

If they wanted to snap at her, she'd bite back. She was big enough and bad enough to sink her teeth in deep.

~

"I DON'T GET IT," Gray said, leaning on the counter of the Moonlight Bar as Sam poured them both a pint of beer. "I thought you and Van fell out years ago."

"We did," Tanner said, then shook his head. "Or we *had*. I don't know. Does it matter?"

"Not really," Gray admitted, taking the glass that Sam slid across the bar and lifting it to his lips. "I'm just trying to work out why Becca called Maddie squealing because she saw you running with some girl you used to be best friends with."

Tanner took a sip of his own beer, closing his eyes for a moment as the cool liquid coated his tongue. The Moonlight Bar was one of the few places in town Gray felt comfortable meeting up with his younger brothers. Sam kept a tight ship and threw out anybody who took photos or asked for autographs. Since he'd moved back to Hartson's Creek and built a home with Maddie Clark, Gray might have had a lower profile than when he was filling stadiums around the world, but he was still famous. And that fame caused him problems almost wherever he went.

"I went running," Tanner said, putting his beer on the counter. "And I saw her out running so we ran together. That's it. You don't have to buy yourself a suit for our wedding or start naming our babies."

Gray laughed. "I'll leave that for Becca. She already thinks you're looking for a house to buy because of Van." He looked at Tanner over the rim of his glass. "You probably want to talk to her at some point. She's a meddler. You and I both know she'll be talking to Van about you."

Tanner shook his head. It made him feel uncomfortable, and yet somehow warm too. At least that meant Van would be thinking about him. "She knows that's all ancient history. There's nothing between Van Butler and me."

"Which is weird," Gray mused. "Because you two were inseparable for years. When was it you met? First day of Kindergarten?"

"Something like that." Tanner sighed. "You want to play a game of pool?" he asked, hoping Gray would get the hint. He didn't want to talk about Van, and he definitely didn't want to spend his evening with his brother talking about all the mistakes he'd made in life. And he was almost certain that Becca would give him the third degree as soon as he let her pin him down.

"Sure." Gray shrugged and the two of them walked across the room to the far side, where an old, battered pool table barely stood upright. He grabbed a cue and passed it to Tanner, then pulled another one from the rack for himself. "You rack them up, I'll take first shot."

"Best of three?"

"As long as I win." Gray winked. "So how's the house hunt going?"

"It's not. There's nothing suitable on the market." Tanner loaded the balls into the triangle, then slid it across the baize.

"Damn. So what are you gonna do? Stay with Dad and Aunt Gina?"

"I might look at renting somewhere for a while." Tanner lifted the triangle away, storing it beneath the table. "I guess I'll go see Fairfax again."

"Maybe you should build somewhere. It's a hassle, but you'll get exactly what you want."

"Maybe," Tanner echoed, taking a sip of his beer, his mind turning to the drive-in theater. The brochure had been sitting in his dresser drawer all week. The land was going for a song. Even if he didn't build on it, it was an investment.

Who was he kidding? There was no way he was building on that place. It held too many memories. Of *her*, smiling at him as they watched yet another movie together. Quoting him all the words to *Twilight* just because she knew how much he hated those damn vampires. He could remember how excited she was to get a new release at the drive-in when most of their movies were at least a decade old.

God, he missed those days.

Ten years later, and he still thought of her every time he smelled sweet buttery popcorn. Or when a black and white movie came on the television, because they were always her favorites. She loved Cary Grant and Doris Day, laughed like crazy at Katharine Hepburn. Then there was the summer of Tom Cruise, when they'd shown his old, retro movies, and she'd fallen for Maverick in a big way.

He'd been fifteen when he first noticed how she was changing. It had been almost imperceptible at first. Things like her lips becoming fuller, her eyes looking wider. Then her body followed suit, blooming like a flower. She wasn't Van, his best friend anymore. She'd become Savannah. The girl who drew guys' stares. The one they whispered about in the locker room after practice.

It had just about killed him not to say anything to his teammates as they talked about her tits.

"You playing or what?" Gray asked.

Tanner looked up. "Huh?"

"I just missed the first ball. Man, you're distracted. Come on, let's get it over with so I can win."

Tanner pushed the memories away. "Shut up. I beat your ass every time."

Gray shook his head. "You realize we'd always let you win when you were a kid? We got so sick of hearing your bitching, we just let you think you were good."

"Nice try." Tanner potted a yellow stripe ball in the middle pocket. "But I always knew you cheated." He lifted his cue up and surveyed the table. "I mean, you weren't as bad as Cam, but who is. That guy's a sore loser."

"You see his final game last season?"

"Yep. I saw him try to start a fight with that lineman. He needs to control his temper." Tanner softly kissed his cue against the white ball. "I swear it's getting worse, on the field at least."

"Cam was always uber competitive. You have to be to play football." Gray shrugged.

"So how about you?" Tanner asked him. "How are you finding living back here after so long in L.A.? Is it driving you mad yet?"

The corner of Gray's lips quirked up. "Yep, living in the house I've always dreamed of with the best girl in the world is a real bind. I'm longing for the days of misery on the West Coast."

Tanner grinned as he sunk an orange striped ball smoothly into the middle pocket. "So when are you going to make it official?"

"With Maddie?"

"Yep." The next shot was going to be tricky. All the striped balls left were pressed against the side or blocked by solids. He walked around the table, scanning it carefully.

"That's between us."

"But you're gonna do it, right? I mean you're not getting any younger. You don't wanna be an old dad."

Gray shook his head. "Have you been talking to Aunt Gina and Becca?"

"I might have overheard a few conversations." Tanner

gave him a wicked grin. "If I'm being honest, I might have encouraged it. I've always preferred the spotlight being on you."

"Thanks, bro. And for the record, I'm only three years older than you."

"Four."

"Three right now," Gray pointed out, his brow lifted.

"Ah yeah, but your birthday's coming up and that'll make it four." There was a time when those years felt like a gulf. As the youngest brother, Tanner had longed to keep up with Gray, Cam, and Logan as they sat and plotted their next escapades. Maybe that's why he'd been so drawn to Van on their first day at school. She was like the Hartson brothers on speed. The ultimate plotter of pranks.

"And not that it's any of your business, but I'll be asking Maddie to marry me in my own sweet time. Now are you gonna play that shot, or what? Watching you walk around the table is excruciating."

"Watch and weep, bro," Tanner said, finally taking his shot. And when it careened off the cushion and potted Gray's blue solid instead, he tried really hard to ignore his brother's laughter.

CHAPTER NINE

*V*an hadn't blinked when she walked out of her mom's bungalow that morning, and spotted him standing there by the old oak tree. Instead, she'd done her usual stretches, her limbs long and lithe as she curled over them, and started her run along the lane toward the town square. He'd kept up easily, neither of them saying a word as the buildings gave way to fields and farms.

He'd spent at least half of their run looking at her from the corner of his eye, hoping Van wouldn't notice. Out here, on the dusty road, with the sun shining down on her, she looked completely like the girl he used to know. Strong and determined, yet with a vulnerability only he could see. Of all the people in Hartson's Creek, he was pretty sure only very few knew who she really was.

It had always felt like the most special of gifts, being Van Butler's best friend. She'd been the sun his world had orbited. Without her, the world had felt colder. Lifeless. One of the reasons he threw himself into work the same way Gray threw himself into music. It was a way of pretending the pain wasn't there.

Beneath her black shorts, her legs were firm and lean, the line of muscles beneath her tan skin illuminated by the sun. She was wearing that sports bra again, and he couldn't help but glance at her stomach, his eyes roaming the lines of her abs until they reached the grey fabric covering her breasts.

Shaking his head at himself, he dragged his gaze away. "You wanna take a break here?" he asked, as they reached the old entrance of the drive-in.

"If you're tired, I can wait with you." She shrugged. Then she saw the bright white sign somebody had hammered into the field. "Sold?" she said, her brows pulled together. "I didn't even know it was for sale." She leaned on the old fence and looked at him. "Do you think a developer bought it? Ready to plow over all our childhood memories?"

His mouth felt dry. "No. I don't think they did."

Her eyes were pulled back to the sign again. "Fairfax Realty," she murmured. "They're everywhere, aren't they?"

"I bought it," he told her, waiting for her response.

Her head whipped around. "What? Why?"

"To stop a developer from plowing over all our childhood memories," he said dryly.

She laughed. "Jesus, Tanner. How rich are you?"

"Enough that buying this didn't make a dent in my account."

The smile slid off her face when she realized he was serious. "I don't get it. I know software pays well, but…"

"I sold my company."

Her eyes widened. "You did? Why?"

"Because it would have been crazy to do anything else. And my co-owners wanted to take the money."

"Wow. I didn't know." She shot him a smile. "Congratulations. And now you're set for life." She shook her head, the ghost of a smile playing on her lips. "I knew I should have paid more attention in school."

"I did tell you that," he pointed out.

She laughed, and he loved the way it transformed her face. God, she was beautiful. "We both know you're the only reason I graduated at all," she said, her eyes warm as she looked at him. "All those times you made me study when all I wanted to do was have fun. Those nights when you'd explain the same damn equation over and again until it finally clicked."

"I had an ulterior motive."

She lifted an eyebrow. "And what was that?"

"I didn't want to go to college without you."

The smile slid from her lips. Yeah, well look how that turned out. She looked away, over her shoulder, at the field as it stretched toward the screen. The grass was almost knee high. Beneath it some of the little wooden markers remained, that guided the cars to the right spot for them to park and watch the show.

"So what are you going to do with this place?" she asked.

"Fairfax thinks I'm planning on building a house here."

She eyed him carefully. "But you're not?"

He slowly shook his head. Then he put his hand on the top of the peeling fence and vaulted over it, landing on the field with a soft thud. "Come on," he said, holding his hand out to her.

A wicked grin formed on her lips. "Are you getting brave, trespassing in your old age, Hartson?"

"It ain't trespassing if I own it, *Butler*," he said. "Now are you coming or what?"

She rolled her eyes and started to climb the fence, clearly preferring that to vaulting over. Impatiently, he grabbed her waist when she reached the top, then lifted her over until she was in front of him.

Damn, she was light. And warm. And now his hands wanted to feel more of her. The long grass was swaying like corn in the field, the fresh smell wafting up as they made their way through it.

"You're gonna need a good lawn mower," Van told him. He reached for her hand, and she slid it into his without protest, her head moving from left to right as she took it all in. The ticket booth, whose roof had fallen in, the white wooden screen which was covered in graffiti thanks to the youth of Hartson's Creek. Even the swing set remained, though it was so rusty it looked like it could crumble at any moment.

"I can't believe you bought this," she said. "What a dump."

This time he laughed, low and deep. "You have no vision," he told her.

She lifted her chin up and looked at him with narrow eyes. "Good thing you're rich," she said softly. "Otherwise I'd feel sorry for you wasting your money. What are you going to do with it?"

"I'm going to restore it."

She blinked. "As in make it a drive-in again?"

"Yep."

"Jesus, Tanner, you're crazy. Who the hell wants to go to a drive-in anymore?"

He shrugged. "If we build it, they will come."

She eyed him carefully. "Did you just misquote *Field of Dreams* to me?"

"I might have."

"And who's this *we* you speak of?"

"You and me."

The amusement drained from her face. "There is no *you and me*," she said quietly. "There hasn't been for a long time."

And he wanted to change that. So badly. The only thing worse than losing his best friend would be to lose her all over again. "I need you, Butler. I can't do this on my own. You were always the ringleader, the one with the ideas. I was your sidekick." He gave her a lopsided smile. "The muscle."

She shook her head. "You don't need me. You could do this in your sleep. You have enough money to employ somebody to restore it. People who know what they're doing."

"I don't want someone who knows what they're doing. I want you."

The words sent a shot of pleasure through her. Ugh, he didn't mean it like *that*. She let out a laugh, trying to recover her equilibrium. "Don't sweet talk me."

"Wasn't going to."

"You're crazy, Tanner Hartson. Completely and utterly twisted. Have you thought of getting some therapy?"

He leaned forward, tucking a lock of hair behind her ears. "Say yes," he said softly. "Work with me. Let's make this place into something amazing."

She looked around again, her eyes widening as though she was seeing the field in a different light. That's when he saw it. The spark of interest that made her lips part and her chest lift up and down.

How many times had he seen that before – when she had an idea and couldn't wait to share it with him? It was her tell, the same way a bad poker player would give away the fact they were holding two aces. He had her, he knew it.

"I still think you're crazy," she said softly, licking her bottom lip as she brought her gaze back to his.

"Is that a yes?"

She laughed. "I have no idea if it's a yes, a no, or a stay the hell away from me." She breathed out heavily. "Do I have a choice?"

"There's always a choice."

Van wrinkled her nose. "Not with you there isn't. When we were kids you always knew how to wrap me around your little finger. Just a little bat of those pretty eyelashes and I was a goner."

He gave her a speculative look. It was the first time since he'd been back that she'd admitted he had a hold on her. It was hard to ignore the hope flaring up in his chest.

Leaning in closer, he kept his eyes trained on hers. "Say yes," he whispered, curling his fingers beneath her chin, lifting it until their mouths were only a breath away from each other.

Van swallowed hard, her skin flushing as her gaze remained on his.

"I'll think about it."

CHAPTER TEN

*V*an hated the way her stomach kept contracting as she stood on the Fairfax's doorstep, waiting for somebody to answer the bell. Somebody – Regan, probably – had decorated the porch with yellow streamers and balloons. Shifting on her feet, Van looked up as the door opened, and Nora Fairfax was staring at her, her face impassive as she stepped to the side.

"Come in."

Van smiled at her, but Nora's expression didn't move an inch. "I have a gift, is there anywhere to put it?" She held up the sparkly gift bag she was carrying. It was filled with soft toys and toiletries – the type of things she could remember her mom getting when she was pregnant with Zoe.

"We said no gifts," Nora said tersely.

"I know. But I felt wrong arriving without something in my hands. Oh, and I brought a bottle of wine to say thank you for having me." She lifted the green glass bottle from her bag and passed it to Nora, who took it but held it at arms' length, as though it was a grenade.

"Come in." She sighed. "Everybody is in the living room.

77

Would you like a glass of lemonade?" She glanced at the bottle again. "Or I can open this if you'd like something stronger?"

"Lemonade will be fine."

Giving her an unsmiling nod, Nora led the way down the hallway. Van could hear the low-level buzz of conversation echoing from a room at the back of the house. As Nora peeled off into the kitchen, Van walked inside, taking a deep breath when she saw how packed it was in there.

Her skin prickled up as everyone turned to look at her. Walking into that living room with its perfectly polished wooden floor and whitewashed walls felt like walking into her senior homeroom. She caught one of the women in the far corner looking her up and down as though she was something the dog had brought in.

"Savannah! You made it." Regan struggled to standing, and Van had to grit her teeth together when nobody offered to help her. "Girls, you remember Savannah Butler, right? From school?"

"I brought you a gift," Van said, trying to ignore the way some of them were leaning in and whispering to each other. "I know I'm not supposed to, but you deserve something for carrying a baby around for nine months."

"That's so sweet. Thank you." Regan gave her a quick hug. Why don't you take a seat? There's a free one over there." She pointed at a chair by the fireplace.

Nora chose that moment to enter the room, carrying a glass of iced lemonade in her right hand. "Savannah," she said, passing the glass to her. "I expect you remember Chrissie." She inclined her head to her daughter. "I know she remembers you. Or her face does at least."

Van took a deep breath and formed a smile onto her lips. "Hi."

"Hello." Chrissie was sitting between two women Van

recognized from school – though she couldn't recall their names. "I heard you were back in town."

"It's kind of like a reunion, isn't it?" Regan said, oblivious to the way Chrissie was staring at Van. "You must remember Sarah and Marianne." She pointed to the girls on either side of Chrissie. "Why don't you sit over there, Van? Next to the fireplace?"

"Sure," Van said softly, sinking into the chair and taking a sip of the lemonade. She glanced at her watch. It was just after one in the afternoon. Maybe she could escape in an hour if she was lucky.

She could last that long, couldn't she?

"Hey, did you hear Tanner bought the drive in?" Chrissie asked Marianne. "According to Dad, he's planning to build on it."

"Tanner Hartson?" Marianne said. I thought he was something big in technology."

"Well he was. But he sold and now he's deliciously wealthy." Sarah raised an eyebrow.

"Is he single?" Marianne asked, and they all laughed.

Van wished Tanner was here. He'd be making faces surreptitiously as they all talked about him. She thought she was beyond this feeling of complete inadequacy by now. What did it matter that she wasn't as educated as them, or that her mom didn't have a perfectly beautiful house in which she loved to play hostess? She was twenty-eight years old, that stuff shouldn't matter.

Yet she still found herself shifting on her seat, her chest tight, every time one of them looked at her.

"I'm Ellie," the girl on the other side of the fireplace said, leaning forward and holding out a hand. "Regan's cousin. And I don't know a single soul here."

Van smiled and slid her palm into Ellie's. "I'm Van. I went

to school with Regan about a hundred years ago, and I haven't spoken to anybody in here for about ten years."

Ellie lifted an eyebrow. "Thank god you're here."

❧

VAN ALMOST MANAGED to escape without anybody noticing, if it wasn't for her damn adherence to Southern manners making her walk into Mrs. Fairfax's kitchen to thank her for hosting.

Nora was standing in the corner, a glass of something that looked suspiciously like wine in her hand, leaning forward to talk quietly to Chrissie who was scrolling through her phone.

"I'm heading out. I just wanted to say thank you for hosting," Van said, hovering in the doorway. "It was a lovely afternoon."

"Come in." Nora turned her hand and beckoned her.

Van took a deep breath and stepped inside.

"I was just talking to Chrissie about you. We were wondering if you had a boyfriend."

"No. I'm happily single." Van kept smiling, no matter how much her cheek muscles fought it.

Chrissie looked up from her phone, her eyes flickering over Van. "You never got married?"

"No."

"Hmmm." Chrissie lifted her phone to show her mom something. "How about this one."

"That's pretty," Nora said, leaning over the screen. "But too short." She gave Van a smile. "It'd make you look cheap, sweetie." She glanced at Van from the corner of her eye. Standing completely still, Van smiled back, refusing to give her the satisfaction of seeing her pull at the hem of her dress. Yeah, it fell at mid thigh, but it was pretty.

She *felt* pretty, and she wasn't going to let the Fairfaxes ruin that.

"Speaking of short skirts, I heard Doctor Tamlyn came out to see your mom yesterday." Nora's lips curled up, but it couldn't be described as a smile. "I guess all that hard living has finally caught up with her."

"It was nothing important." Van's hands curled into fists, her arms hanging by her side. "But I'll be sure to pass on your kind wishes."

Nora said nothing. Just looked at Van the way she always had.

"I'll see you out," Chrissie said, flipping her glossy dark hair over her shoulder. Slowly, she rose from the high stool she'd been sitting on, and walked around the oversized kitchen island. "I'll be right back, Mom."

"Okay, sweetie."

When Chrissie held the kitchen door open, Van stole a glance at her face. It was beautiful, the same way it always was. At school, Chrissie had been the first to get a figure – okay, the first to grow breasts. And boy did they all know it. In gym, she and her friends would giggle in the corner at the 'pancakes' who hadn't developed yet. Van had been one of them, and it had aggravated her to no end.

To be fair, Chrissie had always made Van feel small. It wasn't the fact that she had more than Van, nor that she had two parents who were sober and loved her. It was that it wasn't enough. She had to rub it in Van's face, make fun of her. Her happiness depended on others' misery.

And that made Van dislike her. The day her fist connected with Chrissie's face had been a culmination of years of frustration. Yes, she'd said some awful things about Van's mom that day, but Van was used to that. It had only been the excuse to do the one thing she'd always dreamed of.

To hit back at those people who thought they were better than her.

It had been worth it, too. Worth the two-week suspension, worth being lectured for hours by the principal, even worth having Tanner being disappointed with her.

"We have a plan," he'd said when he climbed through her window that night. "You need to study and keep your grades up. That's the only way to get into college."

"So are you and Tanner Hartson still close?" Chrissie asked as she unlatched the front door.

Van blinked the memories away, and looked at Chrissie, who was holding the door open.

"Um. Kind of. Why?"

"I just heard he was back in town." Chrissie shrugged. "And according to popular opinion he's more gorgeous than ever. Is he seeing anybody, do you know?"

"I've no idea." Van shrugged. "You'd have to ask him."

Chrissie laughed. "I might just do that. Thanks, Savannah."

"No problem." It was an effort to smile, but she did it anyway. "Bye, Chrissie." Then she walked down the steps and the path, not looking back once.

Even if she did feel like punching Chrissie's face all over again.

CHAPTER ELEVEN

*V*an was kneeling on the front lawn doing yard work when she heard a voice call out.

"Savannah Butler, I heard you were back in town. I hope you were intending to come say hi to me at some point."

She turned to see the smiling face of Tanner's Aunt Gina leaning out of her car, and her own lips lifted into a grin. Growing up, Aunt Gina had been like a second mom to Van, the same way she'd been to the Hartson siblings. Feeding them, talking them through their problems, making sure they felt loved.

Her welcoming smile was such a stark contrast to Nora Fairfax's the previous day at Regan's sprinkle. It felt like a balm to Van's ruffled soul.

"Of course I was going to come see you." Van ran over to the car and hugged Aunt Gina through the open window. "How are you?"

"I'm doing fine. Even better now that some of my babies are back in town." Aunt Gina winked. She was perfectly turned out as always, her white hair elegantly coiffed. She was wearing a pink-and-white patterned tea dress and it complemented her still-svelte figure. "And that includes you in case you're wondering," she told Van. "Now when are you coming over to my place so I can feed you up? There's nothing left on those bones of yours."

Van glanced at her body. She was wearing a pair of cut-off jeans and an old grey t-shirt she'd knotted at the waist to keep it out of the dirt as she weeded her mom's flower beds. "I've been eating plenty. But I'd never turn down one of your meals."

"That's good. Because we're barbecuing this evening. Bring your family with you. Your mom and your sister, Zoe, is it?"

"That's right. And we'd love to, or at least Zoe and I would. Mom's not feeling the best." Van's heart swelled just a little. Aunt Gina never left anybody out.

"I'm sorry to hear about your mom." Aunt Gina's voice was soft. "And about her marriage troubles. That's never good for anybody. Is she doing okay?"

Van let out a mouthful of air. Her mom hadn't gotten up today at all. Not even when Van and Zoe cooked pancakes and bacon, giggling in the kitchen as they danced to old eighties music. "She's been better. But she'll pull through."

Gina nodded, but said nothing. She didn't need to. Her eyes were full of understanding. She'd never pried about Van's mom, not even when she was younger. But she always made sure Van was okay.

"Okay then. Come over any time after five. And don't bring a thing. We already have too much food. Even with Tanner and Gray there it won't all get eaten."

Van's heart clenched at the mention of Tanner. She hadn't had time to run at all this weekend, and she missed seeing him. It was stupid, because she'd managed for all these years without him. Yet a couple of days and her heart was galloping at the thought of seeing him again.

"I can't turn up empty handed," Van told Gina. "What would they say at *Chairs?*"

"*Chairs*, schmairs. Just come and make an old woman happy." Gina blew her a kiss. "Now I have to go, I have a bridge game in ten minutes. And if I get there late they'll replace me with Della Thorsen." She widened her eyes in horror. "That woman could cheat her own mother."

Van laughed, making a shooing motion with her hands. "Go. And I'll see you tonight."

Gina put her foot on the gas, and her old brown station wagon lurched forward. The grin was still on Van's face as she watched the car disappear around the corner, the roaring sound of the engine still audible above the sweet singing of the birds in the trees.

Five o'clock. That's when she would see Tanner again, if she didn't see him running first. Van was more than aware she owed him an answer about helping him with the drive-in. She'd been thinking about it for days, after all.

"So there are five of them?" Zoe asked, as Van lifted the old brass knocker on the Hartson's front door. "Wow. I can't imagine having five brothers and sisters."

"It was always chaos at their house," Van admitted, biting down a smile. Memories of sitting at the Hartson's oversized dining table washed through her. Aunt Gina always managed to make sure there was enough food no matter how many of them were sitting around there. Often Gray would bring his girlfriend, and Logan and Cam would have two or three friends with them, along with Becca and their dad. It had been such a contrast to the meals Van would eat at home, which were usually a piece of toast and whatever canned goods she could manage to get open, while her mom was who knew where.

The Hartsons' house had been her sanctuary growing up. She'd been envious of Tanner's family, and overjoyed that they'd treated her like one of their own. She'd genuinely fallen for them all. Gray and his singing. Logan and his cooking. Even Cam's obsession with football, which meant every Monday night was spent with the game blasting out from the television in the den.

"Hey!" Becca shouted from the side of the house. "What's with you knocking on the front door? You always used to come around the back."

Van let the knocker fall back into place. She felt Zoe nestle a little closer to her. "I didn't want to presume," she told Becca.

"Gah, you're one of the family. Come on 'round." Becca grinned at Zoe. "Hey, kiddo. Anybody told you that you look just like Van did when she was younger?"

Zoe blushed. "I do?" she asked with wide eyes. She looked at Van as though she couldn't quite see it.

"Yep," Becca said, as they made their way to the side of the house. "She had that whole angelic thing going, too. Though she was really naughty. Did she tell you about the time she spiked the communion wine at church?"

"That one wasn't me," Van protested. "It was Gray."

"What was me?"

"Is that Gray Hartson?" Zoe whispered, her hand sliding into Van's.

Van nodded. "Yeah." There he was. The boy she used to know standing six feet three inches tall, his arms covered in tattoos, his hair artfully disheveled. And he was grinning at her, his handsome face lighting up as he caught her gaze.

Gray walked over to them, leaning forward to hug Van tightly. "Maddie told me you were back in town. You should've come to see me." He stepped back and smiled at Zoe. "And you must be Van's sister." He held out his hand and Zoe took it, swallowing hard. Van tried not to laugh at the awe on Zoe's face.

"Hi," she squeaked out.

"You guys want a drink?" Becca asked. "Aunt Gina made iced tea."

"I'd love one." Van glanced down at Zoe who nodded, still star struck.

The next few minutes were taken up with hugs and greetings. Though Cam and Logan weren't there, the garden still felt full. Maddie's mom was there, and Becca's friend, Laura, and her family. "We decided to eat outside since it's so nice," Becca told her, nodding at the table set up on the freshly cut lawn.

"Where's Tanner?" Van asked, trying to keep her voice nonchalant. When Becca shot her a questioning look, she lifted her iced tea to her lips to hide the way she couldn't help but grin.

"He sassed Aunt Gina so she made him go to the store to pick up marshmallows." Becca wiggled her eyebrows. "We're having 'smores for dessert."

"'Smores?" Zoe asked tipping her head. "What are those?"

Becca shook her head. "Kid, you've got a lot of learning to do." She pointed at Van. "This sister of yours isn't doing her job if you don't know what 'smores are." She hunkered down until her face was level with Zoe's. "'Smores are like the best thing you'll ever taste. Like eating heaven and hell all mixed in one. And the cool thing is you get to make them yourself. With a stick, over fire."

Zoe shot Van a look over her shoulder. Van grinned and nodded. "Yep. They're pretty good."

"Somebody get me a beer," Tanner called out, rounding

the corner with overstuffed brown bags in his arms. "I just got goosed by Lucy Sanders in the grocery store."

Becca coughed out a laugh.

He put the bags on the table next to the grill. When he turned back, his eyes met Van's and his grin widened. "You came."

Becca slid a cold beer into his hand. "Of course she did. We have 'smores."

"Thanks to me." He lifted an eyebrow. "I'm going to be traumatized for the rest of my life just because you wanted marshmallows."

"Shut up." Becca shook her head. "We all know you have a thing for the older ladies."

Van bit down on her lip, trying not to laugh. There was such a feeling of warmth in the backyard that had nothing to do with the evening sun or the burning grill. Spending time with the Hartsons had always felt like pulling the warmest, coziest blanket over herself.

From the way Zoe was grinning from ear-to-ear as Becca shoved a marshmallow in her mouth, her sister felt exactly the same way.

Maybe things were going to be okay after all.

THE SUN WAS SLIPPING down past the treeline, casting long shadows across the burnished grass. Aunt Gina was carrying the last of the dishes inside, batting away everybody's offers of help. "You young folk stay out here. I'm going to sit in my chair inside and read my book for a while." Her eyes crinkled as she moved her gaze from Gray and Maddie around to Zoe and Van. "It warms my heart to have you all here again."

Van checked her watch. "I guess we should go," she said,

pressing her lips together in a regretful smile. "It's past Zoe's bedtime."

"No! Don't go yet." Becca's eyes were imploring. "I promised Zoe I'd show her how to play chubby bunnies."

"She'll be here all night," Tanner teased. "You have the biggest mouth of all of us."

Becca slapped his arm. "Shut up. And don't think I've forgotten the time you shoved a boiled egg in my mouth when I was trying to beat my record. I still haven't gotten the taste completely out of my mouth."

"That was Van's idea," Tanner said, sliding his gaze to hers.

Van lifted an eyebrow. "It wasn't my idea to do it to *Becca*," she pointed out. "I did it to you, then you just had to share the fun."

"Still makes you a bad influence." He winked at her. She looked so damn beautiful tonight it made his heart hurt. Her golden hair tumbled past her shoulders in soft, easy waves, catching the light of the setting sun when it peeped between the trees. She was wearing a white, embroidered sun dress, the bodice tight against her chest, drawing his eye every time he looked over.

"Come on, let's go eat the marshmallows over there," Becca said, grabbing Zoe's hand and leading her to the garden chairs set up next to the pond. "We'll be at a safe distance from your sister and my brother. It's the only way to avoid their dastardly plans."

On the other side of the table, Maddie and her mom were playing cards with Laura and her family, while Gray strummed his guitar and hummed, occasionally writing something down on the pad in front of him.

Tanner grabbed a half-full bottle of white wine, and walked back to where Van was sitting. He topped up her glass then took the seat next to her, stretching out his long legs.

"Thank you." She took a sip. There was a light in her eyes that made him want to get lost inside of them.

"Are you okay?" he asked.

She tipped her head toward him, her skin glowing in the dim light of the sun. "I was just thinking how lovely this all is. I've missed your family. I can't remember the last time I sat in this yard and laughed so much."

"They've missed you, too." He ran his tongue across his dry lips. "You being gone for so long is my fault. I took this from you." His chest tightened. "I'm sorry."

"It's okay." Her eyes were soft. "It's old news."

No it wasn't. It still felt new and painful. It was the reason he'd lost his best friend. But she didn't want to talk about it, that much was obvious. He poured himself a glass of wine and took a sip. "I heard you talking about your job to Aunt Gina. I didn't know you went freelance."

"Yeah. A couple of years ago." She smiled at him.

"Do you like being your own boss?"

"Yes." She nodded. "I like being able to pick and choose my clients. Especially being able to say no to those ones who are difficult." Van leaned back in her chair, her body angled toward his. His hand was close to hers, enough that if he straightened his arm he could touch her. He had to curl his fingers away to stop himself from doing just that. "And then there's the flexibility," she continued, as if she was oblivious to the chemistry building between them. "It meant I could come here when I was needed without being afraid of getting fired."

"There are some perks to being in charge," he agreed.

"Sure are."

It was crazy how often their gazes were meeting. He'd never get tired of the way she'd make his body feel electric with a simple glance. It was a special kind of torment. Like a kid being tickled until he could barely breathe. He loved it and he hated it.

"How about you?" she asked. "Do you miss your work?"

He lifted his glass to his lips, thinking through her question. The truth was, in the past few days he'd barely thought about New York. His mind was too full of her.

"I miss being busy," he admitted. "I'm not built to sit around doing nothing."

She glanced at his body. "I don't believe you do nothing. You run, you shop for Aunt Gina." She smirked. "And you buy drive-ins on a whim."

He couldn't help but laugh. "Yeah, I guess that's kept me busy." He licked his lips, still studying her. "Will you go back to Richmond at some point?"

She still hadn't mentioned his offer of a job. He wanted to talk to her about it, but right now their conversation was so easy, so flowing. He hated to interrupt it.

"I don't know," she admitted. "It depends on Zoe, I guess. And Mom." She pulled her bottom lip between her teeth, and he recognized that expression right away. He'd seen it too many times when they were kids not to know it. He'd been the closest person to her then. He knew her tells, the same way a poker player would.

"Is Kim bad?" he asked.

Van nodded. "Like she used to be." Her voice dropped as she told him.

"Shit."

"Right?" She gave him a sad smile. "I can't leave Zoe when she's like this. So I'm here for a while."

"Can you get child services involved?" Tanner leaned forward, his face earnest.

"Mom would never forgive me if I called them. She'd probably throw me out and refuse to let me see Zoe. I figure it's better if I approach this softly. Maybe she'll even surprise me."

"Maybe." He smiled at her. He loved the way she had it all together. There was something so alluring about the way she never faltered. With her perfectly fitting dress, her golden hair, and sunkissed skin she looked like a little piece of sunshine sitting next to him. It made his body ache for her. He wanted to peel that dress off her, inch by inch, and see the perfection underneath.

Wanted to taste her, touch her, make her sigh.

It had been way too long since he'd touched a woman. That's what being a workaholic did to you.

It's been way too long since you touched this *woman.* His lips curled at the sound of the voice in his head. It sounded way too much like Logan for comfort.

Her eyes caught his again, and widened, as though she could read the thoughts rushing through his brain. He didn't blink, unafraid of his thoughts. He wanted her to know them.

And to reflect them right back at him.

"Tanner…"

"Yeah?" he asked, shifting so he was facing her. His knees grazed hers. Even through his cotton pants, he could feel the heat of her skin. Could smell her, too. Sweet and floral.

Damn it, he couldn't ignore the need to touch her anymore. He slid his fingers between hers, curling his palm around her hand, swallowing hard at the softness of her skin. Her chest was rising and falling rapidly, her eyes fixed on his. If they weren't surrounded by people right now…

"I win!" Maddie shouted, standing and doing a twirl. "Did you see that, Tanner?"

Van immediately pulled her hand from his, her cheeks flushing as though afraid somebody might have seem them touching. Tanner smiled at Maddie, then glanced back at the beautiful woman next to him.

"You okay?" he asked.

This time she didn't quite meet his gaze. "I'm fine. I should see how Zoe is doing." She glanced at her watch. "It's late and we both need some sleep." She exhaled softly as she stood, putting down her empty glass of wine. "Maybe I shouldn't have been drinking either. I feel a little light headed. Good thing we walked over."

"I'll walk you back."

"There's no need." A calmness seemed to descend on her, like she'd flipped a switch and turned everything off. "Zoe?" she called out. "Are you ready to go?"

CHAPTER TWELVE

*A*s she walked across the soft lawn, Van could feel her cheeks blazing. Even though her back was to him, she could still picture Tanner perfectly. His dark hair falling over his brow, his strong jaw covered with the perfect amount of scruff. And his mouth. All night her gaze had been drawn to it. Remembering how sweet his lips had felt against hers all those years ago. How he'd known just the right way to touch her, until her skin was on fire and her heart was clammering against her chest.

It had been a struggle to keep her cool in front of him.

"Aunt Gina? We're going. Thank you for a lovely evening." Van hugged her tight.

"Don't be a stranger, sweetie," Gina told her. "You and Zoe are always welcome here. No need for an invitation."

"Van, can we make s'mores at home some time?" Zoe asked, skipping over from where she'd been sitting with Becca by the fire. "They're so good."

"Sure." Van ruffled her hair, then wrinkled her nose. "You smell like smoke. You're gonna need a shower when we get home."

"Oops, sorry. My fault." Becca shot her a smile.

"Ah, she needed one anyway."

One by one, Van and Zoe said their goodbyes to the Hartson family, all smiles and hugs as they promised to come back soon. And then she was standing in front of Tanner, his warm eyes gazing at hers.

"Can I call you tomorrow?" he asked. "We need to talk about the drive-in."

"I thought you'd forgotten."

He slowly shook his head. "Just didn't want to rush you. Or talk about business at a social occasion."

She took a deep breath in. "Yeah, you can call me."

"I'll need your number." He handed her his phone.

Taking it, she quickly entered her number in the contacts and passed it back. Their finger tips brushed, and she felt a jolt of electricity rush through her. She smiled shyly at him, and he winked back, as though he knew exactly the reason for her shiver.

"Okay then. We need to go. I'll speak to you soon." She glanced at him again. Should she hug him? It would look weird if she didn't when she'd hugged every other member of his family. Yet she still hesitated. Not because she didn't want to, but because it meant too much. She was already on edge. It could tip her over.

"Come here," his voice was velvety soft. He reached for her, his arms circling around her shoulders and his palms flat against her back as he pulled her against him. The sudden movement took her by surprise. She wasn't ready for it. She didn't have her defences up. Her heart started to hammer in her ribcage so hard she swore he must be able to feel it. She was so aware of the way his fingers felt against the fabric of her dress.

Slowly, she lifted her head, looking up until her gaze met his. For a moment his eyes burned into hers. He swallowed, the prominent lump in his throat undulating with the action. All she could think about were his lips. The need she had to feel them on hers. He'd kiss her hard, the way he once had, then slide his mouth softly down her throat. Her body tensed at the thought, her nipples hardening against his ribcage.

If he'd kissed her, she would have let him. In spite of everybody around them. His family, Zoe, all of them. But instead he stepped back, releasing his hold on her, shifting awkwardly.

"Bye, Van."

Her body felt icy without him pressed against her. Still, she forced her lips into a smile. "Bye." And if her body felt like it was on fire? Well she'd have to live with that.

She wanted him. The exhilaration rushing through her was enough to tell her that. But she also knew what that kind of need brought. The low after the high.

She'd let herself fall for him once, and look what happened. This time, she was determined they'd stay friends.

"Can I ask you something?" Zoe said as they turned the corner into their street. It was almost nine o'clock, past Zoe's bedtime, and she looked suitably excited that Van let her stay up late on a school night. The sun had dipped below the mountains and the street lamps had come on, flooding the road with light.

"Sure. Shoot." Van glanced at her sister from the corner of her eye.

"Which one was Tanner and Becca's mom? Was it Aunt Gina?"

Van shook her head. "No. Their mom died when they were little. Aunt Gina is their mom's sister. She moved in to take care of them."

"Is she married to their dad?"

The moon was glowing softly above the tree line. "No," Van told her. "They're just friends, I guess. But she's taken care of all of them like she was their mom."

"He's scary."

"Tanner's dad?"

Zoe nodded. "He looked angry all night."

It was strange how perceptive kids could be. "Yeah, he's never been very happy. Not since their mom died."

"Did you know their mom?"

Van's brow wrinkled as she thought. "Sort of. We were just kids when she died, so I can't remember her that well." She could remember the night she died though. The frantic rapping of Tanner's knuckles on her window in the middle of the night. His tear stained face as he climbed into her bedroom, sobs wracking his tiny body as he tried to tell her what had happened. It had been the middle of the night, and Van was dressed in her favorite sheep pajamas, her brain full of sleep as she tried to make out his words.

His mom had died less than an hour earlier. Tanner had been the only one of his brothers not to sit by her bedside as she passed. It had taken him years to admit he'd been too afraid to watch his mom die, and instead he'd run away and hidden in the summer house, his eyes scrunched closed as he prayed to a god he hoped was listening.

He'd only known she'd died when he heard Gray walk into the garden and let out a haunting scream. Gray had been almost twelve. The oldest of the five. Tanner had never heard him cry until then.

That's when Tanner had run to her house. And without asking, she'd lifted her covers and they'd curled up together on her bed, their tiny frames nestled together in the scant comfort he'd sought.

His dad had knocked at the door some time before dawn

and somehow Van's mom had been sober enough to let him in. He'd grabbed Tanner's hand and scolded him for running away, not hugging him, or ruffling his hair, or asking if he was okay.

At least Aunt Gina had changed all that when she moved in with them. She'd turned out to be like their mom but on acid, constantly chiding, chasing, and feeding them.

"If mom died, would you look after me?" Zoe asked. "Or would I go and live with Craig?"

They'd reached the bungalow. Van stopped and turned to Zoe, smiling softly at her as she reached to cup her sweet face. "Mom isn't going to die," she told her. "But I'll always be here for you. No matter what happens. And I know Craig hasn't been here much recently, but he loves you, too."

Zoe's bottom lip wobbled. She was such a deep thinker. "I don't want to be alone."

Van reached for her, hugging her tight. "You never have to. I promise. We'll always take care of you."

It was the one thing she knew, more than anything else. She'd protect her sister forever, the way she'd never been protected. From nastiness, from speculation, from gossip. She'd never have people teasing her because their mom brought home a random guy, or because the rumor about her stealing from the Fairfaxes had finally reached the school gates.

Kissing her sister's head, Van promised herself she'd always be Zoe's protector. Nothing else mattered. Not the way their mom was almost certainly still curled up in bed, nor the way her heart skipped every time she saw Tanner Hartson.

She was here for Zoe. Nothing else.

"How about you call your brother once in a while?" Logan complained over the phone to Tanner later that night. "I just spoke to Becca. She told me you bought the drive-in. How the hell didn't I know this?"

"It only happened last week. The ink on the contract isn't even dry." Tanner shook his head, though he couldn't help but smile. Of his three other brothers, he'd grown closest to Logan over the years. Maybe because Gray had been so busy touring the world and Cam had been chasing his football dreams, leaving Tanner and Logan to spend more time together. It had been Logan who was there for him when Van had told Tanner she never wanted to see him again and followed through with her threat.

And as they both built their own businesses – Tanner in New York, Logan in Boston– they'd become confidants. Bitching at each other about how hard it was to please their employees. Talking through business options when they needed somebody they could trust.

It was natural Logan was a little taken aback that Tanner hadn't discussed the drive-in with him. Tanner couldn't help but feel bad about that.

"I bought it on a whim," he confessed. "I don't have a business plan or anything. Just signed the contract and now here I am."

Logan laughed. "That doesn't sound like you."

No it didn't. "Yeah, well I had money burning a hole in my pocket. And I was bored."

"There's always a job for you in Boston," Logan reminded him. "I could use somebody I trust."

Tanner lifted a brow. "I think I'll stay in Hartson's Creek for now, but thanks anyway."

"So what are you planning to do with the drive-in?" Logan asked.

"I'm gonna rebuild it."

"Seriously?" Logan sounded skeptical. "How the hell are you gonna do that? You don't have any experience of the hospitality industry."

"I know. But I know some people who do." He grinned. "Like you."

"Yeah. I'm a bit busy to be playing movies with you. Seriously, bro. I thought you weren't supposed to be doing any work for a year? Wasn't that part of the conditions of your sale?"

"Only in a competing company," Tanner told him. "And I'm not planning on doing much work anyway. I'm going to get somebody to do it for me."

"Who?"

"Van Butler."

"What?" Logan chuckled. "As in Van Butler the girl you used to hang around with, then you dicked over until she was in pieces?"

"Shut up."

"Come on," Logan said, his voice disbelieving. "I heard you tell Becca you weren't interested in seeing Van again. And now you're talking about employing her? How long have I been gone? When did the two of you reconnect?"

"It's a small town." Tanner shrugged. "We're friends, that's all."

Logan was silent for a moment. "Friends?" he asked, as though he couldn't quite believe it.

"What else would we be?"

"You tell me? She's always felt like the one who got away." There was a shrug in Logan's voice. "There was a point I thought you'd never get over her. Or what happened. It just feels... I don't know... weird, that you're talking about her like you don't have a past."

"Maybe I grew up," Tanner said. "We've bumped into each other a few times. At the diner, running... that kind of thing.

And then Aunt Gina invited her to dinner this evening. We're okay. What happened between us is water under the bridge. I think we can be friends again." And if he wanted more? Well, they'd see what happened.

"Just be careful, man," Logan said softly. "I remember what you were like ten years ago. The situation broke you. I don't want to see you get hurt again." He cleared his throat. "And she doesn't deserve to get hurt either."

"I won't hurt her." Tanner was certain of that. "We're both adults, we know what we're doing. And thank you. It's good to know you've got my back."

"Always."

"You okay?" Tanner asked his brother.

"Yep. Busy as hell at work, but surviving."

"Any women on the horizon?" he teased.

"Nope." Logan's voice was sure. "No time for one if there was. The women of Boston are probably sighing with relief."

"I doubt that." Logan was a good looking guy, or at least that's what Tanner's female friends told him. "But whatever gets you through the day."

"Talking of which, I'd better go. We got a party of forty in this evening. And the wine is flowing a little too fast. You take care of yourself, bro. And don't go breaking anybody's heart. Especially not your own."

"Wasn't planning on it," Tanner said, his voice light.

"Yeah well. We never do."

CHAPTER THIRTEEN

"*H*ey," Tanner said, his voice warm as it echoed through her cellphone. "I was wondering if you're free for lunch today. To talk business," he added quickly. "I thought we could meet at the diner around one."

Damn. "I can't make lunch. I have to take my mom for an appointment. Can we meet later?" Because she really wanted to talk to him. "Maybe four?"

"At the diner?"

"Why don't we grab coffee and walk?" she suggested. "It's a beautiful day." And maybe if she was surrounded by fresh air she wouldn't be quite so aware of him. All those gas molecules might dilute his essence.

"Sounds good to me. I'll get the coffees and meet you in the town square. We can walk down to the creek."

"I'd like that a lot."

"See you at four." His voice was soft, and it held a promise that made her heart ache.

"See you there."

"ARE YOU READY?" Van called out to her mom, grabbing her car keys and purse. "We have ten minutes to get there."

Kim walked out of the bedroom in a pair of tight, bleached jeans and a navy tank, her light blonde hair tumbling over her bare shoulders. She wasn't wearing any make up, but she looked better than she had in days. Van gave her a tentative smile, and Kim smiled back.

This was already going better than she'd expected.

The drive to town took less than five minutes. Van would have suggested they walk, but she knew her mom wouldn't have gone for it. She was too fragile to deal with meeting people in the street. They'd head straight for the doctor's office, then home again.

"Here goes nothing." Kim followed Van out of the front door and down the steps. A warm breeze rustled through the trees and lifted her hair, the golden tips dancing in the wind. Van looked at her mom, taking in her warm, smooth skin and pale blue eyes. Right now she looked like she was in her twenties, not her forties.

She'd always been a good looking woman. And she'd relied on those looks to get her through life. They'd been her blessing and her curse, bringing her joy and pain at the same time.

Parking outside the doctor's office, Van opened the car door, then walked around to help her mom out. Kim blinked as she emerged into the bright afternoon sun. "You can wait here," she said, her voice low. "I won't be long."

"You sure you don't want me to come with you?"

Kim shook her head. "I only need a prescription. It'll take no time."

Van watched her mom walk into the doctor's office, then leaned on her car, enjoying the feel of the sun against her skin. She was wearing a dark blue shirt dress, belted at the waist, the hem skimming her mid thighs. Like her mom, her hair was freshly washed and flowing. She felt good today. Maybe it was the fact that things were finally falling into place. Her mom was feeling better, Zoe seemed happy, and she had a job offer that she was almost certain she was going to take.

"Look at you leaning on that car like some kind of model."

Van grinned as Becca walked toward her. Tanner's sister was wearing a sleeveless blouse and a black skirt, her dark hair twisted into a messy knot.

"Hey. What are you doing here? I thought you worked at the distillery."

"I do." Becca held up a piece of paper. "I've been sent on a lunch run. Because my boss is an asshole and thinks I'm his assistant." She rolled her eyes. "On the plus side, it means I can enjoy the sun instead of being cooped up inside. And if it takes Murphy an hour to make up the order?" She shrugged. "I guess they'll have to deal with that."

Van couldn't help but laugh at Becca's expression. It was somewhere between disgust and satisfaction. "Well enjoy the break. I'd recommend sitting outside while he makes up the order."

"I might just do that." Becca winked. "Thanks." She pulled her lip between her teeth, her brow dipping as though she was thinking about whether to speak. "So, it was good to see you on Sunday."

"It was good to see you, too. Thanks for spending so much time with Zoe. She enjoyed it."

"You and Tanner seemed close." Becca shifted her feet awkwardly. "It was nice... seeing you talk again like old times." She looked up at Van. "Do you think you two can be friends again?" she asked.

Van felt her chest tighten. "Yeah," she said, nodding. "I think we can." Even if part of her yearned for more.

"Do you have a boyfriend?"

Van started to laugh. She couldn't help it. Becca was so damn obvious. "No, I don't."

"Nor does Tanner." Becca frowned at her own words. "I mean he doesn't have a girlfriend," she added. "You're both single. That's interesting."

"Is it?" Van chuckled.

"Yeah. Why are you laughing?"

"I don't know," Van said, swallowing hard. "It just struck me as funny. That's all."

"I just think it would be nice if you two… I don't know… maybe thought about dating or something. I always thought you would when we were younger. You two look good together. And that would make you my sister." Becca grinned. "I'd like that a lot."

"We're just friends, Becca. That's all." Van's voice was soft. She'd always had a soft spot for the younger girl.

Becca nodded, her hopeful expression dissolving. "I guess I should go get this food."

"Sure. I'll see you around."

Giving her a half-smile, Becca said her goodbyes and walked into the diner. When Kim emerged from the doctor's office ten minutes later, Van was sitting in her car, the windows down, listening to soft music playing on the local country radio station.

"Well that was a waste of time," Kim said, sitting down and slamming the door. "He won't up my dose of happy pills. Not unless I agree to go to AA." She shook her head. "I told him I'm not an alcoholic. I just like a drink occasionally."

Van let out a lungful of air. "You drink most nights."

"Yeah, to take off the edge. Maybe if he upped my dose I

wouldn't need to." Kim shook her head as Van pulled away and drove toward home. "I told him it's just temporary. To get me over losing Craig. And then he started talking about therapy." She huffed. "Like I need therapy."

"Everybody could benefit from therapy," Van murmured, her knuckles tight as she turned the wheel.

"I'm not crazy. I've just been left by my husband." Kim leaned her chin on her hand, staring out of the passenger window. The air was rushing through the gap at the top. "I don't know why I bother."

"Because you want to feel better?" Van suggested.

"Yeah. Well now I feel worse." Kim slumped down. "I think I'll go to bed when we get home. I'm exhausted."

"You do that," Van said, her teeth clenched as she pulled the car into the driveway and put it in park.

Two steps forward and one back. At least her mom had gotten dressed today. But the way she swung between moods made Van feel distinctly uneasy. In so many ways, it felt like she was eighteen again.

Her mom was drinking and volatile, the same way she'd been before she got pregnant with Zoe.

And then there was Tanner.

He was gorgeous, unforgettable, and made her heart skip way too many beats.

She was almost certain she was going to take the job at the drive-in.

And it felt like Van's world was tipping on the edge, out of reach no matter how hard she tried to hold onto it. If she'd let herself think about it for too long, she'd be scared to death.

As soon as he saw her his body tensed up. Not in a bad way, just a 'damn, I'm a goner, and I really don't want her to know it' fashion. Van was walking toward him, her golden hair rippling in waves as the afternoon sun hit it, her bare legs tan and lithe from all the running she did. She was wearing a dark blue dress, belted at her slim waist, a few buttons at the top unfastened so he could see the dip between her neck and her chest.

"I got you a latte," he said, passing her a takeout cup. "I hope that's okay."

"It's perfect." She smiled at him, her red painted lips curling up. "Thank you." She lifted it to her mouth, closing her eyes for a moment as she took a sip, then let out a long, deep sigh. "Oh, you don't know how much I needed this," she said, looking up at him through her dark lashes.

He swallowed hard, even though his coffee remained untouched. Did she know what she sounded like when she sighed?

Like sex.

Shut up.

Was his mind really arguing with itself right now?

"Bad day?" he asked, as they walked out of the square and crossed the road. One of his aunt's friends was scrubbing the steps of the First Baptist Church. He lifted a hand in greeting, and she waved back.

"Something like that." She inhaled deeply. "But I'm feeling better now. Thank you."

"I didn't do anything." He shrugged. "But I'll take your gratitude anyway. " He winked. "If you'll take my job."

"Okay."

He blinked. Her sudden acceptance shocked him. "Seriously?"

"Yeah." She nodded. "I need a job if I'm staying around a while."

"I had this whole speech memorized." He grinned at her. "I was prepared to beg you. I'm kinda disappointed now."

She pouted. "So am I. You want to do it anyway?"

He laughed. "Nope. Not when you're such a pushover."

"Shut up. And I haven't told you my terms yet." Her voice was almost cocky. He loved confident Van.

Loved? What the heck?

"I accept them," he said smoothly, ignoring the thoughts whirring through his brain.

"Stop it!" Her bottom lip dropped open. "What if I told you I wanted to be paid a million dollars and have half the shares in the company?"

"I'd tell you that you're underselling yourself." They turned the corner, walking past the big houses that led to the creek. "You might have to wait a while for the million though. Until we're turning a profit."

"I don't want a million." She took another sip of coffee. Some foam clung to her red lips, and she licked it away. Tanner tried to pull his eyes away, but he couldn't. It was too mesmerizing.

"What do you want?" he asked, his voice thick.

"I just want people to know I got this job under my own merits. Because I'm good at what I do. I don't want the gossips saying you gave me a job because you feel sorry for me or..." She sighed. "Or that I'm sleeping my way to the top."

"But you're not."

"That's not how they'll see it. People are already talking about us."

"They are? Who?" His brows pulled together as he looked at her.

"Your sister for one."

"Becca said something to you?" His frown deepened. "I'll speak to her."

"No, don't." Van shook her head. "She was just being silly. Asking me if I was single. Telling me that you were."

He took a deep breath. His chest felt strange. As tight as it did the last time he finished a marathon. "Are you single?" he asked her. His breath caught in his throat as he waited for her answer.

She tipped her head to the side, her hair falling over one shoulder. "I am." She nodded.

Good.

They'd made it to the edge of the creek. Van lifted her hand to her brow to block out the sun. "Remember when we tried to build a raft?" she asked him.

He smiled. The water was glistening, reflecting the solar rays that hit it. "Yeah. I remember how it sunk as soon as you climbed on it."

She laughed, and it looked good on her. Way too good. "I only climbed on it because you were too scared to."

"Too sensible, you mean."

Her gaze met his. "You always were the one with more common sense."

"I wanted to be like you. Fearless. You were never scared of anything."

Her lips parted. He could see the tip of her tongue peeking through. "I was scared," she said. "I just hid it well. I find that harder to do as time goes on."

"What are you scared of now?" he asked. He could feel the blood pumping through him, heating up his skin. A gust of wind lifted her hair, leaving a tendril stuck to her lips. He reached out to pull it away, tucking it behind her ear.

Her skin was warm. Soft. Everything he remembered.

"How long have you got?" she asked him. "The list is long."

His eyes met hers again. "I can listen for as long as it takes."

God he loved the way she smiled. The sun dipped behind a cloud, the shadow cooling his skin. He could feel his heart pumping in a steady rhythm against his ribcage. Standing there by the creek, she looked like the image of a country girl. Golden and tanned, her pretty dress doing nothing to hide the delicate curves of her body. He wanted to scoop her up and pull her against him, then kiss her so damn hard until they were both breathless.

The moment flickered between them, sending a pink flush to her cheeks. Her lips parted, as though she was trying to catch her breath.

There was no point in fighting it, this aching need he had for her. It had taken on a life of its own. It made him feel emotions he hadn't felt in a long time. Things he'd told himself he didn't need. And yet now they felt like air to him.

"Savannah," he said, his fingers unfurling as he reached out to cup her cheek. Her skin was so damn warm and soft. He brushed the nape of her neck with his fingers, and she swallowed hard.

"You never call me Savannah," she whispered, her voice almost a sigh.

"You never used to let me." His thumb traced the line of her cheek, down to the corner of her full lips. "You refused to answer to it."

"It's a weak name."

His eyes dipped to her mouth. "No it's not. It can't be. It's your name and you're the strongest person I know."

He slid his hand to her neck, her soft hair brushing against his knuckles. She swallowed hard, her neck undulating, her eyes trained on his. He couldn't tell if she was breathing. All he could hear was the soft rustle of the leaves as the afternoon breeze danced around them, and the pounding of the blood as it rushed through his ears.

Her eyes dilated as he bent his head toward her, his lips a breath away from hers. She parted her mouth, her breath catching in her throat, and he felt the need to taste her in every inch of his body.

"I'm sorry." She stepped back, her chest rising and falling rapidly. "That was weird. I don't know what just happened." She pulled her coffee cup to her chest, as though it was some kind of shield. "Maybe it's Becca's fault. For talking about us being single." Van shook her head. "It's been a long day."

Tanner's brow pulled down. "It wasn't you. It was me." He'd wanted to kiss her. Ached for it. Still did. But there she was, her expression full of regret, her body set in a stance that screamed keep away. "I'm sorry, too."

"Maybe I should add something to my terms," she said, lifting her lips into a smile. One that didn't quite reach her eyes. "No weirdness between us. Just a boss and employee relationship."

"No weirdness, right." He nodded slowly. "I'll be sure to write that into your contract."

"Seriously, though." Her smile softened. "I don't want to do anything that affects our working relationship." She looked down at the dry grass growing around their feet. "I haven't ruined it before it's begun, have I?"

"Of course you haven't." He offered her a small smile. "We're all good here."

Van blew out a mouthful of air. "Thank goodness. Because I need this job. Almost as much as I need for the whole town not to be talking about me." Her eyes finally lifted to his. "And as much as I need you to be my friend."

He could see the plea inside her stare. "I'll always be your friend. And nobody's going to be talking about you," he promised. Her shoulders visibly relaxed. "Come on," he said, reaching for her hand. "Let's go for a walk."

If she wanted him to be her friend, then that's what he'd be. Even if it killed him from the inside out.

He'd lost her once because of poor judgment. He wasn't planning on doing it again. He'd be her friend, her employer, whatever else she wanted him to be.

For now, that was enough. It had to be.

CHAPTER FOURTEEN

"Hey, I heard you were back in town." Tanner looked up from his phone to see a tall blond guy standing next to his table in the diner. He blinked for a moment, before recognition finally dawned. Nate Daniels hadn't changed that much, after all. His hair was thinner, his face more weathered but he'd recognize that wide smile anywhere.

He and Nate had been pretty close at school, both playing on the football team. They'd even both gone to Duke. But they'd lost touch somewhere along the way as Tanner grew his business in New York and Nate settled down back in Hartson's Creek, working for his dad's firm of local attorneys. It was strange, seeing him in a business suit instead of their old uniform of t-shirt and jeans. Or on a Friday night, their football gear.

"It's good to see you," Tanner said, standing to shake Nate's hand. "How are you doing, man?"

"Great. Working hard, playing harder." He laughed. "You're the talk of Hartson's Creek right now. My dad told me he's been working on the contracts for the drive-in."

Tanner lifted a brow. Nothing stayed secret for long, but he could have sworn his attorney was supposed to provide him with some kind of confidentiality. Not that it mattered, soon enough everybody would know. "Yeah. I guess I'm back."

"I never thought you'd leave New York." Nate sighed. "I guess we all come back in the end, right?"

"I guess so."

Nate glanced at his watch. "I gotta go. I got a meeting in ten. I just came in to grab a coffee. Hey, you fancy catching up some time? Maybe get some of the old crew together?"

"Sure." Tanner shrugged.

"Great. How about Friday night?"

"As in *this* Friday?"

"Yeah." Nate's face lit up. "It'll be like old times. The guys, the booze, the partying. How about it?"

Tanner tried to think of an excuse, but none came. "Sounds good."

"Excellent. I'll put the word out. It'll be fun. Let's meet at the Moonlight Bar at eight." He slapped Tanner on the back. "It's so great to see you, man. I feel like I'm eighteen again."

"It's great to see you, too." Tanner smiled, though the thought of feeling like he was eighteen again made him want to shiver.

Well that was his Friday night sorted. Maybe he should be happy he finally had something to do. Lots of things, if you included the drive-in, and trying to ignore the way he felt about Van Butler.

VAN WAS CLEANING out her closet when the front door slammed. She still had old clothes hanging in there – bootcut jeans that had long since gone out of fashion, along with checked shirts and sweaters that she'd never be able to wear again, thanks to the late development of her breasts. She looked up and wiped her brow with the back of her hand. The days had become warmer, any remnants of the fresh spring air blasted away by the warm Virginian sun.

"Zoe?" she called out. "That you?" Their mom had left the house earlier, saying something about a job interview. Not that Van had believed her. Who went to job interviews wearing skin tight jeans and a blouse with two many buttons unfastened?

There was no reply. Frowning, Van stood and shook her hair behind her shoulders, pulling open her bedroom door and looking into the hallway. Zoe's shoes were on the floor where she'd kicked them off, her school bag resting against the peeling wallpaper.

Van rapped softly on Zoe's bedroom door. "You okay?"

There was a grunt but nothing else. Van pushed it open, pressing her lips together when she saw her sister laying face down on the bed.

"Bad day?"

Another grunt. At least it was some kind of response.

"Sweetie?" Van said, sitting on the end of Zoe's bed. "What happened?"

"Nothing."

A half smile pulled at Van's lips. "I remember a lot of nothing happening when I was at school. It sucked."

Zoe turned over, revealing red eyes and shining skin. "Yeah, well it would suck less if I wasn't such an outcast."

"You're not an outcast. You have lots of friends." Van ignored the ache in her heart. "Did something happen?"

"No." Zoe swallowed hard. "Apart from all my friends going to see Maroon 5 without me."

"They're going to a concert?"

"Yeah." Zoe's bottom lip wobbled. "They're all going with their moms."

Of course they were. Ten-year-old girls didn't go to concerts on their own. "Didn't they think to invite you?" Van asked her.

"Their moms all know each other. They're *friends*." Zoe shrugged, trying to look nonchalant, though her red-rimmed eyes betrayed her. "Their moms don't know our mom. She's not one of their crowd. And they're all so excited. They're going out on Saturday to buy new outfits and have lunch." She took a deep breath. "I'm not invited to that either."

"I can talk to them," Van suggested, smiling at her. "See if there are any tickets left. I'll take you."

"It's sold out. And anyway, you don't know them either. It'll be lame if we tried to tag along." Zoe picked at the cotton on her bedspread. "I'll be even more of an outcast than I already am."

Van gave her a tight smile. Why was growing up so damn hard? She hated the way she couldn't fix everything for Zoe. It felt like history repeating itself. "It gets better," she said softly. "Right now, I know it feels awful. But I promise you it won't always be like this." She laid down on the bed next to Zoe, smoothing her hair out of her eyes.

"That's easy for you to say. You don't have to live here any more."

"I'm here, aren't I?" Van pointed out.

"Yeah, but you don't have to stay. You'll leave again, and I'll be left here with mom, and everybody talking about us."

"What if I don't go home?" Van asked her. "What if I stayed here and took care of you?"

Zoe's eyes widened. "What about your job?"

"I've got a job here." Van swallowed hard. "Tanner's offered me one at the drive-in."

Zoe turned on her side. The tears on her face had dried up. "Will you be selling tickets like you used to?"

"No. I'll be setting it up and running it for him."

"Wow. That's a big job." Zoe looked up at her, hope in her eyes. "Are you really going to stay?"

"Yeah," Van told her. "I'm *really* going to stay."

A smile broke out on Zoe's face, Maroon 5 completely forgotten. She rolled closer to Van, circling her arms around Van's neck. "Yay! You're staying. This is so cool."

Van hugged her back, closing her eyes for a moment. Had she really just agreed to stay?

Yeah, she had. And it was either the best idea she'd ever had, or the worst decision she'd made yet.

Right now, it could turn out to be either one.

CHAPTER FIFTEEN

*V*an scrawled her name across both duplicate contracts, sliding one into the envelope ready to hand back to Tanner, leaving the other on the table to file away later. It was almost nine o'clock on Friday night, and she and Zoe were the only ones in the house. Kim had gone out earlier, surprising Van with her blow-dried waves and freshly made up face.

"Don't wait up. I'm meeting an old friend." Kim had air kissed her, the strong aroma of her perfume with an undertone of gin lingering in Van's nose.

"You're looking better," Van had said dryly.

"Don't be mean. I'm trying to get better. You and Zoe have fun without me."

That had been two hours ago. And Van still wasn't sure if she was happy her mom was feeling better, or annoyed she'd left without even asking if Van was okay to take care of Zoe.

Though of course she was. She would have said yes anyway.

"What are you doing?" Zoe asked, walking into the kitchen in her pajamas. She opened the refrigerator and stepped back. "We have sodas," she said, glancing at Van from the corner of her eye. "And chocolate. Can I have some?"

Van nodded. "Go ahead."

Zoe grabbed a can of Coke and a Milky Way. "I love it when you go grocery shopping. You want some?"

"I'll get something in a minute. You want to watch a movie?"

"I can stay up?" Zoe popped the can and took a long sip. "First you let me drink soda and eat chocolate, and now you're not forcing me to bed before nine-thirty. Are you feeling okay?"

Van grinned. "I'm fine. I just want to spend a bit of quality time with my sister. Give me ten minutes and I'll be in. Why don't you find something good on Netflix?"

"Okay." Zoe grinned. "Maybe you can make popcorn, too."

"Maybe." Van wiggled her eyebrows.

Zoe skipped out of the kitchen right as Van's phone rang. She picked it up, frowning when she saw her mom's number.

"Hello?"

"Is this Kim's daughter?" a man's voice asked. Van felt her skin prickle up.

"Yes. Who is this, please?"

"My name's Graham. I'm sitting next to your mom at a bar. She's not feeling well right now."

Van glanced at the kitchen door. "What's wrong with her?" she asked, keeping her voice low.

"Nothing to worry about. She's just a little sick." Graham cleared his throat. "She probably shouldn't have had that last whiskey." He gave a nervous laugh. "Sorry about that."

Van closed her eyes, knowing exactly what this was. Whoever this Graham was, he'd been plying her mom with drinks, thinking she was a sure thing. "What bar are you in?"

"The Moonlight Bar in Hartson's Creek. You know it?"

"Yeah, I know it."

"I'd bring her home, but she's not in a good way." He gave an embarrassed chuckle. "I don't want people talking about me like that."

"It's okay. I'm on my way."

"Great. She's at the bar. I probably won't be here when you get here."

Of course he wouldn't. She didn't expect anything less. Apart from Craig, she'd never met a lover that didn't treat Kim like dirt.

And even Craig had at the end.

He hung up before she could reply. He'd done his duty, after all. Van would feel angry, but the phone call was more than most guys her mom hung around would do.

Sighing, she grabbed her purse and keys, and headed out to the hallway.

"Zoe?"

"Yeah?"

"Mom's sick. I need to pick her up. Let's watch that movie once I'm back, okay?"

The smile slipped from Zoe's lips. "Is she gonna be okay?"

"She'll be fine. I'll bring her back and put her to bed, then make some popcorn." Van winked at her. "Can I trust you to stay here while I'm gone?"

"Of course. Mom does it all the time."

"You have my number in your phone?"

Zoe nodded. "Yep."

"Okay. I'll be back before you know it."

"Sure." Zoe nodded. "See you in a bit." She looked calm, as though she trusted Van to make everything right. And she so wanted to do that. For Zoe and for herself.

Van shot her a tight smile and left the house, climbing into her car and slamming the door closed behind her.

She wished she had as much faith in herself as Zoe did. Because right now she wanted to slap her mom like crazy.

～

"OKAY, IT'S MY ROUND," Nate said, his legs wobbling as he pushed himself off the bar stool he was perched on. There were eight of them in all, sitting around one of the high tables at the rear of the Moonlight Bar. Tanner had only been here for an hour but he was already trying to find an excuse to leave. It turned out that once they'd finished reminiscing about school there really wasn't much to talk about, unless you wanted to hear about Nate's hernia operation or Grant Dubois' divorce.

When he'd said he was rounding up the gang, it turned out Nate meant two guys and a gaggle of the girls they'd hung around with more than ten years ago. Including Chrissie Fairfax and her friends, who all gave him a huge hug as soon as they saw him.

The girls seemed to be getting along better than the guys. Maybe because they'd kept in touch in a way the guys hadn't. They'd all drifted apart after graduation, meeting up occasionally during college vacations or when they were visiting their families in Hartson's Creek, but really there was nothing left between them.

It was the opposite to his relationship with his brothers. That had only grown stronger, even though they were living in different locations across the East Coast. Maybe blood really did call to blood.

Everybody called out their orders to Nate, who looked perturbed when Chrissie and her friend Natalie asked for Pornstar Martinis. "Those are a thing?" he asked, scratching his head.

"Yep. The best cocktails ever." Chrissie smiled at him.

Nate shook his head and wandered to the bar, leaning slightly to the left. Tanner stood and glanced at their group. "I think I'll go help him. I don't like his chances of carrying the drinks back without spilling them."

Chrissie put her hand on Tanner's forearm. "That's a great idea," she said warmly.

Gently, he pulled his arm away and walked over to where Nate was leaning on the bar, lifting one finger up as he tried to remember the order.

"Two pornstar martinis, one white wine and a Coke zero," Tanner said to Sam, biting down a smile as the grizzled barman rolled his eyes. "And four more beers, please."

Sam had put one of Gray's albums on, the low beats echoing out of the speakers fixed to the wall. Tanner tapped his fingers on the sticky bar, smiling as he remembered singing this song with his brother when they'd tried to beat Becca and Maddie at Karaoke.

For some reason the girls won. Becca still hadn't let him forget it.

"I want another drink."

Tanner looked to his left to see where the slurred words were coming from. A woman was half-sitting on a barstool, her long hair spilling out of the clip she'd fixed it in, obscuring her face. Her top was low, enough for her cleavage to be on clear display for everybody to see. Tanner pulled his eyes away.

"Nothing more for you," Sam said, pouring vodka into a stainless steel cocktail shaker, followed by champagne. "You've had enough."

"Just one more." Half her body was on the counter. If she wasn't so drunk, Tanner suspected she'd be climbing over the bar to help herself. "Come on, Sam. Just one more."

He recognized that voice. Tanner tilted his head to the side, stealing another glance. Despite the curtain of bleached hair, he knew who it was. Kimberly. Van's mom. He took a deep breath and turned toward her. "You okay?" he asked.

"Who's asking?" She tucked the curtain of hair over her shoulder and turned to look at him.

"I'm a friend of Van's." He didn't want to tell her his name. He was her landlord, after all, even if she didn't know it. This had the potential to get messy as hell.

Kim slid off the stool and tried to steady herself on the counter. Next to him, Tanner could feel the warmth of Nate's scrutiny. "Hello, friend of Van's," Kim said, her lips curling into a smile. "I don't suppose you want to buy me a drink?"

"No, I don't." Tanner folded his arms across his chest. "You should probably go home."

"Ha!" She tipped her head back, but lost her footing, tottering on her high heels. Tanner reached forward to grab her arm, steadying her.

She snapped her head around. "Don't touch me if you're not buying me a drink."

"Sam's stopped serving you."

She licked her lips, then lifted her head to stare at him. "Do I know you?"

"I'm a friend of Van's," he said again.

Her brows knitted together. "Van. Perfect Van. Don't tell her I'm here, she'll go crazy." Her words were all slurred together. He had to lean his head in to hear her properly. "Oh, you're pretty," Kim said, reaching up to trace his lips with her finger. He could smell cigarette smoke on them.

"I really think you should go home," he told her softly. "I'll walk you back."

She laughed, a glass-like tinkle that cut right through him. "No sex unless you buy me a drink." She attempted to smile. "I'm a lady."

Tanner tried not to shudder.

"Is everything okay?" Chrissie asked, walking to the bar to

join them. Her eyes widened when she realized who Tanner was talking to. "Oh, it's you," she said, looking Kim up and down. "Is she drunk?" she asked Tanner.

"Chrissie Fairfax. Johnny's favorite little girl." Kim lurched forward, only stopping herself from falling by putting her hands firmly on Tanner's chest. He gripped her forearms, looking around for somewhere he could set her. Christ, she was drunk.

If Van could see her now, she'd be mortified. He needed to get Kim home before she embarrassed herself – and her daughters – any more.

Chrissie glanced at Tanner, her eyebrows lifting. "Should we call the police?"

"You're so much like your mom, you know that?" Kim said, still swaying in spite of Tanner's hold. "I bet you're as much of a bitch, too."

Chrissie blinked. "At least she's not a drunk," she replied, her voice full of disgust.

"Yeah well," Kim said, pulling from Tanner's hold as she turned to face Chrissie. "It's a shame she can't keep a man. Your dad's slept with half the women in Hartson's Creek." Her smeared lips curled up into a satisfied smile. "No wonder your mom's such an uptight bitch."

Chrissie straightened her spine. "I'm calling the police. I shouldn't have to deal with this."

He shook his head. "No need to call anybody. I'll get her home."

"I know you, don't I?" Kim said, turning back to him, as though she'd forgotten about Chrissie. "You're Van's friend. Tanner Hartson."

His voice was graveled. "That's right."

"The boy I kept finding in bed with her." She laughed again. "And now you want to take me home."

This was excrutiating. With Chrissie on one side of him

and Nate on the other, he felt like everything he said was being scrutinized. He was acutely aware of the way Chrissie was pulling her phone out of her purse, her fingers poised and ready to call the local cops.

"That's forty-five dollars," Sam said, loading eight full glasses onto a tray in front of Nate.

"Can you take the drinks over to the table?" Tanner asked Chrissie. "Nate's bound to spill them."

She glanced from Kim and back to him. "Are you sure you're okay?"

"It's all good. Kim's going home now, aren't you?"

Chrissie picked up the tray, balancing it carefully as she stood up straight. Tanner turned to take Kim's arm again. But then she stepped forward, her hand reaching out to grab a drink from the tray Chrissie was holding. It was like watching a train wreck in double-slow motion. Kim's hand caught the lip of the tray, her shuddering movement causing it to tip up and spill the cocktails and beer all over Chrissie's cream dress.

A gasp came from the middle of the room, and Tanner felt his spine tingle as he slowly turned to see who was there.

Of course it was *her*. Standing all alone in the middle of the bar, her face pale as a sheet, her hand covering her open mouth. Tanner swallowed hard, his body responding as soon as he set eyes on her.

"Van?"

CHAPTER SIXTEEN

*I*t was like walking into a horror movie, and realizing you were the star attraction. For a moment Van froze, her eyes darting from her mom to Chrissie Fairfax, as she realized she'd arrived too late.

Her heart stopped as she saw Tanner standing there, too. He took the tray from Chrissie's hands and slid it onto the bar as the glasses crashed against each other. Chrissie's dress – cream, of course – was stained brown by the drinks Van's mom had spilled all over her.

Chrissie looked down at her soiled clothes, then back up at Kim. "You bitch, you did that on purpose."

Van's mom staggered backward, her juddery movements only halted when she stepped back against Tanner's chest.

Van swallowed hard, mortified, as they all turned to look at her.

"You saw this, right?" Chrissie asked, turning back to Tanner. "You're a witness. She just assaulted me."

"She spilled beer," Sam interjected. "It happens. I'll get you a towel."

"This is cashmere. It's ruined." Chrissie pulled at the

material around her chest. "She's going to pay for this. It cost three hundred dollars."

"Doesn't look like three hundred dollars," Kim mumbled. "It looks cheap to me."

"I'll pay for it," Tanner said, his eyes sliding to Van's again. She could see pity in them, and it hurt like hell.

"No, I'll pay." Van's feet unfroze from the floor. She walked forward, her spine straight, her jaw set. "I'll wire the money tomorrow."

"We should call the police," Chrissie said, ignoring Van completely. "She shouldn't be allowed to come out and assault people like this."

"No. No police." Van took a deep breath. "I'll take her home." She glanced over at the barman, afraid he might be calling the police himself. "Please ..."

He nodded. "Go."

"Let me help you," Tanner said, his voice so gentle it made Van's chest ache. "You can't get her home by yourself."

"My car's outside. I'm fine." She couldn't look at him. She was so afraid that if she did, she might cry. And she couldn't. Not when Chrissie Fairfax was watching her with narrow eyes.

She didn't even want to think about why Chrissie and Tanner were at the bar together. All she knew was that it hurt. Breathing in a ragged breath, she took her mom's arm. Kim turned as though she was surprised Van was still there.

"Come on, let's take you home," Van told her.

"I want an apology first." Chrissie crossed her arms over the dark stain on her dress. "Then maybe I'll think about not calling the cops."

Van's jaw tightened. "She can hardly talk."

"She could talk enough to call me a bitch. *Twice*." Chrissie shook her pretty head. "She did this on purpose. She hates me and my family." She looked at Tanner again. "You heard her."

Van squeezed her eyes shut for a moment. "Mom," she said, her voice low, "say you're sorry and we'll get out of here."

Kim rolled her eyes. "Sorry."

"You too," Chrissie said, looking straight at Van. "You're as bad as her. You hit me once when it wasn't my fault. You apologize, too."

"Let them go," Tanner said firmly. "That's history."

"Tell that to my teeth. They never recovered."

"I'm not going to apologize to you," Van said quietly. "You hurt me."

"Then I'll call the police." Chrissie lifted her phone up. "Let them sort this out."

Tanner caught Van's eye, shaking his head imperceptibly. Then his lips curled into a slow, easy smile as he turned back to Chrissie. "Why don't you go back to the table?" he said, his voice as smooth as silk. "I'll get another round. Don't let this ruin your evening."

Van wasn't sure what she hated more. The way he'd looked at her with pity, or the way he was looking at Chrissie right now. All she knew was that she had to get out of here. Before the dam that was holding her tears back was breached, and she started sobbing like a baby.

Chrissie sighed. "Okay, but keep her away from me. She's crazy."

Van slid her arm around her mom's back and slowly turned her so they were both facing the door. "Come on, let's go."

She didn't look back. Not when she was crossing the bar with her mom leaning heavily on her, and not when it took her three tries to push the door open before the warm evening air washed over them both.

It wasn't until she'd managed to sit her mom in the passenger seat and climbed into the driver's side and buckled them both in that she let the tears finally spill over.

They rolled down her cheeks as she steered the car toward their little bungalow a few streets down. As she parked, she wiped them away with the back of her hand, determined not to let Zoe see her crying.

Her mom hadn't said a word for the short journey. Kim's head was tipped back, her eyes closed, and she let out a little snore.

She was asleep, and maybe that was for the best. Van would get her to bed, make some popcorn, and hope Zoe would never feel the humiliation that Van just did.

Right now, that was the best she could do.

"CAN YOU BELIEVE THAT?" Chrissie asked when Tanner brought over a new tray of drinks. "This is my favorite dress." He passed her a cocktail and she took a large mouthful. "That family needs an intervention. Now both of them have assaulted me."

Tanner said nothing, passing the drinks around. He hadn't bothered buying himself one. He wasn't planning on staying.

"They always were low key trash," Natalie said, shaking her dark, shiny bob. "Remember the time Savannah stole my lunch?"

"She was eight years old and hungry," Tanner said tightly. He glanced at Nate, who hadn't said a word since he'd arrived back at the table. Maybe there was nothing to say. This whole evening had been a mistake. His stomach was churning like crazy. He wanted to get out of this poisonous atmosphere and breathe again.

"Yeah, well she wasn't eight when she hit Chrissie. Like mother, like daughter." Natalie smiled smugly. "I have no idea why she's back in town. She should have stayed away."

"And taken her mom with her." Chrissie laughed. "You were right, though, Tanner. We should forget about it. Sit down, let's talk about something good instead." She patted the cushioned stool beside her.

"I'm going to head home. It's been a long day." He rubbed the back of his neck with his palm. "I'll catch you all later."

"But what about your drink?" Chrissie's smile dissolved.

"I didn't buy one for me."

Her brows knitted together. "Why not?"

Because all he wanted to do was see Van. "I'm not thirsty," he said, giving them a tight smile.

"Is it because of her?" Chrissie's nose wrinkled. "I know you were friends at school, but I thought you'd grown out of that."

His jaw tightened. "I haven't grown out of anything. She's always been a friend. And now we're working together." He hadn't meant it to slip out, but Chrissie and her friends were so damn smug. He wanted to shake them up and let them see reality. "She's the best person I know."

Chrissie's mouth opened and closed, as though she couldn't think of how to respond. "Well…," she said finally. "I guess you see her differently."

"I guess I do. Good night, everybody." He didn't wait for them to reply. Grabbing his wallet and phone, he stuffed them into his pockets and walked with long strides out of the bar.

It had been a mistake to come here. He was a fool to think this town had changed. Everybody still saw Van the way they always did, making her pay for her mom's mistakes.

Yeah, well this town could go fuck itself. He was sick and tired of the injustice of it all.

~

LEAVING her mom in the car for a moment, Van ran to the front door, unlocking it and pushing it open. "Zoe?" she said softly. "Everything okay?"

For a moment, when she didn't reply, Van felt her heart hammer against her ribcage. But then she stepped into the hallway and looked through the door at the end and saw her sister curled up on the sofa, her chest rising and falling as she slept.

Thankful for small mercies, Van half-carried their mom to bed, taking her high-heeled shoes off before pulling the blanket over her, not bothering to change her clothes.

Kim could do that herself in the morning.

Then she walked back into the living room and gently shook Zoe. "Hey, sweets. You okay?" she asked, when Zoe blinked her eyes open.

"What time is it?" Zoe asked, stretching her arms. "Is Mom home?"

"She's fine. She's asleep in her room." Van checked her watch. "It's almost nine-thirty. You want to take a raincheck on the movie? Maybe we should both make it an early night."

"I'm not that tired." Zoe yawned, and Van bit down a smile.

"I know, but I am," Van lied. "Let's watch a movie tomorrow night instead."

"Maybe Mom can watch it, too." Zoe's eyes lit up. Van's heart almost broke seeing her excitement.

"Maybe." Van smiled tightly. "Good night, kiddo."

"Good night." Zoe hugged her tight, and for a moment Van felt her heart rate slow down. Zoe's hair smelled the same as Van's – she'd begged to use her shampoo that morning. But there was a sweetness there, too. Probably the soda and candy she'd indulged on earlier. Whatever it was, it smelled like peace.

She locked all the doors as Zoe brushed her teeth, and turned out the living room light. Compared to the rest of the house, Van's bedroom felt warm and inviting. She'd bought a new bedspread and pillow shams, and their pale gray and white flowers looked welcoming.

She glanced at her reflection in her bedroom mirror. How many times had she looked in this glass as a kid? She'd lean forward and scrutinize the freckles that dappled the bridge of her nose, wishing her skin was as pristine as Chrissie Fairfax's. She'd scowl at the way her hair always curled into soft waves, wishing it was as straight as her friends'. No matter how many times Tanner told her she was beautiful, she hadn't believed it.

At the age of twenty-eight she'd thought she was beyond those emotions.

And yet… her heart didn't seem to agree. It felt so small right now. Like she was still little Van Butler, Kim's kid. The one who had to go to school and scavenge food from wherever she could because her mom had forgotten to go to the grocery store. Pride had been her shield in those days. She'd always made sure she had the last laugh by pretending not to care.

But the truth was she *did* care. Too much. And now everybody would be talking about her again. How her mom was drunk in the Moonlight Bar and argued with Johnny Fairfax's girl. That she had to slur out an apology to avoid the cops being called.

Van's eyes prickled at the thought of having to walk through the town tomorrow, knowing she was at the center of the gossip. And yet she would, because that's what she did. Pretended she didn't care. Not about Chrissy or Natalie or anybody else that looked down on her mom.

Or about the way Tanner smiled at Chrissie tonight, his eyes soft and warm. Van's stomach churned at the memory.

The tears were rolling down her cheeks. Angrily, she wiped them away and turned from her reflection, grabbing her shorts and tank top from beneath her pillow to take to the bathroom. She had enough of feeling sorry for herself. She wasn't that kid anymore. It was okay, it really was.

Tap tap.

At first she thought it was Zoe or her mom knocking on her bedroom door. But then she realized the sound was coming from her window. Her breath caught in her throat as she turned, half expecting to see the police standing on the other side of the glass.

But instead it was a man. A tall one, with dark hair and thick muscles that molded the lines of his black top. Their eyes met, and for a moment she stared at him, her body flooding with emotions at the sight.

Walking over to the window, her hand shook as she unlatched the lever, pushing the pane out until the evening air rushed in.

"Hey. I saw the light in your window. I wanted to check that you're okay."

"I'm good." Maybe it was even true, because he was here and not with Chrissie Fairfax. God, it was good to see him.

"I'm sorry about what happened." He curled his fingers around the windowsill, leaning in through the open pane. "I tried to get your mom to come home... before you arrived."

Her lips curled into the hint of a smile. "Thank you for trying. I hope she didn't say anything too embarrassing to you."

"She might have mentioned all those times she found me in your bed."

Van let out a mouthful of air. "We were kids. There was

133

nothing to it." Her skin warmed at the memory of the way they'd curled up together.

"She thought I was hitting on her, too." Tanner's lip quirked up. "In case she says anything to you."

Of course she did. A wave of mortification washed over Van again. "I'm sorry. I can't imagine what she said."

"It's not your fault." His voice was soft. But it did nothing to take away the embarrassment suffusing her. She closed her eyes in attempt to stem the tears, *again*. Damn, she hated crying. She didn't want him to see her like this.

"Van, it's not." There was a certainty to his voice that she wanted to believe.

She nodded, her eyes still squeezed shut. Drawing in a ragged breath, she willed the tears to dry up, but she still felt them hot against her lids.

There was a scuffle, then Tanner was inside her room. His hand raked through his hair as he walked toward her, coming to a stop inches from where she was standing. His hot gaze caught hers, and she felt breathless, frozen to the spot as she waited for his next move.

"Come here." He wrapped his strong arms around her shoulders, his hand cupping the back of her head as he pulled her to him.

"It's okay," he said softly, as she let her face press against his chest. She could smell the warm scent of his cologne, and the clean aroma of soap. His shirt was thin enough for her to feel the hardness of his muscles against her cheek.

"It's not okay," she whispered. "It's not."

She felt him press his lips against her head. His fingers tangled in her hair, brushing the nape of her neck, and he tipped her head back until her gaze caught his.

"Don't cry. I fucking hate it when you cry."

"Me too." She gave him a watery smile. "So much."

He wiped the tears away with the pad of his thumb, his

touch leaving a trail of fire across her cheek. "Did you know your eyes change color when you have tears in them?" he whispered. "They look more green than blue."

No, she didn't. But the fact he noticed made her chest feel tight.

She was so aware of the way his body felt against hers. She could feel the denim of his jeans against her legs, the hardness of his thighs against her hips. Taking a deep breath, she blinked the last of her tears away, and he followed their trail with his eyes.

"I've stopped now."

A half smile pulled at his lips. "Good."

"Do you think she'll call the cops?"

He lifted an eyebrow. "Chrissie? Can you imagine? Officer, I'd like to report a stained dress."

For the first time since she'd gotten that phone call, Van felt like laughing. "I don't get why she hates me so much. I know I hit her when we were in school, but that was years ago. What the hell did I do to deserve all that anger?"

"She hates you because you're real," Tanner told her, his jaw tight as he stared down at her. "Because you're stronger, cleverer, and more beautiful than she is." He lowered his head until his brow touched hers. He was close, so close, and he took her breath away. "You're worth ten of her. You always were."

His words felt like a beautiful pointed knife. Cutting her in two, but in such a pleasurable way. "Tanner…" she breathed, feeling the old familiar need engulfing her.

"Shh. Don't say another word." She could feel the warm air of his breath.

"But…"

He put his finger on her lips, and she tried to swallow down a smile. She used to drive him crazy with her talking. But that's how she always thought. Out loud.

135

"Let me have this moment. I just want to look at you." He slid his nose against hers until his lips were a sigh away from her mouth. She waited, swallowing down all the words she wanted to say.

Why was he looking at her that way? What did it mean?

And why did it feel so right after all this time of hating him?

"It was always you," he whispered. "Always." He slid his hands down the curve of her spine, pressing her against him until she wasn't sure where she ended and he began. But still he didn't kiss her. She could see his eyelashes fluttering as his gaze took her in.

It was always you. Her body hummed with the truth of those words. No matter how much she tried to fight it, he'd always been there. In her failed relationships, in her career triumphs, behind her eyelids when she tried to sleep at night.

It was always Tanner she saw, with his crooked smile and warm eyes, and his total belief in her.

"The way you look at me," he whispered. "God, Van."

All her words were gone. Caught in her chest that was squeezed so tight it was a surprise she could even breathe.

It was always him. Yes it was. And no matter how much she fought that, she would always lose.

His hands tightened around her, his fingers digging into her back. "You make my heart race like nothing and no one else," he told her, closing his eyes and breathing her in.

Softly, slowly, he brushed his lips against hers, making her body sing in delight. Sliding his hand to cup the back of her head, he deepened the kiss, his lips needy and demanding, his tongue sliding against hers until they were both aching and breathless.

She looped her hands around his neck, rolling onto the balls of her feet to get closer. He walked forward, maneuvering her until the backs of her knees hit the soft surface of her mattress. Without conscious thought, they bent, until she was laying on the bed, Tanner's strong, long body hovering over hers.

Not once did they break the kiss.

She wasn't sure it was possible. Having his lips on hers felt as essential as breathing. He filled her up, emotions shooting through her chest, her stomach, her thighs.

When he finally pulled back, he looked as dazed as she felt. His eyes were bright, almost manic, his lips reddened by the friction they'd created. His hair was a glorious mess thanks to her demanding fingers, pointing this way and that. The same way it had when they were kids and he hadn't learned to tame it.

She reached up to press the craziest of his locks down. His eyes scanned her face, as though he was looking for the answer to a question he hadn't asked. She felt a jolt of electricity, along with the strangest emotion he'd brought out in her today.

Humor. God, this felt funny. Kissing Tanner Hartson after all these years. She tried to bite down the laughter, but it kept rising up, curling her lips and making her eyes crinkle.

"Are you laughing at me?" He pretended to frown.

She bit her lips together. "No."

He grinned and slid his nose against hers again. She didn't know what it was about that move, but it did something to her. Made every muscle in her body contract with the need for him.

"I think you are," he whispered, tracing a line with his finger across the bottom of her throat. "I think you find me funny."

"Not you, the situation." Another cough of laughter escaped. "One minute I'm arguing with Chrissie Fairfax, the next I'm making out with you on my childhood bed. It's like I fell asleep and woke up in 2010."

"Coming home will do that to you. Make you feel like a kid."

"Or a teenager."

His grin widened. "Touché." He kissed the corner of her lip. "Wanna make out like teenagers all night?"

She slid her hands up his back, pulling him closer. "I thought you'd never ask."

"I'm asking." He slid his hands over the swell of her behind, then pulled her against him, leaving her with no doubt of how excited he was.

"And I'm saying yes." She circled her legs around his waist, anchoring herself against him.

"Okay," he murmured, pressing his lips to hers. "Shut up and let me kiss you again."

CHAPTER SEVENTEEN

Tanner drank Van in with his eyes as she lay on her bed. Her golden hair was fanned out around her like a halo, framing her heated eyes and swollen lips. Lifting himself on the mattress, he caged her in with his arms, kissing his way up her neck, her jaw, until his lips were on hers again.

She tasted so good. Even better than he'd remembered. Her tongue was soft against his, delicately teasing him, making him harder than he'd ever felt before. Sliding her hands beneath his t-shirt, Van feathered her fingers up his skin, making him gasp against her lips.

Much more of this and he'd be in so deep he wasn't sure he'd make it to the surface again.

He needed to see her. *All* of her. Curling his fingers around her t-shirt, he tugged until her stomach was exposed, soft and smooth as he caressed it with his palms. He dipped his head down to press his lips against her skin, smiling when he heard her sigh.

Pushing her t-shirt up further, he kissed his way up her torso, until he reached the edge of her lacy bra. He glanced up, his eyes meeting hers, and she gave the smallest of nods. Her eyelids were hooded as he pulled her t-shirt off, leaving her exposed to him.

"You're beautiful." His voice was rough. Full of desire. He brushed his lips against the swell of her breast, then sucked at her nipple through the black lace of her bra. She arched her back, her breath catching in her throat, and the sound made him throb harder.

The air surrounding them changed. Hissed and fizzed like it was full of electricity. He reached up to smooth her hair back from her face, and pulled her in for another kiss.

She was as needy as him, tugging at his t-shirt until he was lifting it over his shoulders, then pressing his ridged chest to hers. She had the body of a runner. Lithe and firm, with all the right curves. Her ass was smooth and plump, and as his palms traced its contours he groaned into her mouth.

He could feel her nipples pebbling against him through the thin fabric of her bra. With tense fingers he pushed the straps down, then the cups until her breasts were exposed to him. Soft swells with hard peaks, the perfect size for his hands. He captured a nipple in his mouth and sucked hard, causing her to cry out. Damn, he loved the way she responded to him.

Their jeans were the next to go, landing in a heap beside the bed. She was naked now, apart from her panties. With his eyes on hers he slid his fingers beneath the elastic, waiting a moment until she gave an almost imperceptible nod.

"So damn sweet," he murmured against her lips.

He felt the warmth of her against his palms as he slid his hands beneath the cotton. Pressing his fingers into her smooth flesh, he felt her grind against him. Damn, he was hard. Couldn't remember the last time he felt this on edge.

How quickly he could be inside her. His body ached at the thought. He was throbbing, reacting to the steady grind of her hips and her desperate kisses. Sliding his hand down further, he traced her with the tip of his finger, feeling her warm wetness as she gasped against his lips.

When he looked at her, Tanner could see his own need reflected back at him. Her chest rose and fell rapidly, and her gaze never left his. "Please touch me," she whispered, arching her back until her body made contact with his hand again, her pelvis tilting against his palm until his fingers were sliding through to the warmest, neediest part of her.

His finger easily found the swell of her, circling until her hips reflected the rhythm. He swallowed her cries with a deep kiss as he slid two fingers inside her. She was tight and hot and everything he wanted. His thumb pressed against her clit, as he coaxed the pleasure from her. She cried out again, her thighs tightening around his arm as she soared toward the peak.

When she came it was glorious. Her body froze above him, her head tipping back, a long, low groan escaping from her lips. He held her with his free hand, the other still moving against her, heightening her pleasure. As she slowly coasted down from her high, he kissed her softly, wanting to remember this moment forever.

Her hand slid down his chest, her fingers feathering against his hard stomach. Reaching down, he captured her wrist and pulled it to his lips. "You don't need to," he said, his voice thick.

"You don't want to..." She blinked at him, her eyelids still heavy with pleasure.

He looked around her bedroom. "I don't have anything," he said softly. "And when we make love I want us to be alone. Because I intend to make you scream very loud."

She laughed. "So sure of yourself."

"That's what I like for you to think."

She slid her hands down his body, her warm hand encircling him. He squeezed his eyes shut at the sudden shot of pleasure. "At least let me help with this," she murmured in his ear.

He turned his head to capture her lips. "Are you sure?"

"I'm sure." Her grasp was just right. Enough to make his toes curl and his breath shorten. And as her palm moved against him, in a rhythm as old as time, every thought in his brain flew away, replaced by her.

Always her.

No more fears. No more vulnerability. Just the rawness of the two of them together. And when she crawled down the bed, her warm lips stretching around him, enveloping him, there was a bright flash of whiteness behind his eyes. He surged inside her, and she took every drop. And damn if that didn't make him want her even more.

SOMEONE WAS SCREECHING. No, not someone, *something*. It made her head pound, her eyes wincing as she opened them and tried to find the source of the piercing noise.

But instead of rolling onto the mattress, she felt warm, hard flesh beneath her. Tanner was still here. She smiled and poked him.

"Answer your damn phone."

"Huh?" He sat up and looked around, his eyes wide with shock. His hair was messier than it had been last night, pointing every way except the direction it was supposed to.

"Your phone," she said patiently, pointing to the cell poking out of his jeans pocket on the floor. "It's ringing."

"Who is it?"

Her lips twitched. "My mom. She wants to know why you defiled her daughter last night."

"Because her daughter's a damn temptress." He reached

out to grab the phone, bringing it close to his eyes. "It's Becca."

Van laughed. "Maybe she wants to know, too."

He shook his head and accepted the call, putting the phone to his ear. "Wassup?"

"Your car's blocking mine in. Where *are* you? Because I know you're not in your room." Her voice was loud, and Van could easily hear it.

Tanner's eyes met hers, and he smiled. "Nowhere you need to know."

"Did you hook up last night? Oh god, please tell me you're not in bed with Chrissie Fairfax."

Wasn't that a metaphorical cold bucket of water? Van sat up in bed and gave him a rueful smile before reaching for her sleep shorts and tank.

"It's none of your business. And there are a spare set of keys in my bedroom. Top drawer of the dresser."

"I looked in there and couldn't find them." Van could almost hear the eyeroll in Becca's voice. "So get your butt home and move your damn car before I lose my job."

Van pulled on her pajamas and hugged her knees to her chest, watching as Tanner rolled his legs until he was sitting up on the mattress, his feet on the floor. "I'm on my way."

"Thank you." Becca sounded gratified. "And say hello to her, whoever she is. I expect I'll hear all about it at *Chairs* on Friday."

Van went pale. Tanner shook his head and ended the call, turning to look at her.

"That was Becca."

"I know. I heard."

He nodded. "I need to get home."

"Yeah, you do. Before Becca toilet papers your room."

The corner of his lip lifted. "Don't say that. She's probably already planning on it." He reached for his t-shirt, pulling it over his head, then shuffled his legs into his jeans. "I'll go home and shower, get a change of clothes, then I'll be back to pick you up." He glanced at his phone. "Give me an hour."

"You'll pick me up?" She tipped her head to the side. "Where are we going?"

"To the drive-in. We've got the construction team arriving this morning, remember? Then this afternoon we need to talk websites and publicity."

"On a Saturday?" she asked, her eyebrow lifting.

"We're on a tight schedule." He shrugged, standing to button his jeans. "If that's okay with you."

She nodded. "It's fine." Her voice was soft. "I guess I need to shower, too. And make sure Zoe gets up okay." Her eyes shifted from his. "And I'd rather she didn't see you leave." She took a deep breath, remembering Becca's jibe. "Let's not be the topic of conversation at *Chairs* this week."

"I'll climb out of your window like a ninja." He winked, shoving his phone in his pocket.

"A really tall, loud ninja."

He grinned and leaned forward to press his lips against hers. It was unexpected yet familiar. She kissed him back, trying to ignore the way he sent her heart racing.

"Be ready in an hour," he said again, pulling away and opening her window, poised to climb out. "I'll see you later, beautiful."

CHAPTER EIGHTEEN

Van, Age 17

"Did you finish that English assignment?" Tanner was leaning on the side of the wooden box office, his arms crossed over his muscled chest. He'd been playing more football this year and it showed. The coach made them train every night, but he'd still end up at her place as the sun dipped beneath the horizon, covered in mud, his body aching from all the exercise.

"Yeah." She nodded. "I did it when the movie was on." She lifted the sheafs of paper in front of her.

"One advantage of the movie going on forever." He rolled his eyes and took her assignment from her. "How long are they gonna keep showing it? There's only so many times I can bear watching DiCaprio die."

Van's lips twitched. "It's a beautiful scene. He gives his life up for her."

"There was enough room for both of them on the door.

Nobody needed to die." He glanced up at the screen. The credits were rolling. Cars were backing out of their spaces and slowly joining the line to get out of the field. "Can't you persuade old man Chaplin to show something with more action? I'm *sick* of chick flicks."

"Titanic isn't a chick flick." She pulled out the cash drawer to count the takings. "And there's lots of action in the movie. Don't sulk because you're jealous of Leo."

"Jealous of that kid?" He shook his head. "No way."

She stacked the twenties, then the tens.

"Tanner!" someone called from a car. She looked around him to see Chrissie Fairfax hanging out of the window. "We're going to the creek. My cousin's bringing a keg. You wanna come?"

"I dunno." He shrugged. "What do you think?" he asked Van.

"I think I'm not invited," she pointed out. "And anyway, I need to get home. Check on Mom."

He turned back to Chrissie. "Not tonight."

Chrissie batted her eyelashes at him. "That's a shame. Maybe next time."

"Sure."

Van gritted her teeth and rolled the bills into cylinders, wrapping them with rubber bands. "*Sure,*" she muttered. "*Because I'm desperate for a look at your boobs.*"

"I didn't know you were into girls." He leaned closer, grinning at her. "Tell me more."

"Your girlfriend's trying to get your attention."

"What?" He looked over his shoulder.

"Call me," Chrissie shouted, lifting up her cellphone. "If you change your mind. You've got my number, right?"

"Go," Van said to him. "The two of you getting together is inevitable." She had no idea why that thought hurt, but it did.

They were growing up. Having boyfriends and girlfriends was part of that.

"I'm walking you home, remember?"

"I can get a ride off someone. Jack lives over my way."

The smile slid from his face. "You're not getting a ride from Jack."

"Why not?"

"Because he's a manwhore. He'll probably feel you up with one hand and steer with the other. I don't want you getting in any accidents. We have a plan, remember?"

She separated out the coins, putting them into separate clear bags then into the cash box. "Yeah, well maybe I want to be felt up by Jack."

Tanner leaned into the window, his brows knitting together. "What?"

Van shrugged. "I'm not a vestal virgin, Tanner. But everybody seems to treat me like that. Every time I think a guy's gonna ask me out, he always seems to back off. It's frustrating. I'm seventeen years old and I've barely kissed a guy."

"Seventeen's young."

"You're seventeen," she pointed out.

"Yeah, but I'm a guy."

"What's that got to do with it?" She locked the cash box. "Please don't tell me you have this sexist belief that girls shouldn't put out but boys should. I thought you were better than that."

He grinned. "I *am* better than that. And I'm not talking about girls, I'm talking about *you*. Imagine if you go out with a guy and then he breaks your heart. I'm gonna have to beat the crap out of him, and that could end up on my permanent record. So you keeping yourself chaste is doing me a favor. Seriously."

Her mouth dropped open. "Chaste?"

His eyes sparkled. "Virginal. Whatever."

She shook her head. "You're such a loser, you know that?"

"So they tell me." He leaned in and ruffled her hair. "Come on, Van. Let's go home."

She licked her bottom lip, her brows knitted together. Mr. Chaplin drove up in his electric cart to take the money, and their conversation was forgotten.

At least until they were halfway home. They'd walked in silence for the first part, their sneakers kicking up the dust as they passed the growing corn lining both sides of the road. The moon was low in the sky. Heavy, almost, and it cast a pale light that made everything look black and white.

"Tanner?" Van asked, looking up at him.

"Yeah?"

"Did you have something to do with Nathan breaking things off with me last month?"

He stared straight ahead, his tongue pushing against the softness of his cheek. "What makes you ask that?"

"Because I could never figure it out. One minute he was asking me to the Spring Fling, the next he was telling me he needed to concentrate on football." It had been so obvious he liked her. He'd insisted on giving her a ride home from school every day even though it was in the wrong direction. And he'd sent her flowers, too. Nobody had done that before.

Okay, so she hadn't exactly been heartbroken when he'd told her it was over. But it still stung a little. Nobody liked to be rejected.

"You dodged a bullet. Did you hear about him and Lainey Ranger? They did it last month and then he ended things with her the next day." Tanner shrugged. "He's as bad as Jack."

"He went out with Lainey Ranger?" Van stopped walking. "I didn't know that."

"It was after that party at the Fairfax's house."

"Ah. That one." She shook her head. "I guess he really

didn't like me then. He didn't need to lie about concentrating on football though." She swallowed. "Maybe I really am hideous."

"You're as far from hideous as it's possible to be." Tanner winked.

"So why didn't he want to take me to the dance?" Maybe she was more hurt than she thought. God, she hated this whole being a teenager thing. Just a few more months and they'd be graduating, and she could escape from this damn town and its gossip and expectations.

"Because he's an asshole." Tanner let out a mouthful of air. "And because I told him not to."

Her head snapped up. "What?"

"He was talking about you in the locker room and I didn't like it." Tanner eyed her warily. "Kept talking about how you were bound to put out if you were anything like your mom. So I told him not to take you to the dance."

"And he just agreed to that?"

Tanner shrugged. "I might have sweetened the deal with a threat or two."

Heat flushed through her. "Damn, Tanner. I can't believe you did that."

"I'm just looking out for you. It completely sucks, but guys talk about girls in the locker room all the time. They rate them out of ten. I don't want you to be the one they're talking about. Because I'll end up having to fight someone."

"Like I did?"

He almost smiled. "Yeah. Except when you hit Chrissie it wasn't exactly the way guys hit."

"You *are* sexist. I knew it."

"I'm not sexist. I'm a realist. And I'm not going to listen to a guy talk about you like that and not do something about it." He sighed. "So do me a favor and avoid the football team."

"It's clear they're avoiding me, not the other way around."

She tried to feel angry, but it was impossible with Tanner. And as much as she hated the way the world worked, there was truth in his words. She knew how strong he was, could see it in every movement. If he hit Nathan Daniels it would hurt him bad. And Tanner would be in big trouble. "I'm never going to be kissed, am I?"

"Of course you will. By the right guy."

"And who decides if he's right?" she asked, putting her hands on her hips. "You?"

"I know how guys think. And I know that you're not the kind of girl who wants to be thought about like that. We've got a plan, remember? We're gonna study like crazy, get into college, and get the hell out of here. You don't want to mess it up with kissing the wrong guys."

"Maybe I do. Maybe I want to be kissed and touched and shown that I'm more than Tanner's friend. More than the daughter of the town slut. Maybe I want a guy to kiss me so hard I forget my name."

The moonlight sharpened the lines of his face, highlighting the bone structure all the girls went crazy over. "Van..."

"What?"

He stopped walking, grabbing her arm to stop her, too. "You're beautiful," he told her. "You know that. And guys want you. Why wouldn't they? You're like a piece of fucking sunshine that's fallen to the ground."

She blinked. "A piece of sunshine?"

"I'm a mathematician, not a poet."

Still, the words hit her right in the chest.

He reached out to cup the side of her face, her chin tucked into his palm. "You. Are. Beautiful. And the thought of those assholes kissing you kills me."

Her breath caught in her throat, because he was staring at her in a way she'd never thought possible. Like she was the moon and the stars and everything in between. It made her legs feel weak.

"Tanner…"

"You want to be kissed?" he whispered. "Then I'll kiss you."

She said nothing. Just waited for him to start laughing and elbow her in the side. But instead he stared at her with those dark, dark eyes, his lips slightly parted. She swallowed hard, closing her eyes as his fingers caressed her skin, sending a spark of electricity down her spine.

"Do you want me to kiss you?" he asked.

She opened her mouth to answer, but fear stole her words. Because this felt real. Her skin prickled with heat, as though a slow burning fire was engulfing her body.

"Open your eyes," he said softly.

Without thinking, she obeyed, her lids slowly opening. His face was close. Enough for her to see the golden specks in his eyes and the bump on his nose from where he ran into a fence when he was nine.

Her eyes scanned him, as though she was trying to take everything in. This was Tanner. Her best friend. And yet he looked different. His jaw was stronger, more defined. He wasn't a boy anymore; he was on the cusp of being a man. A devilishly handsome man who was impossible to ignore.

"Do you?" he asked, his head dipping until his eyes were in line with hers.

"Yes." Her gaze didn't waver. She waited for him to move closer, but he paused. Enough for her blood to heat up. She was completely aware of him. Of the way he smelled of popcorn and fresh air. Of the breeze that danced through the ends of his dark hair. Of the way his chest rose and fell as he stared at her lips.

He was torturously slow as he inclined his head, then brushed his lips against hers so softly she could barely feel it.

Her stomach flipped like it was on a trampoline. Then he kissed her harder, his hand pressed against the back of her head, angling it to his. She curled her arms around his neck, arching her back as she kissed him, her body taking over as though it knew exactly what to do.

Her soft breasts pressed against his hard, firm chest, and he moaned against her lips, as though she was torturing him. His tongue was soft against her, and without hesitating, she parted them. Their tongues moved together, and another bolt of pleasure flew through her body.

Then she felt it. *Him.* Hard against her stomach. Was that what she thought it was? Dear lord, it was bigger than she'd thought.

Embarrassment mixed with desire, making her blood boil beneath her skin. Her breasts felt tender, as though a simple touch would make her cry out loud.

Tanner pulled back, cold air rushing between them, making goosebumps pepper her skin. Van blinked, trying to work out what happened. Because that kiss wasn't something a friend would do.

It was too real, too skin tingling.

"So that's your first kiss." Tanner's voice was full of grit. "You don't need to worry about Nathan Daniels now."

She ran the tip of her tongue over her lips and looked up at him. There was a twitch in his jaw, and from the corner of her eyes she could see his hands curled into fists. For a moment, in the moonlight, he didn't look like her best friend at all. He looked like a stranger.

A tall, dark, sexy stranger. The big screen hero kind she saw seven times a week.

Her heart was still racing, her blood still rushing, the bleating sound of invisible cicadas filling her ears. She felt like a door had been opened inside her, and no matter how hard she tried, she couldn't close it. It was too stubborn to move. Like her.

Breathing in softly, she straightened her back and looked toward the lights of Hartson's Creek. "I should get home," she told him, starting to walk down the road again.

And though her best friend walked beside her, it felt like he wasn't there at all. As though the kiss had killed him and left somebody completely different in his wake.

She had no idea how to deal with that at all.

CHAPTER NINETEEN

*T*anner wasn't kidding about the construction workers. He pulled his car onto the overgrown gravel track that led to the payment booth – or the box office, as Mr. Chaplin used to call it – veering to the left to park on the grass. They climbed out and walked over to where the huge construction team was standing, huddled around a man wearing jeans and a dark t-shirt, along with a yellow hard hat.

"That's Rich Kelsie," Tanner said to her, walking around the front of the car to where she was standing. "Let me introduce you."

"Sure."

From the corner of her eye she saw Tanner's arm freeze, as though he was planning to put his hand on her back but thought better of it.

"Rich, let me introduce you to Savannah Butler. She's in charge here. Savannah…" He glanced at her from the corner of his eye, as though he expected her to look mad. She grinned at the fact she was disappointing him. "This is Rich.

His team is going to landscape the drive-in and rebuild the structures."

"It's a pleasure." He reached for Van's hand, and she shook it.

"Likewise." She grinned at him. "What's the timeline for completing the project?"

"If the weather stays fine, I think we can get it done in a month." He held out his clipboard, flipping through the papers he had fixed there. "I emailed this over to Tanner last night. It just needs signing off."

Tanner nodded. "Van's in charge of the reconstruction. She'll sign off."

"Van?" Rich looked at him, confused.

"Savannah." Tanner bit down a grin. "Sorry, old habits."

"You can call me Van," she said to Rich, her grin widening when she saw Tanner's brows crinkle up. "And let me take a look at these, if that's okay. I like to know what I'm signing."

"Of course." He handed over the clipboard and Van scanned through it, occasionally looking at the area of the drive-in that day's work would take place on.

"You really think you can get it done in a month? There's a lot to do."

"Yeah. The landscaping and construction are the easy parts. The audio visual and electrical installation are going to be trickier, but we can get it done." He gave her a faint smile. "Especially since there are penalties if we don't hit the deadline."

She glanced at Tanner, who shrugged. "It's business."

Another reminder of how different he was to the boy she once knew. As if she needed it.

"Who's doing the audio visual installation?"

"We've got a subcontractor coming in from Richmond. Virginia Sound."

"I know them. They're good." She nodded and pulled a

pen from her bag, signing the statement of works before handing it back to him. "I guess you can get started," she said with a smile.

"Thank you." He nodded. "And this is your number, right? In case of any problems?"

"Yeah, but I'll be here when you are as much as possible. That way we can minimize delays if you have any questions."

"Great. Okay then," he said, clapping his hands together. "Let's get to work."

The men followed him to the construction vehicles parked on the grass, climbing inside and starting them up. She turned to Tanner, who was looking at her with a smile playing at her lips.

"A month?" she said, raising an eyebrow. "That's ambitious."

"I want it up and running. Hit the summer season. Otherwise we'll have to wait a whole year to make money from it."

"You."

"What?"

"*You'll* have to wait a year to make money from it. I'm just a salaried employee."

"You haven't read your employment contract, have you?" The ghost of a smile passed his lips.

"Of course I have. I gave you my signed copy."

"So you read section six, paragraph eight?"

He was teasing her, she could tell by the way his eyes crinkled up. "What does it say?" she asked, her voice low.

"You must know. You read it." He looked like he wanted to laugh.

"Stop it." She shook her head. "Tell me."

"It says that you own thirty percent of this land. Not in so few words. There's a lot of legalese."

She was dumbstruck for a moment. Unable to form any

words on her tongue. His eyes didn't waver from her face as he waited for her to finally say something.

"I didn't see that." Her voice trailed off. *So lame.* "What does it mean?"

"It means that a third of this whole place is yours." He threw his hand out at the field where the vehicles were driving. Somebody had already unloaded a giant lawnmower and was cutting the grass.

"I don't understand…"

"I can't expect you to do everything without getting some form of compensation."

"You're paying me."

"It's not enough."

She shook her head. "I can't accept this, Tanner. It's too much."

"You already did. You signed on the line. You want me to get it from the car and show you?" His voice was full of humor.

Her eyes shot to his. "How much did this cost you?"

"A lot less than you'd think. Old man Chaplin was desperate to get rid of it. And land around here isn't worth a whole lot." He shrugged. "Renovating it is costing more than the land itself. Then there's the running costs, but I figure we'll make a profit if we play it right."

"And if we don't?"

"Then I'm the most benevolent man in Hartson's Creek." He shrugged. "Stop looking so worried. It's peanuts."

"Not to me."

"Read the contract when you get home," he urged. "You have no liability. That's all on me. And the land itself will be leased to the company I've formed."

She let out a mouthful of air. She still couldn't work out why he'd given her thirty percent of this field. Yet there was a tingle inside her. A frisson of excitement. The construction workers weren't just remodeling a field.

They were remodeling *her* field. Thirty percent of hers if you wanted to nitpick.

"I've never owned land before."

He eyed her steadily. "I know."

She tipped her head to the side, amusement curling her lips. "So what's in this for you?"

"For me?" He raised an eyebrow. "I guess I get to have fun with my best friend again. We can sit on top of the ticket booth and watch movies together like the old times."

"You're a lot heavier than you were back then," she told him with a grin. "You might fall in."

He laughed. "Then it's your job to work with Rich to make sure the roof is reinforced."

"I guess it is." She still wasn't sure whether to laugh or hide. This was so damn crazy. It felt like something she would have thought up as a kid to tease Tanner. Yet here he was, grinning down at her, giving her something she'd never had before.

She owned land. Probably the first Butler in history to do so.

"I'll work my damn fingers off to pay you back," she told him. "I'm no charity case."

"I'm counting on it." His eyes were warm as their gazes met. "I always give my employees a stake in the business. I've learned it can make the difference between failure and success."

Okay then. So now she owned part of this earth. What the hell did she do next?

"Hey!" she called out to the man steering the lawnmower across the expanse of overgrown grass. "You missed a bit over there."

And if Tanner was grinning widely as she stomped over

to the construction team, her arms folded across her chest? Well he could do that. He was the boss, after all.

HEY, bro. I hear you didn't come home last night

Tanner sighed as he read the message from Logan, his fingers curling around his cellphone. *Damn Becca.* Nothing stayed secret around here for long. Thank god Johnny Fairfax had found a few houses for him to look at, even if they were rentals for now. The sooner he moved out the better. His family relationships depended on it.

T - I didn't realize my sex life was so interesting to you.

L - So you were having sex? Interesting ;) Which poor girl am I going to have to console this time?

T - Mind your own.

L - Oh come on. Hartson's Creek isn't that big. I either know her or know of her. Who was it?

T - Get out of here.

L - Was it Van?

Tanner stared at the question. Why the hell did his brother have to be so perceptive? Logan probably knew him better than anybody. Right now that made him feel uncomfortable as hell.

Before he could tap out a reply, his phone started to ring. Sighing, Tanner answered it.

"Van? Seriously?" Logan asked. "Didn't you learn from the last time?"

"I never said it was her."

Logan laughed. "Your silence told me all I need to know. So what's going on? Is she over what happened? Everything you did?"

The question made Tanner's stomach lurch. He leaned

back on the bed. "I don't know," he admitted. "We haven't talked about it."

"What?"

Tanner frowned. "Maybe it's better to forget it all, you know? Leave it in the past. What I did... it was bad. And I learned from it."

Logan's voice turned gentle. "You've been paying for it for years, bro. I still remember the day you called me from Duke. You were broken, she was broken... and all because neither of you knew how to talk to each other." Logan sighed. "I hated hearing you like that."

"Is that why you drove down from Boston to see me?" The ghost of a smile pulled at Tanner's lips. The one enduring thing in his life were his brothers. And when everything had got messed up, he knew that any one of them would have dropped everything to help him. But with Gray taking the music world by storm, and Cam neck deep in the football season, it had been Logan he'd turned to.

"Yeah, that's why I turned up at your dorm room at the asscrack of dawn," Logan said, humor in his voice. "We were worried about you. You and Van... man, you were like twins." He chuckled. "And as much as Cam drives me crazy, I can't imagine life without him."

"Yeah, well apparently life still went on."

"But did you?"

Tanner frowned. "What do you mean?"

"Nothing," Logan said quickly. "Ignore me. I'm grumpy because two of my staff quit today. And the guy who supplies my meat decided to run off with another restaurant owner without making sure I'm stocked up." Logan sighed.

"Come on. You obviously meant something. I want to know." Tanner leaned forward, resting his elbows on his knees.

"We're all messed up in our own ways," Logan said, his

voice quiet. "Look at Gray and Dad, constantly at each others' throats. And there's Cam who only seems to come to life on the football field." He let out a sigh. "You and me, we deal with the crap life throws at us by being workaholics. For the past five years whenever I've spoken to you, you were either at work, coming home from work, or heading there. And I get it, man, I do. Because I do the same. Work is safe. It's our haven. It doesn't hurt us, and we can't hurt it."

"You think I work hard because I'm avoiding emotion?" Tanner shook his head. "That's bull. It's just the way we were brought up."

"I'm just saying it like I see it. Mom's death was like an explosion in our lives. There was before and there was after. Two completely different lives. And there's a part of us that's desperate to have the before again, but its scary as hell. So we bury our heads in work and cling to the after."

Tanner was quiet for a moment, his brows pulled together as he pondered his brother's words. "Logan?" he asked.

"Yeah?"

"Have you gone to therapy?"

Logan coughed, though it sounded suspiciously like a laugh. "I might have."

"Did it help?" Tanner was curious now. He remembered his own experience with therapy as a child. It was scary and made him want to run away.

"It did. For a bit. And then I stopped going." Logan sounded sheepish. "Because work got too busy."

Tanner laughed, because it was so damn typical of his brother. But at least he'd tried. "I love you, bro."

"Ah, stop it with the emotional crap. Tell me, how is the whole employer employee thing going with Van?"

"It's only been a couple of days. But it's fine."

"So it's not just business? Oh boy." Another whistle.

"I don't know what it is," Tanner admitted.

"Well, you need to work it out. Because work, friendships, and relationships don't mix. Ask me how I know."

"I don't need to ask. I know your track record. How did Cam describe it?" Tanner mused, running a finger along his jaw. "Sleeping his way through the wait staff, was it?"

"Three girlfriends," Logan said. "*Three*. And I made sure they weren't kitchen staff."

Tanner laughed. "And you're trying to give me relationship advice?"

"I'm trying to protect you, because you're my little brother and I love you."

"Who's being emotional now?" Tanner's throat was tight, his breath captured inside.

"I'm telling you the truth, bro. Something that not many people do. When everything went down with you and Van, it broke you. And I've watched you fight against that brokenness, the same way you did when Mom died. If this thing… whatever it is… between you and Van implodes again, I'm not sure you'll make it."

The tightness in his throat felt like more of a chokehold. Tanner took a ragged breath in, feeling the oxygen inflate his lungs. "I'm not going to mess things up this time." He couldn't. Because Logan was right, he'd lost too much already. His mom, Van, the life he always thought they'd have. She was his best friend, his permanent companion, and then she was gone.

Just like his mom.

Logan laughed. "Take it easy. And don't do anything stupid."

"I won't." Tanner ended the call, letting his head fall back against the padded board behind his bed.

Logan was right. He'd spent most of his life avoiding the

kind of pain he'd felt the night his mom died. And then when things went south with Van, it had come back tenfold.

But not this time. He was older, wiser, and more determined. And since he couldn't hide himself in work, he'd bury himself in Savannah Butler instead.

CHAPTER TWENTY

Tanner, Age 17

IT HAD BEEN two weeks since their kiss. She'd been avoiding him, and maybe he'd been avoiding her, too, because the awkwardness between them was palpable. On the night after the kiss he'd turned up at the drive-in to walk her home, only to find she'd left an hour earlier with a headache.

Even his brothers had noticed he was quieter than usual. Cam had caught him after football yesterday and walked home with him, obviously primed by Aunt Gina to ask Tanner if there was something wrong. And for a moment Tanner had thought about telling him.

But this was Cam, and if he told him, then soon Logan would know and neither of them would ever let him hear the end of it. They'd tease Van, too, and it would drive her crazy.

Better to keep quiet and wait for everything to go back to normal.

"Hey, Hartson, you coming or what?" Brad Wilshaw asked him. Like Tanner, he played defence.

Tanner looked up from his bag, stuffed with his dirty practice clothes. "Yeah." He zipped it up and slung it over his shoulder, turning his back on the slatted bench that always smelled of sweat, no matter how many times the janitor scrubbed it.

"We're heading over to the diner. Some of the girls are meeting us. You wanna join?"

He thought about Van, who was probably at home working on the English assignment Mr. Draycott had given them today.

"Sure," he said. "Sounds good."

"Great. I'll give you a ride."

Everybody knew Tanner was still saving for his first car. Like his brothers before him, their dad had refused to give him a penny toward it, so he was working weekends at the hardware store. He'd put a downpayment on a rusty old Camaro, but he still had at least three months before he could pay it off.

The two of them walked out to the parking lot. "So, I heard your brother's new single the other day," Brad said, sliding into the driver's seat. "It was pretty sweet."

"Thanks." Tanner was still getting used to the fact that Gray had left town and signed a record contract in L.A.. "I'll let him know."

"You think he'll ever come back here?"

"No idea."

Brad shrugged. "Can't blame him if he doesn't. This town's a shithole. I can't wait for college."

College. Another reason why Tanner needed to get up the guts and actually talk to Van. They were both planning to go to Duke University in the fall, and there was no way he wanted this awkwardness there.

"So anyway, you decide who you're taking to the prom?" Brad looked over his shoulder and reversed out of the space.

"Haven't thought about it." It was the truth. He and Van had always laughed at how seriously everybody took Senior Prom. They'd even talked about doing a Carrie-style prank.

"I hear Chrissie Fairfax wants you to take her."

"Right."

"I… ah… was thinking of asking Savannah Butler." Brad shifted the car into drive, glancing at Tanner from the corner of his eye. "If it's cool with you."

"Why wouldn't it be?"

"She's your friend." Brad shrugged. "And I know you didn't like Nate going out with her."

"Nate's a dog."

Brad laughed. "No argument there." The car pulled onto the road into town. "But seriously, I won't hurt her. I just want to take her out, that's all. She's a cool girl."

"Yeah, she is." Tanner stared right ahead. "And too good for you."

"I won't ask her if you don't like it. Bros before…" Brad trailed off before he could say it. "Well, you know."

"Why wouldn't I like it?"

"Nate thinks you like her. As in actually *like* her. I told him he's talking crap."

Tanner felt a shiver snake down his spine. "Yeah, well he is." He frowned. "She's my friend, that's all."

"So you don't mind if I ask her?"

Tanner opened his mouth to say he minded like crap, but then he closed it again. Because Brad *was* one of the good ones. And Van was already pissed at him for telling Nate to back off. He didn't want to upset her again.

"I don't mind."

Maybe she'd say no. He let that thought warm him for a moment.

"Great. I'll ask her tomorrow." Brad's grin was wide. "Thanks, man."

"Sure."

At least Brad wouldn't get her first kiss. That would always be Tanner's. He ran the pad of his finger along his bottom lip, remembering how good her mouth had felt against his.

"And you should ask Chrissie. Maybe we could even go together," Brad said, pulling into the town square. "We could go in together for a limo or something."

"Sounds good."

As soon as Brad pulled into a space outside Murphy's Diner, Tanner opened the door, climbing out of there like the car was on fire.

His body felt weird. Like every muscle inside of him was coiled up tight, and the only way to get some relief was to hit something.

Or someone.

Watching Brad swagger into the diner like he was king of the damn hill made him realize exactly who he wanted to hit.

But he had a plan. And getting suspended from school for fighting another student didn't figure in it all.

Damn, he hated this. As far as he was concerned, graduation couldn't come fast enough.

CHAPTER TWENTY-ONE

*V*an crossed her arms and looked at the field in front of her. It was a complete mess right now. Where grass had once grown was overturned earth criss-crossed with deep tracks thanks to the heavy construction vehicles the team was using. But even through the devastation, she could see things starting to take shape. The screen was half-constructed, along with the building to the left that would house the refreshment stand on the ground floor, and an office above it for the general manager.

For her. It was still strange to think that. It was like a circle that was finally closing itself. She was back here, in Hartson's Creek, working at the drive in. And at night she lay in Tanner Hartson's arms.

"I got a couple of things for you to sign off on," Rich called out when he spotted her. "The audio visual equipment should arrive next week, so we're concentrating on the screen and the projection room. Once that's all in we can work on the field and finish the buildings. You okay with that?"

She was impressed at how much was getting done. Not

that it surprised her. She'd seen how much Tanner was paying Rich's construction company for such a short deadline. He really was keen on getting this up and running.

"I'm good with that. Is everything still going to plan?"

"Yes, ma'am. No glitches so far. Even the rain two nights ago didn't cause any problems. And I've checked the forecast for next week, it should all be good."

"So the completion date is still achieveable?" she asked him.

"Yes. For sure."

Van nodded, her lips pressed together. She and Tanner had already agreed that Saturday July fifth would make the perfect opening date. It was a holiday weekend, everybody would be in a party mood, and she had just enough time to organize an opening gala before they showed the movie. Hopefully that should get them some publicity and bring the movie-lovers out.

She'd held off sending out invitations until she checked with Rich. She'd been burned too many times planning events like this. But she knew Virginia summers. They were hot and humid, with only the occasional storm that passed almost as soon as it arrived. It would rain thick and heavy for an hour at the most, then the sun would come out and dry it all up again.

If the construction was finished on time, that gave them some leeway to have a rehearsal where they could run all the systems and the refreshments, inviting a few friends to try the drive-in out, before the gala. She made a quick calculation. They could have the rehearsal the weekend before the opening. That would give them a week to iron out any issues.

"Oh, hey, Tanner," Rich said, looking over her shoulder. Van felt her skin warm up, the way it always did when he was around. She turned to see him walking up the field, his jeans low, his t-shirt tight against his muscles, with a blue football cap pulled low over his thick hair.

Her stomach gave a tug as he smiled at her, his eyes crinkling. It felt new and old at the same time. She smiled back, glancing carefully at Rich, hoping he didn't know what was going on between her and Tanner.

Right now she was happy keeping things on the down low. Gossip still hadn't died down about her mom's appearance at the Moonlight Bar, and she certainly didn't plan on adding any fuel to the fire.

Her relationship with Tanner wasn't anyone's business. It was too precious to be tainted by wagging tongues. Too new for her to do anything but protect it. Even if she did want to go and shout about it to everybody, she was too busy anyway. With the drive-in, Zoe, and Tanner, of course. The perfect triumvirate.

Tanner skimmed his fingers across the top of her bare arm, then reached forward to shake Rich's hand. Even that briefest of touches was enough for the goosebumps to rise on her skin. Van swallowed hard, trying to slow her heart down. Why was it so difficult to keep a poker face?

"Everything under control?" Tanner asked.

"All good. I was just telling Van about the audio visual installation next week. Once that's done, we have a couple of weeks to finish up the parking area, buildings, and the playground. We should be good to go by completion day." Rich shrugged. "Of course it does mean working weekends."

Tanner lifted a brow. "Whatever it takes." He gave Rich a nod then turned to Van. "You got time for a meeting?" he asked her. "I have lunch in the truck. I thought we could go over the opening plans while we eat."

"Sure." Van nodded. "Let me sign these papers and I'll be with you."

Five minutes later, she was climbing into Tanner's rental

car, an oversized beast of a truck that probably ate fifty gallons of gas for breakfast. He was still trying to decide which new car to buy, since he'd had to give up his old one when he sold the company in New York. "I see your taste in cars hasn't improved," she said, biting down on her lip as he started up the engine.

"What do you mean?" he asked, his brows knitting together.

She looked around the interior. "This is pretty much a penis extension in vehicular form," she told him, grinning at his raised eyebrow. "And I have to tell you, you don't need one."

He grinned. "This was all they had left in its class. I'll get something better soon. And for what it's worth, you used to love my old Camaro."

"I loved the way it meant I didn't have to walk to school or the drive-in anymore," Van told him, remembering the rusty orange sportscar with a smile. "But it stank like ditch water and was so unreliable."

"I have a lot of good memories from that car." Tanner pulled out into the main road. "A few of them with you."

Her face heated up as she remembered prom night. They'd both gone with other people, though the four of them had traveled in the same limo. One paid for by her date, Brad. They hadn't gone home together, though. After a few drunken fumbles, Brad had finally gotten the message that she wasn't planning on giving him her virginity on prom night, no matter how much he'd paid for the limo. He'd gone off in a huff, leaving her without a ride home.

"Remember prom night?" Van murmured, as Tanner pulled onto a dirt road. The same one his Camaro had juddered along as they drove to the overlook together. Him in the black dinner suit he'd inherited from Logan, who'd inherited it from Gray. Van in one of her mom's more demure dresses, that somehow looked anything but demure when Van put it on.

"Yeah, I remember." Tanner nodded. "I hadn't wanted to go at all."

Van blinked. "So why did you?"

"Because Brad Wilshaw told me he was taking you. I wanted to be there to make sure he didn't take advantage of you."

"Yeah, well he tried."

"It's a good thing I went then," Tanner said simply.

"What happened between you and Chrissie that night?" Van asked. "One minute you were dancing, the next she wasn't talking to you anymore."

"Nothing." He pulled up next to a tree. The outlook was empty. From here you could see all of Hartson's Creek, from the sparkling blue water that gave the town its name, to the vibrant green grass of the town square and the glinting white roof of the First Baptist Church.

"I thought you liked her."

"Yeah, I kind of did. But it turned out, there was somebody I liked more." His eyes met hers, and she felt her chest tighten.

"Is that why you didn't get a ride home with her?"

"She offered me a ride. I asked if you could come, too. She told me to choose between her and you." Tanner shrugged. "There was no competition. It was always you."

Those words again. They warmed her and made her afraid at the same time. If it was always her, what had happened over the past ten years?

"It was sweet, the way you made me wait at the school so you could run home and get your car."

"I didn't want you to ruin those shoes you were wearing." He winked at her. "They were hot." He cleared his throat, a smile lifting his lips. "I also had an ulterior motive. I wanted to get you up here and I couldn't do that without a car."

The air was sparking between them. Despite the cold blast of the air conditioning, her body felt overheated as she remembered that night. Their second kiss. Less fumbling this time. More sure. They'd lain on the grass together, looking up at the stars sparkling in the dark sky. Then he'd touched her, until she saw stars behind her eyes, swallowing her cries with his warm, wanting mouth.

"Is that why you've brought us up here now?"

He grinned. "I really do want to talk to you about the drive-in," he told her. "But I also don't know if I can talk to you without kissing you, and I figure you don't want Rich and his crew seeing that."

The way he was looking at her made her stomach do a flip. Intense, dark, needy. "I don't," she said softly. "I hate it when people talk about me. About us. This thing that's happening between us." She gestured at the space between them. "I want it to stay between us. And I'm grateful that you're thinking of my needs."

"I know you," he said, a half-smile pulling at the corner of his mouth. "I know how you think. And though I want to go and shout about you to the world, I'll take this at your pace."

"Even if it means playing it cool in front of everybody else?"

"I hid my feelings for you for years," he said, biting down a grin. "I can do it for a few more weeks." He leaned forward to brush his lips against hers. "At least in public."

She curled her hand around his neck, sighing softly as he deepened the kiss. "I just don't want people judging me. They'll say you gave me this job because I'm sleeping with you."

"They're not as judgmental as you think." He brushed the

hair from her face, his fingers lingering on her jaw. "You're not your mom, Van."

"That's not how they'd see it." She closed her eyes as he leaned in to kiss her neck, his mouth sending tingles down her spine. "Like mother like daughter. The town sluts."

"Anybody calls you that, I'll make sure they can't speak again." His voice was low.

She laughed at his words. "You're my hero, you know that?"

"I'll be whatever you want me to be," he told her. "But I need you to know this is serious. I want you in my life and in my bed, Van. No messing about, no mixed messages. This is it for me."

His gaze was deadly serious. Her breath caught at his intensity. "I feel the same. Just give me some time to get used to it."

"Okay." He nodded. "Agreed."

"And in the meantime, we can sneak around like teenagers," she said, grinning. "And make out in cars." She cupped his jaw with her hands, brushing her lips against his. He kissed her back, hot and hard until they were both breathless.

"Sounds good to me."

CHAPTER TWENTY-TWO

"Van! Hey!" Maddie Clark walked out of the diner kitchen, waving at Van as she leaned on the counter. "How are you? And your sister? Is she okay?" She walked along the counter and picked up the coffee carafe. "You want some?" she asked. "It's decaf, I'm afraid. Murphy messed up the real stuff."

"Sure." Van watched, amused, as Maddie filled up two mugs with the bitter liquid, then put them on the counter along with a few containers of creamer and a container of sugar. Then she walked around and sat on the stool next to Van's.

"Maddie Clark, how many times have I told you not to help yourself to my coffee," Murphy, the diner's owner, grumbled as he shook his head at her cup. "You don't work here anymore, remember?"

"I was saving you the hassle. I hear Cora Jean's not feeling well." Maddie shrugged. "And I did say hello."

"Well unless you want to put an apron on and run a shift, I suggest you stay on that side of the counter."

Maddie blew him a kiss. "I miss you like crazy, Murph,

but I'm never working for you again. You're too bad humored."

"Humph." He shook his head and walked back into the kitchen, the door swinging shut behind him.

"He loves me really," Maddie told Van. "Even if he doesn't show it."

"I didn't know you used to work here," Van said, taking a sip of coffee.

"Yeah, before Gray and I met." Maddie grinned. "Well after, I guess, since we met when I was a kid. But this was where we met for the second time."

"Right." Van didn't try to hide her confusion.

Maddie laughed. "Sorry, I'm talking too much. Gray's been in the studio all week and I've had nobody to talk to. That's why I came to see Murphy, but then I remembered that he doesn't talk much." She shook her head and put her hand on Van's wrist. "Am I holding you up? Do you have somewhere to be?"

"Only the drive-in. But I can stay and drink this coffee. It's good, by the way."

"I forgot you were working with Tanner." Maddie lowered her voice. "How's that going? If he's anything like Gray, he's making you work all the hours god sends."

"I'm enjoying it," Van admitted, smiling at the petite brunette. "I'm busier than I've ever been, but it's really starting to come together." And yeah, she was enjoying being with Tanner, too. Even though when they were at the drive-in he kept his promise and was all about business.

When he climbed through her window at night, though, he was anything but.

"I can't wait to see it when it's done." Maddie clapped her hands together. "I'm so excited about making out with Gray at the movies. It'll be like I'm a teenager again."

Van laughed. "A lot of people have said that to me. It's

making everybody around here nostalgic. How about you? And how's Gray?"

"I love him to death, but he's such a damn perfectionist. He's been recording the same song for a week, and keeps asking me to listen to the latest version so I can hear the difference." Maddie leaned forward. "And I have to lie and say I do, because it's exactly the same."

"Is this a new album?"

Maddie nodded. "Yeah. And I think the pressure's got to him. He said the last one wrote itself, but this one..." She sighed and shook her head.

"Wasn't the last one about you?"

"Apparently." Maddie grinned. "Anyway, I was wondering if you're free on Sunday? We're having everybody over to watch the documentary about Cam's team. You and Zoe are invited, and your mom if she's free." She glanced at Van from the corner of her eye. "And Tanner will be there, of course."

She could imagine Zoe's excitement at visiting Gray Hartson's house. Okay, so he probably came below Adam Levine, but he was still a huge rockstar.

"I didn't know Cam was in a documentary."

"It's one of those Netflix ones. They followed his team around for all of last year. I was hoping he could come and join us, but he's having to do publicity for it. So the next best thing is that we all watch and give him hell over the phone."

Van laughed. She could just imagine the ribbing Cam's brothers would give him. "That sounds like fun. Zoe and I will be there. I'm not sure it's my mom's kind of thing though."

"No worries. And if she changes her mind, feel free to bring her. We'll be cooking up a feast, since Logan will be there." Maddie smiled warmly at her.

"I guess I'd better go," Van said, finishing her coffee.

"Thanks for this," she said, lifting the mug. "How much do I owe you?"

"It's on me." Maddie told her. "Or on Murphy, technically. I'll see you Sunday."

Yeah, she would. And Van wasn't sure why that made her body feel all warm and gooey inside, like chocolate left on the window sill on a warm Virginia day.

She stepped outside the diner, glancing at Fairfax Realty across the bright green of the town square, and took a deep breath.

Maybe it was the fact that some people in town accepted her and wanted to spend time with her.

This place was starting to feel like home again.

"Stop staring at her," Logan murmured. "Unless you want everybody to guess what's going on." He'd flown down from Boston the previous night, and the three of them – Tanner, Gray, and Logan – had spend yesterday evening at the Moonlight Bar, catching up and shooting pool.

While Gray had been buying his round, Logan had taken the opportunity to ask Tanner how it was going with him and Van. He'd caught him up quickly. They were together, but trying to keep it on the downlow.

That was easier said than done now that he was sitting on the sofa in Gray's beautiful den, following Van's every move. She was looking hot today, in a little pink-and-grey checked sleeveless dress, tight on all her curves and stopping at mid thigh, her golden waves tumbling over her bare shoulders.

"I'm not staring," Tanner told him. "I'm just looking around, taking everything in."

"You're right. You're not staring. You're ogling. And

possibly panting." Logan grinned. "Damn, have you even had sex with her yet?"

"Not that it's any of your business, but no," he said, his voice short.

Logan raised an eyebrow. "No?"

Truth was, they'd done everything *but* sex, and right now that felt pretty good. Especially since neither of them had their own place – something he was working pretty hard on resolving. And the sleeping was awesome. He'd curl up behind her and she'd curl her back against his chest, his arms wrapped around her like he was her human shield. He slept so deep his alarm barely woke them in the morning. It was as though his body was finally able to relax after all this time.

But today he didn't feel relaxed. He felt excited and needy and full of desire. Every time she walked past him while they were sitting watching the movie, he'd wanted to reach out and slide his hand up her leg.

She knew exactly the effect she was having on him. Now and then their eyes would meet, and her lips would curl up, her face flushing. And he'd swallow down the urge to stand up and tell everybody that this gorgeous, funny, beautiful woman was his.

She was talking to Maddie right now, the two of them laughing at something Van just said. Her eyes caught his for the hundredth time. Then she touched Maddie's arm briefly, and walked through the open glass doors to the expansive deck Gray had built, leading to the wide grass lawn, and the wooden bar stocked with every flavor of liquor and beer.

"I'm going to grab another drink," Tanner said, standing.

"Sure you are." Logan smirked, and turned back to the TV, where the first game of last season was flickering on the screen.

Tanner shook his head and followed Van's path through the doors and down the lawn to the wooden tiki bar. She poured a glass of soda, throwing some ice into the mix, completely oblivious to the fact he was a few feet away from her.

"I need to talk to you." He kept his face impassive.

Her head shot up. "Jeez, you scared me." Her lips curled into a smile. "Hey you. What do you want to talk about?"

"Not here," he said, curling his fingers around her wrist. "Somewhere private."

Her eyes widened. "Is something wrong?"

"Yeah." He pulled her around the back of the bar, toward the copse of trees that had been there long before Gray had built his house. When they were in the center, he checked to see that nobody else was there, then pushed Van's back against a thick trunk.

"What is it?"

"This dress," he murmured, tracing the line of the bodice across her chest. "It's very, very wrong."

Her breath caught in her throat as he lowered his head to kiss the swell of her breasts, where they met the top of her dress.

"As your employer, I'm going to have to issue you a formal warning. Don't wear this dress and expect me not to kiss you."

She laughed as he slid his lips toward the dip in her throat. "I'd like to appeal that warning."

He curled his hand around her bare thigh, the way he'd been dreaming about all afternoon. "No appeals," he murmured. "Though you can beg if you really want."

Her eyes sparkled as he kissed his way up her neck, along her jaw, pressing his mouth to the corner of her lips. She tipped her head back against the tree, letting out a soft moan as his lips met hers, his fingers brushing the tender skin of her inner-thigh.

"Do you know what you do to me?" he asked, tracing the

edge of her panties. "All afternoon I've been looking at you. Thinking about how you taste."

"I know." She grinned. "I've been kind of enjoying it."

He slid his hands over her hips, pulling her against his thighs until she was under no illusion how hot she made him. "Did you wear this dress to tease me?"

She shrugged. "I might have."

"Wear it tonight. In bed. I want to peel it off you."

"Who says you're coming to my bed tonight?"

He blinked, his eyes meeting hers. "That wasn't a request. Don't forget you're under disciplinary review."

She tipped her head to the side, her eyes still on his. "Discipline, hmm?"

He grinned, sliding his hand behind her butt. She arched her back, pressing herself to him, and the sensation sent a shot of desire through him.

"Careful," he warned her. He wasn't sure how far his restraint could stretch.

"Maybe I don't want to be careful."

He gave her a crooked smile. "You do, I know you do. Even if I want to drag you out and shout to the world that you're mine."

"Is that what I am? Yours?"

"Yeah." His voice was rough. "You are."

She traced a line from his open collar, up his neck, to his hard jaw. "That makes you mine, too."

Damn, he loved that. He swallowed hard, as she traced his bottom lip. "It does." He kissed the pad of her finger.

Her smile widened. "And that means I can do what I want with you, right?"

"Right."

"Great." She leaned closer, until he could feel the warmth of her breath against his skin. He waited for her to close the gap, to press her lips to his.

But instead she pushed him away, laughing as she dodged around the trees into the open lawn. Then she turned and stuck her tongue out at him, the way she did when they were kids.

He chuckled, not just because she was funny as hell. But because it was so damn good to see her carefree, running with her golden hair flowing out, her eyes crinkled with humor.

She was his. Maybe she always had been. All he knew was he couldn't let her go again.

"Okay, so there's another reason why I asked you all to come here today," Gray said when the documentary was over, and they'd finished raising their glasses to Cam. They were all sitting in the soft leather chairs Gray and Maddie had custom-made for their over-size den. They were big enough to fit three families on, which was a good thing, because there were a lot of them. Van looked around with a smile, taking in Tanner's dad and Aunt Gina, plus his brothers, along with Maddie, her mom, and her sister and her family. Then there was Becca, who was sitting with Zoe, trying to teach her how to do a cat's cradle.

Van couldn't remember the last time she'd felt this content. And her happiness had an enticing edge to it, thanks to the way Tanner kept shooting dark looks over at her.

It was strange how easily she'd slipped back into this life, this family.

"Don't tell me. You're getting your star on the Hollywood Walk of Fame," Logan said, grinning at his older brother.

Gray sighed. "No. And shut up."

"Play nice," Maddie said, smiling at them both. "Just tell them, Gray."

"C'mere," Gray said, holding his hand out to her. "I don't want to do this alone."

"What's this about?" Aunt Gina said, frowning. "You're not going to tell us she's pregnant, are you?"

For a moment there was complete silence, as everybody took in Gray and Maddie's expressions.

Gray cleared his throat, his eyes meeting Maddie's. "Uh, yeah. We were."

Tanner coughed down a laugh, as Aunt Gina's face turned white, and she covered her gaping mouth with her hand. "Oh my," she said, her voice muffled. "I'm so sorry. I never dreamed…"

"You're pregnant?" Becca asked, her eyes wide. "As in having Gray's baby?" She stood up and ran to hug them both. "I'm going to be an auntie."

"Congratulations, man," Logan said, then he walked over to give Aung Gina a hug. She was all jittery, a combination of embarassment and excitement.

"Way to go," Tanner said, walking over to shake Gray's hand and hug Maddie. "I'm so pleased for you both."

"That'll explain the decaf coffee," Van said, joining them. She grinned at Maddie.

"Yeah. I didn't make it because it tastes good, that's for sure." Maddie wrinkled her nose. "I miss caffeine."

Van felt a finger trace her spine. She turned to Tanner, who gave her an innocent stare.

"Stop," she mouthed.

He winked back at her.

"Let's hope your pregnancy doesn't last as long as Regan's," Becca said, looking at Maddie's stomach as though she was trying to discern a bump. "I swear she's got the gestation period of an elephant. Is she ever going to have that baby?"

"It probably likes it where it is," Maddie murmured. "It's

quiet and safe, compared to her house. I visited the other day. Her kids are louder than one of Gray's concerts."

"How far along are you?" Maddie's sister, Ashleigh asked. Van had been introduced to her when she arrived at Gray's house, though she remembered her from the old days. She didn't look much different, apart from the wrinkles and the fact she wasn't constantly wearing a cheerleader outfit.

Okay, so that was a bitchy thought. But then again, Ashleigh had never been nice to Van, either.

"Sixteen weeks," Maddie said, her face glowing.

"So there'll be a baby in five months?" Becca was almost shaking with excitement. "We have so much to plan. Where do you want your baby shower? What nursery theme are you going to have?" Her eyes lit up. "Have you started a registry yet? It's never too early."

"Becca," Tanner said, his voice deadpan. He put his hand on her shoulder.

"Yeah?" Becca sighed and looked up at him.

"This isn't your baby. It's Maddie and Gray's."

Becca shook her head. "You're such a spoilsport. Have you thought about going back to New York?"

"Not really." He smirked, and his eyes slid to Van's again. "I like it here too much."

"Is that why you sneak out of the house every night once we're all in bed?" Becca asked him.

Tanner shot her a dirty look. So much for sibling support.

"You sneak out of the house?" Gray asked. "Where are you going?"

"Or who is he going to?" Becca said, lifting a brow.

Maddie looked at Van, and she felt her face flush. She knew. Or at least, she'd guessed. Van could tell by the expression on Maddie's face.

"Why are you so interested in Tanner's love life?" Logan

asked, shaking his head at Becca. "Is it because you don't have one?"

"I don't have a love life because I have four brothers," Becca told them. "Everybody in town is scared of you. It's so damn annoying."

"Maybe that's why they call them the Heartbreak Brothers," Van said, smiling at her.

"Did they do that to you, too?"

"All the time. Tanner pretty much scared off every guy who asked me out."

"Isn't it annoying?" Becca said, crossing her arms over her chest.

"Hey, I didn't scare off Simon," Tanner protested, lifting a brow at Becca. "You did that all by yourself."

"I didn't scare him off. I broke it off. That's different."

"Yeah, well he wasn't good enough for you anyway." Tanner blew Becca a kiss.

"You see what I have to deal with?" Becca sighed. "Maybe you can invite a movie star or two to the opening of the drive-in. Preferably one with ripped abs who isn't scared of a few brothers."

"When are you planning on opening?" Gray asked Tanner. "Do you have a date?"

"Yeah." Tanner nodded. "We're having the opening in three weeks. Saturday July fifth. We figured we may as well cash in on a holiday weekend. You'll all be getting an invitation from Van very soon."

"I can't wait." Becca smiled at them both. "This is such a good year. With the baby and the drive-in. Plus Cam's team is looking hot. It's so good to have you all home." She tipped her head and lifted a brow at Tanner. "Except for you."

"I know you love me."

Van felt a tug at her hand, and she turned to see Zoe standing next to her.

"You okay, kiddo?" she asked.

Zoe nodded, then she leaned closer. "Van?"

"Yeah?"

"Will I be able to come to the opening night at the drive-in?" Her eyes were wide. *Hopeful.*

Van glanced at Tanner and he nodded imperceptibly. "Of course you can."

"And can I bring my friends? They'll be so jealous that you work there. And they'll love me for inviting them."

"You can bring whoever you want," Tanner told her. Then he tipped his head to the side. "Or even better, why don't you invite them all to the rehearsal? That way we can have a test audience to make sure everything goes as planned." He glanced at Van. She nodded at him, her eyes bright.

"Would you like that, Zoe?" she asked.

"My own private screening at the drive-in? Before it's even open?" Zoe broke into a grin. "I love it!" She threw her arms around Tanner's waist, hugging him tight.

Van watched them with a half-smile. Her chest felt funny to see how happy Zoe was. How easily Tanner had charmed her. It was like they were two pieces of the puzzle that was her life, slotting together easily. Maybe it was time to finally relax.

CHAPTER TWENTY-THREE

 an, aged 18

"Mom? You home?" Van glanced over her shoulder at Tanner standing on the porch. "I guess she isn't," she said. "Big shocker."

"You want me to come in with you?" Tanner asked, leaning on the door frame, his head tipped to the side. "Check for boogeymen?"

"I'm pretty sure you'd be more scared of them than I am." She rolled her eyes. "Thanks for the ride home."

He brushed his lips against hers, curling his fingers around her neck. "I'll call you later. And don't forget that math assignment. It's due on Monday."

"I won't." She watched as he clambered down the steps to his new car. He'd saved for months for that old Camaro, but even then it wasn't quite enough. Luckily, Gray had sent him some money for his birthday, enough to make up the short-fall. He started up the engine and it roared into life, spluttering as he pulled away. He honked the horn, and it made her jump. Van shook her head and walked inside to her bedroom.

Opening her closet, she knelt down, reaching out to pull out the old shoebox she'd stashed at the back. Pulling the lid off, she looked at the rolls of bills she'd put inside. Her wages from the drive-in. She didn't have to count them to know exactly how much there was. Two thousand, three hundred and sixty five dollars. Taking her latest envelope from the back of her jeans, she sorted through the bills, then added them to the appropriate rolls, fastening them with a rubber band.

Two thousand, four hundred and fifteen dollars now. By the end of the summer it should be more than three thousand. Enough for her to pay her rent and to afford food for her first term. Maybe more if she could find a way to make it last.

That money was her ticket out of town. Her chance to be like every other kid around here. Sure, Tanner and their friends would all get help from their parents, but it didn't matter. She didn't need her mom's help, she could do this by herself.

"Van?" The front door clicked open, and Van hurriedly replaced the lid on the box and pushed it back to its hiding place in the closet.

"In here, Mom." She stood and brushed the dust from her jeans, walking over to her bedroom door. "Everything okay?"

"Not really." Her mom sighed. "I'm heading to bed. Did you get paid?"

"Yep." She pulled five bills from her pocket. "There you go."

Her mom nodded, then leaned forward and ruffled Van's hair. "You're a good girl, you know that?"

Surprised by the uncharacteristic show of affection, Van

blinked. For a moment she felt bad, thinking about her college money. She knew it would help, but she couldn't bring herself to give it away. Not when she knew her mom would spend it on drink and good times.

"Thanks, Mom," she said, pressing her lips together. "Good night."

"Night, honey. Sleep tight."

Van closed the door again, and slumped on her bed, grimacing at the way the mattress sunk down in the middle. Just a few more months and she could leave this place – *and her mom* – behind forever.

Strange how that made her feel more than a little nauseous right then.

CHAPTER TWENTY-FOUR

"Hey, Tanner!" Johnny Fairfax called out as he hurried across the verdant town square. The flowers were blooming in their beds, a pool of color at the base of each oak tree. "Hold up a minute. I want to talk to you."

Tanner glanced at his watch. He was due to meet Van at the drive-in. "Everything okay?" he asked.

"Everything's great." There were dark circles of sweat beneath Johnny's armpits. "I drove past your site yesterday. It's coming on. I heard on the grapevine you've set the opening date. July fifth, is that right?"

"Yeah." Tanner nodded.

"When are you sending the invitations out?" Johnny asked, a hopeful smile on his face. "I know that Mrs. Fairfax is hoping one will land in our mailbox."

"They should be going out this week. And you'll be invited, of course. Everybody in town will." Tanner gave him a short smile.

"And how's young Savannah getting on? I have to say I was surprised when I heard you'd employed her to manage the place." Johnny lowered his voice. "Her mom once stole a lot of money from me. I think it's laudable that you're trusting her with your business."

"She's working out great." Tanner took a deep breath and checked his watch again, this time making a show of it. "I need to go. Have a good day."

"Wait!" Johnny grabbed his arm and Tanner did his best not to shudder. "Just keep an eye on her. That's all. Take it from me. There are certain families around here that would steal the coat off your back if you let them. I always check my staff's work. Even Regan's, and she's so stupid she couldn't steal money if she tried."

God, he was odious. "I trust Van implicitly," Tanner said, shrugging him off.

"Wait! Did you check out that house Regan emailed you? I've had a couple of other interested parties."

"I'm thinking about it," Tanner told him. Without saying goodbye, Tanner stalked across the pathway, past the band-stand and the benches, to where his car was parked on the far side of the square. Wrenching the door open, he sat down heavily in the driver's seat and let out a sigh.

Is this what Van dealt with every day? Sneaky words and pointed judgement? People comparing her to her mom? No wonder she wanted to fly under the radar.

He hated that they didn't see her the way he did.

Switching the ignition on, he pulled from the parking space onto the road, steering his car in the direction of the drive-in. And as the town disappeared behind him, he felt his muscles relax and a slow, steady breath escape from his lips.

Every roll of the wheels took him closer to her, and though it had only been a few hours since he escaped from her room, he couldn't wait to see her again.

She was worth a hundred of all of them – the judgers and the haters.

She was everything.

And now that he had her, he wasn't planning on letting her go.

∿

"Hey," a soft voice broke through her dream, making Van blink her eyes as she sat up in bed. "You fell asleep."

Tanner was walking across her bedroom, her curtain still swaying from his climb through the window. She stretched her arms up and smiled at him. "What time is it?"

"Only eleven. Am I wearing you out already?" He pulled his shoes off, then his t-shirt, followed by his jeans. She lifted the bedcovers and he climbed in, wearing only his shorts.

"I was up early this morning," she reminded him. "Thanks to your alarm."

"Yeah, well Aunt Gina's getting suspicious. And I can't stand the way Becca smirks every time she looks at me. I need to get home before any of them are up."

He pulled her against him, then rolled her over on the mattress, adopting their usual position with him spooning her. His arms were warm, his biceps hard against her sides. She tipped her head back and breathed him in.

"And it doesn't look at all suspicious when you saunter in at six a.m.? I'm sure you're fooling every single one of them."

"You're the one who insists I leave before the town wakes up," he pointed out. She could feel him grin against her hair. "And anyway, we won't have to do this for much longer. I've found a place to rent."

"You have?" She tipped her head back to look at him.

"Yup." He lifted an eyebrow. "No more sneaking out, no more banging my head every time I climb through your damn window."

"You should have stopped growing at fourteen. You wouldn't have that problem then."

He chuckled. "I might make you climb through my window. Just for fun and giggles."

"Who says I'm coming to your place?" she asked, biting down a grin. "Maybe I prefer staying here."

"I say you are," he told her, pressing his lips to her shoulder. "I can't sleep without you."

"Just what every girl dreams of hearing. That she puts the guy she likes to sleep."

He kissed her neck. "I like the things we do when we're awake, too." Sliding his fingers beneath the hem of her tank, he feathered them up her side. He was hard against her, his desire a reflection of her own. He only had to touch her and she felt like she was on fire.

So far they'd done everything, with one exception. The big one. The one that set her heart racing and her mind reeling. At twenty-eight years old, it made her feel like a teenager afraid to take that final step. Teetering on the edge, then stepping back, so afraid that when she let go she'd tumble.

Until she met rocky ground.

"Where'd you go?" Tanner murmured, brushing her soft hair from her face. "I lost you for a minute."

"I was thinking."

"What about?"

"Sex."

He coughed out a laugh, and she turned quickly, slapping her palm over his mouth. "Shh," she reminded him. "Zoe's across the hall."

"You surprised me," he told her, his lips caressing her hand. "I wasn't expecting such a blunt reply." She released her hold on his mouth, and his lips immediately curled into a grin. "Tell me exactly what kind of sex you were thinking about."

God, he was beautiful. He had the kind of face ancient greeks would have killed for. Strong nose, defined jawline, full lips. He wouldn't look out of place at the Met. She reached out, tracing his bottom lip with her finger, watching as his eyes darkened.

"I was wondering why we haven't done it yet," she told him.

He captured her hand with his, pressing his lips against her palm. "I was waiting for you to be ready."

"How do you know I'm not?"

"Because you have a big mouth. And when you're ready you'll tell me." He winked.

"That's exactly the kind of talk that'll get a girl going." She rolled her eyes at him, and he kissed her hand again, before releasing it and cupping her face with his palm.

"Seriously," he said, keeping his voice low. "If you're worried that I don't want you, stop it right now. I want you, Van. I always have." He glanced at the space between them then grinned. "Touch me if you don't believe me."

"Oh I believe you."

"Good. Then I have a question for you." He paused, then continued, "Actually, I have three."

She ran the tip of her tongue across her dry lip. "What are they?"

"First, are you okay with condoms?"

"Yeah." She was completely okay with them. And touched that he wanted to check with her. "What's the second?"

"Can you wait until I move into my new place? Because when we have sex you're gonna want to make a lot of noise. And we don't want to wake up Zoe."

"You're very sure of yourself," she said, her voice teasing.

"I'm more sure of you. You can be loud when you're having a good time."

She shook her head, biting down a smile. "You're an idiot, you know that?"

"Yeah, but I'm *your* idiot."

"I'm almost afraid to ask what the third question is." She wrinkled her nose. "Am I gonna hate it?"

"Probably." He gave her a soft smile, brushing her hair with his fingers. "But I need to ask it anyway." The smile melted away, and his serious expression made her chest feel tight.

"Okay then." She took a deep breath. "Hit me with it."

"Do we need to talk about what happened at Duke?"

Her muscles tensed. Without realizing it, she'd pulled away from him, the inches of air between them a cold barrier. "I…"

"Because I think we do. It's like a huge dancing elephant in the room, and no matter how hard we ignore it, it's always there. And I don't want it to be there, Van. I don't want that reminder of how I hurt you so much. I want it gone, and the only way is to talk about it."

She closed her eyes for a moment, remembering that day. The one when he tore her heart out of her chest and trounced it all over the ground. She tried to breathe in, but her lungs wouldn't expand, forcing air out in short pants that provided no oxygen at all.

"Breathe, Van," Tanner urged, grabbing her hands and holding them against him. "It's okay. We're here in your room. And I'm not going to hurt you again."

She opened her eyes, and he was staring right at her. He winced, as though he could see the pain in her eyes.

"I'm so fucking sorry I hurt you. I've thought about it every day since, and it's pretty much killed me. I called you and left voicemails. I sent you emails, letters…" his voice trailed off.

"I got them." Her voice was thick. It hadn't been easy to

ignore them. It had crushed her already-broken heart even further. In the end, she'd changed her number and her email address, and told her mom to burn any mail once she'd moved out. It had been the only way she could cope.

A one-eighty turn. Forget he existed.

Although that had been impossible, of course.

"What I did was wrong. I could give you excuses about being angry with you, about being too young to know how to deal with my emotions. But that's all they are. Excuses," he told her. "And I'll never stop apologizing for hurting you in the worst way."

He looked distraught. His face was close to hers, his eyes searching as though they were trying to find all the answers. She leaned forward, gently pressing her lips to his. "I forgave you a long time ago," she whispered. "I just never knew what to do with that."

"You forgave me?" Warmth rushed through him. He didn't deserve it, not one bit.

She nodded, and the tension melted from his face.

"Because I'd understand if you didn't."

She scooted closer to him, until her breasts molded against the hard planes of his chest, her thighs intertwining with his. "It was such a long time ago. We were kids. Too naïve to understand that things aren't always black and white." She took a deep breath. "I owe you an apology, too."

"You do?" His brows knitted together. "Why?"

"I'm the one who ruined our plans. Who broke our promises. I told you I'd go to Duke with you, and I didn't."

He swallowed, his Adam's apple bobbing in his throat. "Yeah, but I know why you did it." His smile was sad. "Or at least I know now. I didn't then."

"Yeah. That's what makes it so sad. I didn't know how to talk to you, and I didn't want to listen. I was so afraid of what everybody thought of me, when the only opinion that mattered was yours."

"I've always thought you're amazing," he whispered, pressing his lips to her cheek. "And funny, and beautiful, as well as the strongest woman I know. And every time I see you smile at me, I feel like the luckiest bastard in town. Not everybody gets a second chance."

She smiled at him, a soft, hazy kind of smile, and he leaned forward to press his lips against hers.

"Are we done talking now?" she asked, sliding her arms around his neck and deepening the kiss.

"I am," he rasped, as he broke away. "If you are."

"Yep. Completely done."

CHAPTER TWENTY-FIVE

"What're you doing?" Zoe asked, leaning on the doorjamb. Van was pulling out all the dusty old boxes that had languished at the back of her closet for years.

"Sorting through my old memory boxes." For too long she'd ignored them, the same way she'd tried to push down the memories of that time. But since it was a Saturday morning, and she'd already checked in with the contstruction team, it felt like a good time to clear out the cobwebs. Get rid of the things that didn't give her joy.

"Can I look?" Zoe asked, kneeling down beside Van and taking a box, sending dust flying into the air. "Oh god, these are ancient." She sneezed, then screwed her face up. "How long have they been in there? Centuries?"

"Don't be rude." Van shook her head, then passed a photo to Zoe. "This was me at your age. Or maybe a little younger."

Zoe glanced at the photo, her eyes wide. "Oh my god, are those flares? Why is the waistband so low?"

"They're bootcut jeans, not flares. I wasn't born in the

seventies, thank you very much. And it was the fashion to have low waistbands."

"Who's the boy with you?"

"That's Tanner."

"As in Tanner Hartson?" Zoe's mouth gaped. "But he's shorter than you. And his jeans are even worse."

Van laughed. "He was shorter than me until seventh grade. I hated it when he grew and I didn't. Felt like I was losing a race or something."

"What's that?" Zoe asked, pointing at an egg-shaped piece of plastic.

"A tamagotchi."

"A what?"

"It's an electronic pet. You had to keep it alive by feeding it and cleaning up after it. I used to sneak it into my pocket at school, because if I left it at home it'd be dead by the time school was finished." She pressed the tiny button at the top, but nothing happened. "I guess the battery's dead."

"And the pet," Zoe pointed out.

"Touché." Van put the tamagotchi back in the box, and replaced the lid. "Actually, while you're here, there's something I want to talk to you about."

"What?"

"Tanner's found a rental house to live in. And he's asked if I'd like to stay over with him sometimes." Her words came out in a rush, like she couldn't wait to be rid of them. "But that would mean leaving you here with mom. Unless you want to come with me. He has lots of rooms."

Zoe frowned. "Why would you want to stay over with…" Her words trailed off, as realization covered her features. "Is he your boyfriend?" she whispered, her eyes wide.

"Um, I don't know. Sort of. Though it's early days and we're just getting to know each other again." She gave Zoe an awkward smile.

Zoe nodded and looked away, her face serious as she took it all in. "Are you planning on moving in with him forever?"

"No. Absolutely not. It's too soon, and neither of us are ready for that." Van flashed her a smile. "We just want to spend a bit of time together. And I don't want you waking up and being scared because I'm not here. Though if you do, you can call me. I'll always have my phone on."

Zoe pressed her lips together, then looked at the photo in her hand again. "I like Tanner," she said. "He's always nice to me."

"Yeah, he's a good guy."

"So, it's okay with me if you want to have sleepovers at his place." Her expression was so serious it made Van want to laugh.

"Thank you. It won't be all the time. Maybe twice a week."

"Does Mom know about him?"

Van shook her head. "No, I haven't told her yet. I haven't told anybody, really. Except you."

Zoe smiled. "Wow. So now I know all your secrets. You're gonna have to bribe me with chocolate."

"It's not a big secret. Just something I don't want people knowing about yet. I'll talk to Mom and tell her. I don't want you feeling like you need to keep things from her. But I'd prefer it if you didn't share it with anybody else just yet. We're both getting used to being close again, and I'm not ready for the whole town to stick their nose in."

"A bit like when I learned to ride a bike. I didn't want anybody knowing in case I failed." Zoe pressed her lips together. She put the old photograph carefully back in the box and pulled another one out. "Is that me?" she asked, pointing at a photo of an eighteen-year-old Van holding a baby.

"Yeah. The day Mom brought you home." Van smiled. "You were so tiny, I was scared to even touch you. Eventually she persuaded me to hold you, and it felt perfect. Can you see how happy I look?"

"I look happy, too."

"That's because you were full of gas. You were always burping."

"Hey!" Zoe mock-pouted. "That's rude."

"And true." Van winked. "Come on, let's finish sorting through these, and then I'll take you out for ice cream. It's too nice of a day to stay inside for long."

"CAN you meet me at the drive-in in twenty minutes?" Tanner's voice echoed down the phone line, like he was on speaker.

Van lifted her head from the book she'd been reading. Zoe was playing a game on Van's laptop, and their mom was staring at Alex Trebeck on the TV, her hands curled around a cold mug of coffee. She showered today, and washed her hair. With no make-up on, and just a cute top and jeans, she looked young and beautiful. It made Van's heart ache.

"Sure. Why? What's happening?"

"They installed the audio visuals earlier. I want to check them out."

Van caught Zoe's eye. "I need to head to the drive in," she said, covering the mouthpiece. "Will you guys be okay if I'm gone for a couple of hours?"

Zoe bit down a smile and nodded, her eyes never leaving the laptop screen.

Their mom looked up from *Jeopardy*. "Fine by me." She lifted the remote control and turned the volume up, curling her legs beneath her on the sofa.

Ten minutes later, Van pulled her car up at the entrance to the drive-in. It was still unpaved – that would be the last thing done once all the heavy vehicles no longer needed access. The construction team had started to erect a brand new overhead sign that could be seen easily from the road. She and Tanner had gone back and forth about whether to change the name or not, but in the end nostalgia had won out.

The Chaplin Drive-In Theater, Virginia's First and Best was outlined in bulbs on the pale-blue painted wooden sign. Once the electrics were finished, they'd illuminate the way they had back when she'd worked here as a kid. Looking up at it made her chest feel all tight.

"You staying in there all day?"

She looked up to see Tanner walking toward her, wearing jeans and a black Henley, his dark hair hidden beneath a grey Boston Bobcats hat, no doubt given to him by Cam.

"I was just admiring our handiwork." She grinned at him, climbing out of the car. "I can't believe we've got so much done in such a short time."

He pulled her into his arms, pressing his lips against her brow. "Everything okay at home?"

She knew what he really meant. Is your mom sober? "Yeah, it's all good. Mom and Zoe are in the living room watching a *Jeopardy* rerun."

"Here's your question for two hundred. What's the most boring program on television?"

"Stop it." She smiled up at him. "Just because you never get any of the answers right."

"They're not answers, they're questions." He pressed his lips to hers, making her toes curl in delight. "And for the record, I always beat you in quizzes."

"Because I let you." She kissed him back, already breathless at his touch. "Otherwise you'd cry like a baby."

"I don't cry."

"You did when you lost that chess tournament."

He slid his hands into the hair at the nape of her neck, tipping her head back. He had one eyebrow raised, his expression amused. "I was seven years old, Van. And that other kid cheated."

"It's okay," she told him, tracing her finger along his bottom lip. "You're allowed to cry. Just not over stupid stuff like chess."

"Did I tell you I've been playing against Becca?"

"And how's that going?"

"She pretty much hates me and wants me to move out. Which is a good thing, since I paid the deposit for the house on West Street this evening. I can't wait to get the keys and take you there."

She loved the way he was looking at her. There was wonder in his eyes, as though he couldn't quite believe his luck that she was standing there in his arms. But right now she felt like the lucky one. As though she'd spent the last ten years in some kind of hazy limbo, unwilling to build the bridges back to him, yet standing on the other side, staring longingly at the life she once had.

"I have to pinch myself everytime I realize you're mine," he told her. "You were the wisp dancing in the wind. I've spent most of my life trying to capture you in my hands."

Her mouth felt dry. Every time she looked at him, emotion flooded her body. Not just because there was all this history, but because he was everything she'd pretended she didn't want.

A man who looked inside and saw the real her. Who knew that sometimes she would smile even though she wanted to howl. He peeled away the masks she wore and still liked what was underneath.

He'd always been her guiding light. She'd known it from the moment he'd written her name for her, meticulously tracing the three letters of her name, his tongue pressing against his cheek in concentration. They'd been children. Innocent of the knowledge they had now. The world had felt unfair, but it still had a logic to it. A logic that had disappeared the day she'd told him she never wanted to speak to him again.

And now it was back. Her sun rose and set on him. He was the fulcrum to her see-saw life. Always there, always steady. Holding onto her whenever she wavered.

He was changing her, day by day. Making her want things she'd never allowed herself to consider. She felt bold and afraid all at the same time.

"When you look at me like that…" Tanner's voice was low, thick. "It makes me hope so damn bad, Van."

"Hope for what?" she whispered.

"Hope that you feel the same way about me that I feel about you."

She grabbed his hand, placing his warm palm in the dip between her breasts. "Do you ache so bad, right here, that you wonder if your heart might have something wrong with it?" she asked him, sliding her fingers between his.

He nodded, his eyes not wavering from hers.

"And when you see me," she continued, sliding his hand down until it was warm against her belly. "Does your stomach feel like you've just fallen off a rollercoaster?"

"Every damn time."

Her lips curled up. "And here?" she said, feathering his fingers against the center of her. "Do you feel like you're on fire?"

He grabbed her hand and pulled it against him. She blinked at his hardness. "What do you think?" he asked, his voice guttural.

"I think you've got it bad."

He laughed. "I do. I've got it something awful for Van Butler. Every time I see her it feels like my world's tipped over." He lifted her hand and kissed her fingertips, his throat undulating as he swallowed hard. "I've loved you from the moment we first met. Before, maybe. It's like there's always been a Van-shaped hole in my life. And it grows bigger every year. Sometimes you filled it, heck sometimes you were way too big for it." He smiled at her, his eyes crinkling. "But now, you fit it just right." He dropped his head to hers. "You make me happier than I have a right to be."

Her throat felt scratchy, as though it was trying to swallow a sob. The air between them felt thick, full of meaning. She breathed in a ragged mouthful of air, her eyes still captured by his. "You make me happy, too."

He loved her, and it was everything. It was bright like the sun, eclipsing everything that tried to compete with it.

"I'm glad to hear it. Now get in my car and I'll make you happier still."

She laughed at his abrupt change in conversation. "Are you talking about car sex?"

"Nope. I'm talking about movies." He slid his hand around her waist, steering her around the back of the half-constructed ticket office.

She blinked when she saw what was there. An old orange Camaro, white stripes painted down the hood, rust clinging to it like a lover. "Is that what I think it is?" Van asked, not sure whether to laugh. It looked exactly the same as Tanner's first car. He'd been so proud of it.

"I saw it three days ago in the grocery store car park." He led her to the passenger door, pulling it open. "Paid the kid who owned it three times what it's worth."

She laughed, running her finger over the split leather upholstery. "I can't believe it's been in Hartson's Creek all this time. How many kids do you think have driven it?"

"Since I sold it?" He shrugged. "I guess at least three more owners. I can check."

"No, don't." She shook her head. "I kind of like the mystery."

He tapped his hand against the wheel. "She still drives like a dream."

"A nightmarish kind of dream?" she teased.

He grinned and started up the engine, both of them holding their breath in the long second between his turning of the key and the motor catching. He pressed his foot on the gas, a loud growl rumbling from the hood.

She leaned forward to turn on the radio. It crackled and hissed, but no music came out. "The stereo's still kaput. And it still smells like the creek. But god, it's good to see it."

"Buckle up," he told her as the Camaro lurched forward, the complete lack of suspension flinging her body up and down as Tanner steered it across the freshly cut grass toward the gravel drive. "It's movie time."

CHAPTER TWENTY-SIX

Tanner unlocked the Camaro's trunk, tugging at the stiff lid until it finally gave way and opened with a groan. Lifting the box he'd hurriedly put together before leaving the house, he carried it back to the driver's seat, laying it on the torn leather. "Stay here," he told Van, who was watching him with an amused smile. "I just need to start the movie."

"What are we watching?"

"Wait and see." He winked and closed the door. He walked across the gravel parking lot toward the projection room, following the directions the audio visual team had given him, starting the digital screen and loading up the movie. As he sauntered back to the car, his cap pulled down low on his brow, his hands pushed into his jeans pockets, he looked at the Camaro, feeling a flash of warmth as he saw Van's blonde hair spilling over the cracked leather seat.

He'd meant every word he said to her when he'd held her in his arms. He was in love with her. And if she hadn't said it back yet? Well he could wait. He'd been waiting for ten years, after all.

Ten years of being without her and he could barely remember how that even worked. How had he woken up without her being the first thought in his mind? How had he slept without her curling her warm body against his?

The opening credits had started. Production companies' logos flashed on the screen, one after another. He'd parked the Camaro in the front row, around thirty feet from the screen. To the right was the playground that kids could use whenever they got bored of what was being shown that night. To the left was the refreshment stand, though it hadn't been completed yet. When it was, it would have state-of-the-art equipment to make popcorn, burgers, hot dogs, and fries.

Pulling the car door open, he lifted the box of food and slid inside.

"Is this the movie I think it is?" Van asked, as a big globe came on the screen, along with a little satellite orbiting around it.

"Almost certainly."

"Jerry Maguire?" She looked at him, smiling. "What made you choose it?"

"It reminds me of Cam." He shrugged. "And we watched it back when we were kids, remember?"

"The Tom Cruise summer series. I can't tell you how many people complained that year." Van sighed. "He's a love-hate kind of actor."

"He's made some good movies though."

"Yeah, he has." She leaned forward to lift his baseball cap off, raking her fingers through his hair. Sitting back, she jammed the cap onto her own hair, her golden waves spilling out beneath it.

He looked at her and his stomach clenched. It was stupid and infantile, but he loved that she was wearing something of his. And of course, his girl rocked it.

His girl. Was that what she was?

He pulled up the Chaplin Drive-In Theater app on his phone, opening it up and linking it to the Bluetooth speaker he'd stashed in the glove compartment. The sound came on, synced perfectly to the screen.

He'd had to pay for the app to be designed, thanks to the contract he'd signed when he'd sold his business. It had rankled him to fork out for something he could have coded himself in less than a day, but those were the terms he'd agreed to.

Sometimes it sucked to be a grown up.

"Are there still only six billion people on the planet?" Van asked, as Tom's opening monologue blasted out of the speakers.

"Around seven and a half billion now," Tanner told her. "This was made almost twenty-five-years ago."

"We were three-years-old." She grinned. "Hadn't even met yet."

"We probably had and didn't know it. Hartson's Creek is so small we had to have passed each other in our strollers."

"I'd have known it," she said, her voice sure.

He opened a can of Coke and passed it to her. "How?"

"Because when I look at you, you turn my world upside down. You always have. Especially the first time we met."

"When I knocked you over?" He grinned.

"Yeah. That time was literal."

"Do you think there was always something between us?" he asked, tipping his head to his side as he looked at her intently. Tom was still talking, though neither of them were paying attention to him.

"You mean *something* something?" she asked, her eyes dancing. "Because I don't know if I was thinking about *something* when I was six. I just knew my life didn't work unless you were in it."

"How about the last ten years?" he asked, wondering if she'd come to the same conclusion as him. "Did they work?"

She pulled her bottom lip between her teeth, her gaze moving to the screen. Jerry was walking into a sports bar, his hair slicked back, his suit expensive and perfectly cut. "I don't know," she admitted. "I mean I thought they did. I thought I was doing okay. And then I came back here and saw you and everything I believed in was a lie."

"How about guys?" he asked softly. "There must have been some."

"A few."

His stomach tightened.

"But nothing serious."

The band around his gut loosened a little. "Did you live with anybody?" He wasn't sure he wanted to hear the answer.

"Nope. You?"

He shook his head. "No. I was too busy working to think about relationships."

"I don't believe you were a monk for ten years."

"I didn't say I was. I had… needs." He winced. "God, that makes me sound like a dirty old man."

"There's nothing old about you," she said, leaning forward to cup his cheek. "Though you are kinda dirty."

He laughed, and knocked the cap up from her brow, pulling her closer until their lips met. Kissing her made his heart hammer in his chest. God, she was perfect.

"Ow." Van winced and rubbed her side. "Damn gear shift."

"You okay?"

"Yeah. Just remembering why making out in cars is uncomfortable."

He leaned over to the backseat and grabbed a blanket and the speaker. "Let's go sit on the grass. It'll give us some more space."

She joined him at the front of the car, watching as he laid

the blanket out, then offered her his hand. She was still holding her Coke can, and she took a sip, smiling at him as Tom visited his concussed client in the hospital.

"How many concussions has Cam had?" she asked Tanner as the camera panned out to show a football player in a neck brace.

"Too many. Five, I think."

"Ouch. I saw the one he got against Chicago. It looked awful."

"Yeah, I flew up to see him that time. He was unconscious for more than twenty-four hours." Tanner sighed. "I'm hoping he thinks about retiring soon."

"He's too young for that, isn't he?"

"I guess so."

"Does he have plans after he stops playing?" Van asked. "Maybe he could become an agent like Jerry Maguire."

"Ha! That would involve having to actually talk to people."

"It's funny how often people got him and Logan mixed up at school," Van mused, smiling at him over the rim of her can. "And yet you could tell the difference as soon as they opened their mouths. He'd mumble a few words…"

"And Logan would never shut up." Tanner laughed. "I guess they've always been that way. A bit like you and me."

"As in you're the talkative one, and I'm the strong silent type?" Van asked, her brow arching.

A bolt of pleasure shot down his gut. He loved her like this, all smart mouthed and strong. "As in, you never shut up," he said, grinning.

"You're cruising for a bruising, Hartson," she murmured, biting down a grin at her own pun.

He mock-winced. "Maybe I am."

She put down her can and rose to her knees, then launched herself at him, pushing his back to the wool blanket. She landed on him, her thighs on either side of his, her hands grabbing his wrists and putting them over his head.

He was hard almost immediately. She scooted forward, her body brushing against him as he let out a sigh. Then she was kissing him, her hands still tethering his wrists to the ground, her body wriggling all over his.

He could have pulled his hands away easily. Could have flipped her over and ground his body into hers until she was gasping with pleasure. But he was curious as to what she'd do next.

"Hmm," she breathed, his nose brushing against his. "I kind of like being in control."

"When it comes to us, you're always in control," he said, swallowing a groan as she laid herself over him, her groin pressing into his.

"If I'm in control then I can do this, right?" She tugged at his Henley, pulling it up until his skin was exposed to the cool evening air. Then she slithered down, pressing her lips against his stomach, her mouth warm against his skin.

He was achingly hard. So aware of her lips as they slid down his abdomen, reaching the thick leather of his belt. Her fingers pulled it loose, then deftly unfastened his jeans, her hand sliding under the waistband of his shorts, until she closed her fingers around him.

Slowly, she slid her palm up, the friction oh-so-good yet not nearly enough. He thrust his hips against her and she looked up at him with a smile. "Am I torturing you enough yet?" she asked.

"Oh yeah."

Without saying another word, she slid her hands beneath his waistband and released him, sliding her lips around his plush head. He closed his eyes, Jerry Maguire and his money long forgotten, as he submitted himself to the pleasure only she knew how to give.

∾

THE MOVIE WAS COMING to an end. Van was laying back against Tanner, his arms circled around her as he leaned back against the grill of the car. His fingers were tracing circles along her abdomen, his lips pressed against the top of her head as they watched Jerry walk into his house. It was full of women. They all stared at him as he declared his love for his wife.

Jerry's voice cracked as he told Dorothy that his life wasn't complete without her, and it made Van's breath catch.

Tanner shifted her slightly on his lap, leaning forward until his chin was against her shoulder. "Are you crying?"

"Not yet." She bit her lip. "Give me a minute." Jerry told his wife that he missed her, and Van felt her throat tighten as tears pooled in her eyes.

"Don't cry, baby," Tanner said, kissing her cheek.

"I can't help it. It's just so beautiful."

"You think Tom Cruise crying is beautiful?"

She shook her head. "I think a man admitting he's lost without his woman is just…" Van sighed. "It's just everything."

"I was lost without you."

She sniffed. "Stop it."

He brushed his lips against her ear. "I was. I fucking missed you. Every day. I'd meet new people – friends – and wonder if they could ever fill the space you left." He scooped her hair over her shoulder, then kissed her neck. "And they didn't. Not one of them."

He splayed his fingers across her stomach, pressing her closer into him. "It was always you, Van. *Always*. And I'm so damn glad you came home."

She was crying now. Hot tears trailed down her cheeks to

her chin, dropping onto her chest. He turned her around until she was straddling him, his hands cupping her face.

"Don't cry."

"I can't help it. You're beautiful, too."

He shook his head. "I'm a cartoon next to an old master."

"I missed you, too," she whispered. "So much." And maybe she hadn't realized how much until now. All those victories when she'd turn to tell somebody, but he was never there. The sad movies and the happy parties, the wins at work and the nights she couldn't sleep. He was her ghost limb, a memory that never left. And now he was here, in beautiful Technicolor.

"You're mine," she whispered, as much to herself as to him. She was full of wonder as she touched him, tracing the line of his nose, the swell of his bottom lip.

"Damn right I am." He leaned his face into the crook of her neck, kissing her skin. "So now will you let me tell everybody?"

"I already told Zoe."

He chuckled against her neck. "You did?"

"Yeah."

"That's good. Because I told Logan," he said sheepishly.

She grinned at him. "I think Maddie's guessed as well. We're such terrible liars, aren't we?"

"Nah. Some things are just too good not to share. So when are you going to let me parade you through town?"

She shook her head. "Not happening, Hartson. But maybe we can start, I don't know, being seen together or something? After the opening gala, maybe. Let's get through that first."

"The day after the gala." He nodded seriously.

"Yeah. We can go for brunch or something. Keep it casual."

He slid his hands beneath her, his fingers cupping her

behind as he dropped his lips to hers. "One thing you need to know, babe, is that there's nothing casual about us." He kissed her hard. "I'm serious as hell about you. Just so we both understand."

She leaned forward to kiss him again. "Understood and reciprocated," she whispered against his soft lips.

For the first time in forever, it felt like her life was sliding into place. Piece by piece, things were getting better. Zoe was happy, her mom was sober, and she was in love with Tanner Hartson, the first boy to ever steal her heart.

Maybe it really was possible to have it all.

CHAPTER TWENTY-SEVEN

"Zoe, your friends are here," Tanner called out, pulling open the office door. As soon as he saw her sitting with Van at the brand new desk they had delivered yesterday he grinned. "And the refreshment booth is officially open. Show time is in twenty minutes."

Van had been showing Zoe around the drive-in while they waited for her friends to arrive for the dry run. And of course she'd been most excited by the refreshment stand. The construction team had finished the installation three days earlier, and this was the first time they were trying everything out in real time.

"They're here? Oh boy!" Zoe's face lit up as she looked up at him. Van was pretty sure he had a fan for life.

She was still choked up that Tanner had been so thoughtful to let Zoe's friends come to their dry run. Last weekend they'd all gone to Maroon 5 without her, and Tanner had taken Zoe and Van over to Gray's studio, where he'd played her some of his new songs, and put a photograph of the two of them on his Instagram account. For the past week, Zoe had been like a superstar at school, especially now that her entire class was invited to watch the newest Troll movie with free refreshments.

"A few of the parents are hanging around," Tanner told Van as Zoe rushed out of the office and down the metal stairs. "I told them I'd give them a backstage tour and grab them refreshments. I figured the kids won't want them cramping their style."

Van smiled at him. "You're pretty good at this, aren't you?"

"At what?"

She slid her arms around his neck, pressing her lips against his. "This almost-uncle thing. You have Zoe wrapped around your little finger."

He kissed her back, his hands sliding down her hips. "Yeah, well you Butler girls have me pretty much whipped. I live to make you happy." He slid his lips down her neck, pushing her hair away with his hands. She let out a little gasp as the sensation overtook her.

"Van?"

Tanner pulled back, a horrified expression on his face. Van turned to see Zoe standing at the doorway, the sun spilling in behind her.

Van swallowed hard. "Um… I didn't know you were there."

"Obviously." Zoe wrinkled her nose. "I was just wondering if you guys were watching the movie with us. But now I'm really hoping you're not because if you do that in front of my friends I'll die of embarrassment."

She could hear Tanner chuckle softly behind her. "You weren't meant to see that." Shooting Tanner a warning look, she smoothed her hair back over her shoulders.

"I'm not a kid. I know that you two kiss." She wrinkled her nose. "And do other stuff."

Van's mouth dropped. "You *are* a kid," she pointed out. "And what do you know about other stuff?"

"Emily Mayburn's mom has a book. We've all seen it." Zoe shrugged, as if it was no big deal.

"What kind of book?" Van asked, alarmed.

"Let's hope it's not the kind of books you read," Tanner murmured. Van bit down a grin.

"*The Girl's Guide to Life.* It's about periods and stuff." Zoe looked over her shoulder, as though she was afraid people were listening. "And babies."

Tanner let out another laugh. This time Van spun around to glare at him. "Hey," he said, lifting up his hands. "That was an embarrassed giggle."

"You didn't sound embarrassed," Van told him, her eyes narrow. In fact, he looked like he was enjoying every minute.

"Um, can I go now?" Zoe asked. "How long until the movie starts?"

Tanner checked his watch. "Fifteen minutes until showtime."

"Okay, I'm gone." Zoe gave them one last glance. "Do you think you can stop the kissing thing. At least until my friends have left?"

Tanner gave Van a lopsided grin. "I'll try," he promised, looking back at Zoe. "But your sister needs a lot of kissing. She's that kind of girl."

Zoe rolled her eyes and ran down the stairs again, and Van let out a deep sigh.

"Why does she have to grow up?" she said, shaking her head. "Before we know it she'll be getting her period and crying over boys."

"She won't cry over boys," Tanner said, stepping up behind her and sliding his arms around her waist. "I'll beat them up before they can hurt her."

Van put her hands against her chest and pretended to swoon. "My hero."

His lips curled against her neck. "I like to think so. Now let's go put on a movie."

It was almost ten o'clock by the time everything was closed up and they were ready to leave. Zoe had gone to her friend's house for a sleepover. Van climbed into Tanner's car and pulled the seatbelt across, watching as he walked across the grass after locking up the refreshment booth.

"So that went well." He smiled at her. "Apart from the popcorn burning."

"And the sound turning off halfway through." Van shook her head.

"Oh, and don't forget that kid throwing up after she ate too many hotdogs." Tanner wrinkled his nose. "That's something I could do without seeing ever again."

Van grinned at him. "At least we know what's inside a hotdog now."

"Yeah. That's enough to put me off them for life." He turned the ignition key then looked at her, a soft smile playing at his lips.

"What?" she asked, loving the way he was looking at her.

"You want to come back to my place?" he asked her, his eyes dark. She swallowed hard, loving the way he was looking at her.

"You got the keys?" she asked eagerly.

"Yep." He nodded. "I thought you'd want to be the first one over the threshold."

"I'd be honored."

Five minutes later, he pulled into the driveway of a huge Victorian house. Her mom's bungalow could fit in it three times without blinking. It was one of the old-style two-stories, with a wraparound porch and a brick chimney standing proud from the slate-tiled roof. The kind of house she used to dream of when she was a kid.

Because that kind of house always had a mom who took care of you and a dad who came home every evening and played games with you until bedtime. Or at least it did in her childhood imagination.

"Fairfax thinks the owner might be willing to sell it after the six month lease is over." Tanner inclined his head. "Ready?"

She was already halfway out of the car. He laughed at her enthusiasm, locking the car up and following her along the brick-lined path.

Even in the dark it was beautiful. There was a tree in the expansive front yard with an old rope swing tied up to it. If it wasn't completely dark, she would have launched herself on it.

"Later," Tanner said, as though he was reading her mind. "Let's go inside first."

He grabbed her hand and pulled her up the steps. There was an old rocking chair on one side of the wraparound porch, and a wicker love seat and coffee table on the other. The kind of place where you could sit out in the evening with a glass of iced tea and watch the world go by.

Tanner unlocked the door and pushed it open, stale air escaping through the crack. "It's been empty for a while," he told her. "Fairfax didn't even show it to me at first. He thought it wasn't modern enough."

Van followed him inside, her footsteps echoing in the empty hallway. It stretched for two floors, a grand staircase curving around the right wall, with enough room for a grand piano beneath it.

"You're going to rattle around in here," she murmured, as

he flicked a lightswitch. A chandelier lit up, casting patterns across the tiled floor.

"I'm hoping I won't be here on my own much."

She smiled at him. "I guess your family will visit."

"And you?" he murmured, tracing her collarbone with his outstretched finger. "Will you be here?"

"If you buy some furniture."

"I'll take that for now." He brushed his lips against hers, sending a shot of electricity through her body. "Come on, let me show you around."

The house was everything she thought it would be. Full of character, from the old sanded floorboards on the upper level, to the gas stove that dominated kitchen. But it was the living room that took her breath away. Even without furniture it was impressive, with its high ceilings, beautifully carved molding, and huge wood-and-glass doors that led out to the backyard.

"It's an acre in all," Tanner told her. "There's a brook at the end that leads to the creek. The neighbors tell me there's a herd of deer that sometimes run along it."

"And it's all yours."

"For now." He was looking at her with dark eyes. The smile had melted from his lips, replaced by a hungry expression that made her thighs clench together. He reached out to trail his fingers along her jaw, tipping her head up so he could press his lips to hers.

"I'm hoping it will be yours, too. Sometime," he murmured, his mouth moving against hers. Then he deepened the kiss, making her toes curl with delight as he pulled her close against him, their bodies arching together.

She slid her hands into his hair, scraping her fingers against his scalp as he moaned softly against her.

She could never get tired of kissing him. It was like he'd flipped a switch and brought her back to life.

His hands slid down the back of her jeans, cupping her behind as he plundered her mouth. She pushed her hands inside his shirt, feeling his warm skin against her palms, her fingers tracing their way to the hard ridges of his stomach, then to his chest.

He moaned again. Lower and rougher this time. It sent a thrill through her, pleasure knotting in her stomach as he moved his hands to the hem of her shirt, pushing it up.

He cupped her breasts, his thumbs brushing against her nipples. It was her turn to gasp as he pushed the lace cups down.

She pulled her t-shirt over her head, exposing her sensitive skin to the cool nighttime air.

"You're beautiful," Tanner told her, reaching out to trace the swell of her breast. Then he was leaning down, capturing a nipple between his lips, and she had to bite down as to not let out a cry.

It took everything she had to keep standing as he kissed and caressed her, moving from one breast to the other as if he couldn't get enough. His tongue was slow and sensuous, his lips hot and demanding, and every time he pulled at her flesh she felt her legs tremble with desire.

"Can I undo your jeans?" he asked her.

She nodded. It was crazy that he even asked. He had to know what he was doing to her.

He deftly unfastened the metal button, then pulled at the zipper. "Any time you want me to stop, you tell me," he said, his voice rough. He dropped to his knees, pulling her jeans down, past her thighs, her knees, before she stepped out of them.

"I don't want to stop." Her voice was sure. He looked up at her, his eyes shining as they connected with hers.

"We're not kids anymore, Van," he said thickly. "I want to have sex with you."

"I want it, too."

"But before we do, you need to know something. This is it for me. *You're* it. There's no running away, no hiding. Once you're mine, you're mine."

She nodded, breathless. Not just from the way his fingers were tracing the edge of her panties, but from the way he was staring at her. As though he might die without her.

It sent shivers of delight down her spine.

"Don't move," he said, standing and walking over to the hallway.

"Where are you going?" She felt vulnerable, almost naked compared to his fully-dressed state.

"To grab a blanket from the car. You're not lying on the dusty floor."

"Can you hurry?" she asked urgently. She didn't want him to leave her for even a moment.

He laughed. "I'll run like I've never runned before."

He was back within a minute, shaking the blanket out and helping her down to the floor. He pulled his t-shirt off, and she stared up at him, her eyes scanning his sculpted chest.

We're not kids anymore. That was for sure. Back then they were playing at being adults. Their few attempts at sex had been furtive, fumbling, yet still the most amazing thing she'd ever done. But now, it was deeper than that. And more practiced, too.

Tanner leaned over her, kissing her hotly, unfastening her bra and throwing it to the side. He moved his lips down her throat, kissing her collarbone then the swell of her breasts, kissing her nipples, her stomach, then pulling at her panties. She arched up, watching as he slid them down her shaking thighs, then he crawled between them, pushing them up to give himself room.

As soon as he took her into his warm, practiced mouth she was gasping. He put a hand on her stomach to hold her down as he sucked and licked at her again and again. She could feel the pleasure coil inside her, snapping and fizzing as he grazed her with his teeth, sliding two fingers inside her to heighten her desire.

"Tanner…" His name came out as a gasp. She didn't know how much longer she could last.

"Shh." He dipped his head again, his tongue tracing a languorous line to her aching core. Then he sucked at her, making her cry out, her thighs tensing, her body arching as the pleasure burst from inside her.

His fingers dug into the soft skin of her thighs, his mouth still licking and sucking as she rode the wave of desire. As she slowly came down, he was pulling his jeans off, followed by his boxers. Her breath caught in her throat as she took in the thick lines of muscles on his thighs. He pulled a condom from his jeans and passed her the silver disk. "I want you to put it on me," he told her, looking down at his thick hardness.

She nodded, tearing the packet open and throwing the foil to the side. She wrapped her fingers around him, loving the way her touch made him gasp. Moving her hand up and down, she watched as his eyes closed, his mouth dropping open as he gasped in time to her movement.

"The condom," he said roughly. "Now."

Slowly, she unrolled it onto him, sheathing him before laying back on the blanket. He moved his powerful body between hers, bracing his arms on either side of her shoulders as his hardness slid against the neediest part of her.

"You're beautiful when you come," he told her. "I want to see it again. With me inside you." He dropped his head to hers, kissing her hard.

His words sent a fresh shot of excitement through her. She could feel him begin to enter her, and she closed her eyes.

"Open them," he said roughly. "I want to see you."

He was overwhelming, filling her body and soul. She gasped as he stretched her, inching slowly inside, then stopping to give her time to accustom herself to him. He began to move, muttering an oath about how good it felt. Van slid her hand down his back, to his ass, her fingers pressing against his hard flesh in encouragement. She could already feel the ache starting to throb inside her again, her body moving against his as he increased the rhythm.

"Van…" he said roughly, dipping his head to suck at her nipple. "You're everything, you know that?"

She nodded, too full of him to speak. He sucked at her again, the tugging sensation making her thighs tighten around his hips, as pleasure started to steal at her once more.

"Are you close?" he rasped out.

"So close."

"Thank fuck."

She laughed softly, then gasped as her climax began to peak. It was slower this time, more intense, her body shaking as he moved in and out of her. Then he was coming, too, his eyes staring right into hers. She thought she could see stars in them as they both gasped out loud.

It took a minute for him to get his breath back enough to pull out of her, tying the condom and putting it aside. He pulled her into his arms, kissing the top of her head as she spooned into him, pleasure still warming her body as her eyes began to droop.

"I love you," he murmured. It was so soft, she wasn't sure she was supposed to hear it. So she closed her eyes and let her breathing slow, trying not to think too much about those words.

He loved her. And it was beautiful. But it was scary, too. Because he'd loved her once before and look how that turned out. Love was a fluffy cat with claws, it soothed and it cut in equal measure. She hoped to god the claws stayed hidden this time, because she had no idea what she'd do if they didn't.

We're not kids anymore. Damn, she hoped that was true. Because she'd been in love with Tanner Hartson her whole life.

CHAPTER TWENTY-EIGHT

"Guys, I gotta head over to the drive-in and get everything ready for tonight," Van called out, walking out of her bedroom into the hallway. When she reached the kitchen, she gazed out of the window, checking for the twentieth time that morning that the sun was still out. The clouds needed to stay away. There was no way she wanted the grand opening party to be a wash-out.

"Mom?" she called out. "You and Zoe need to get there by six, okay? I've reserved you a space at the front." She grinned at Zoe who was sitting at the kitchen table, spooning Rice Krispies into her mouth. "And you get all the popcorn you can eat."

Zoe grinned back. "I can eat a lot."

"I know." Van winked at her. "Mom?" she called out again. "Where are you?"

"She's in the bedroom." Zoe inclined her head toward the hallway. "She came out about ten minutes ago to pick up the mail, then disappeared again."

Van walked back into the hallway and knocked at her

mom's bedroom door. "Mom, I gotta go. Did you hear what I said?"

No answer. Van sighed. Don't let her be like this. Not today of all days. She needed everything to go perfectly. It wasn't too much to ask, was it?

"Mom?" she said again, trying to keep the impatience from her voice.

"Come in." Her mom's voice was thick. Croaky.

Van pushed the door open, and tried not to wince at all the clothes strewn over the floor. "I was just saying I gotta go." She looked over to the bed. Her mom was curled up, facing the wall, papers in her hands. "Are you okay?" Van said softly.

Her mom rolled over. Her eyes were red, her hair a mess. She held out the papers to Van. "He's divorcing me," she whispered. "I just got this."

Van took the papers from her mom's outstretched hands and scanned through them. "It's a letter from his lawyer. He wants to discuss separation terms, not a divorce," she said, looking up. "It's not that bad."

Her mom's lips trembled. "It's the first step. A separation agreement and then a divorce after a year. He really isn't coming back."

"But it's a good thing, right?" Van said, forcing a smile onto her face. "It says here he's going to pay you enough money to cover the rent. And he doesn't want any of the furniture." She turned over the page. "Look! He wants to see Zoe every other weekend. She'll be happy about that."

"I'm not letting my girl go and stay with him and that bitch," Kim hissed. "They don't get to play happy family with my kid." She shook her head. "Zoe isn't even his."

Van's phone buzzed in her pocket. She pulled it out to see Tanner's name on the screen. "Can we talk about this later?" she asked. "After the gala? I have a thousand things to do at the drive-in. And you don't have to do anything about it right away."

Her mom said nothing, just took the papers from Van and turned back on her side again.

"You need to be there at six," Van said. "I've saved you a spot. Just give your name at the booth and they'll direct you. Everybody else arrives at seven, so don't be late."

"Okay," her mom whispered.

Van leaned forward to rub her back. "It's going to be okay. Nothing's changed. We're all still good, right?"

Her mom sniffed.

Van's phone rang again. This time she answered the call. "I'm on my way," she said.

"Good. Because I miss you already." Tanner's voice was warm. The tension immediately seeped out of her. They'd get through tonight, then tomorrow everything would be easier. Her mom, her relationship, all of them could be dealt with.

But now she had a party for five hundred people to finalize. Everything else would have to wait.

"IS THIS OKAY?" Van asked, walking into the office later that day. She'd spent most of the morning and afternoon running around getting everything ready, before heading to the salon to get her hair done and pick up her dress.

Tanner leaned back in the chair, taking in the sexy red gown that clung to her every curve. Her hair was down, freshly waved to make her look like some kind of old-style movie actress, and her full lips were slicked with a scarlett gloss. Tanner pushed the chair back and walked over to her, his mouth dry as he looked her up and down.

"You look beautiful," he said, reaching out to touch her

face. "Why don't we skip this party and head straight to my place?" His voice was low. Needy.

She smiled. "For one, you still don't have any furniture."

He leaned forward to brush his lips against her cheek. "I'm working on that," he murmured. "We've got an appointment at the store tomorrow. I want you to help choose it."

He slid his lips to the sensitive skin below her ear, right where her jaw met her neck. She sighed as he kissed her. "It's just a couple of hours," she said, her chest rising up as he kissed her again. "We can't miss our own party. I've been working on this for weeks."

Curling his hand around her waist, Tanner gave her a lopsided grin. "I guess I can wait. If you promise that I can peel that dress off you later."

Her eyes caught his. "It's a deal. And now I need to go check on the band and the refreshments." She glanced at the slim gold watch on her left wrist. "One hour before the guests are due to arrive."

"I'd better get my suit on." Tanner raised an eyebrow hopefully. "Unless you've changed your mind and I can stay in my jeans."

"No can do. The dress code is Hollywood glamor." She looked at his frayed jeans and checked shirt. "I don't think that will work."

It had been fascinating watching her organize tonight's event. She'd taken care of every detail, working so hard with the caterers, the entertainment, and the ground staff they'd recruited. It was another side of her he hadn't seen before, but he liked it. A lot.

"I love you," he told her, kissing his way down her neck.

"I..." Her phone buzzed. "Damn. This thing never shuts up." She grinned at him, then checked the screen. "It's Mom. Hang on." With her eyes still on his, she answered the call, lifting the phone to her ear. "Hey, Mom, what's up? You guys on your way?"

He took advantage of her distraction to kiss his way along her shoulder, breathing in her floral scent. He could never get enough of her. Not even if he were to kiss her for the rest of their lives. He wanted lifetimes. Eons. Long days filled with only her and nobody else. Damn, he wished this party was over already.

"Zoe, calm down." Van frowned, and he lifted his head up, a questioning look on his face. "What time did she leave?"

He couldn't hear Zoe's words. Just a low murmur as Van held the phone to her face. He leaned back on the desk, watching her as she took a deep inhale, her chest rising up in that magnificent dress.

"Okay, just stay there. One of us will come and pick you up. Are you in your dress? Good. Don't worry, she'll be okay."

She covered the mouthpiece and looked at Tanner. "Mom left the house at lunchtime. She hasn't come home. Zoe's panicking."

"You think she's gone to a bar?" Tanner asked her. Van had told him about the separation papers. And It was typical of Kim to go drown her sorrows when she could be supporting her daughter.

"Probably."

"I'll get Becca to go pick Zoe up," Tanner told her. "And I'll ask Logan to drive to Moonlight and see if she's there."

Van nodded, her lips pressed together, then uncovered the phone. "Honey? Becca's gonna come to get you. And we'll get somebody out to look for Mom. Try not to worry, okay? She'll be fine." Van's eyes caught Tanner's. She tried to smile at him, but it looked like a losing battle.

He sighed, and started calling his sister. If Kim spoiled Van's night, she'd have him to contend with.

~

VAN TOOK a deep breath and looked out at the crowd. Women in elegant dresses laughed with men wearing dark dinner suits, rolling their heads awkwardly, unused to starched collars and bow ties. Waiters weaved their way in and out of the cars carrying trays of champagne and hors d'oeuvres. Mini hotdogs and little cardboard boxes of truffle-oil fries carried on the movie theme, and in front of the stage the orchestra she'd hired was playing movie themes.

Becca had brought Zoe an hour ago. When she saw her sister, Van felt the tension seep out of her like air from a balloon. Logan was still looking for her mom – apparently the Moonlight Bar was empty – but it didn't matter. Maybe it would be better if she wasn't here.

The hum of the crowd increased, and Van tipped her head to the side, watching as Gray and Maddie drove up in a shiny old Cadillac. Gray stepped out of the car, looking every inch a superstar, his strong, muscled body encased in the finest wool suit. He opened the passenger door and held his hand out to Maddie, helping her stand on her heels. She looked beautiful with her dark hair caught in a side-chignon, her baby bump visible beneath her champagne silk dress.

"That's Gray Hartson," she heard somebody say. "Did you hear his latest album? It's amazing."

"I know Gray. I went to school with his sister. Have you seen his brothers? They're as gorgeous as he is. They sure know how to breed handsome in that family."

"Hey." Tanner was smiling at her. Van turned her head to take him in, suddenly feeling breathless. "You okay?"

"I am now." She stepped forward, curling her fingers around his lapels. "You look amazing," she whispered, rolling on her toes to kiss him. "Promise me you'll let me peel this off you tonight."

He laughed. "I promise," he said solemnly. "I just left Zoe and her friends. They started screaming when they saw Gray and I couldn't take it anymore."

Van laughed. "They all have a huge crush on him."

"I got that impression." He rolled his eyes.

"Tanner Hartson!" a deep voice boomed. Van's stomach dropped when she saw Johnny Fairfax heading their way, wearing an old-fashioned powder blue dinner suit. Nora was dressed in a peach knee-length dress, her hair perfectly coiffured. Van looked over their shoulder for Chrissie, breathing a sigh of relief when she couldn't see her.

She'd sent their invitations with gritted teeth. Part of her had wanted to slide them into the shredder, but that would have caused more gossip. She could put up with the Fairfaxes for one night.

And maybe she'd enjoy them seeing everything she and Tanner had achieved.

"Good evening, Johnny," Tanner said, sliding his arms around Van's shoulders as if he could sense her unease. She didn't pull away. Didn't want to. Maybe she didn't care what the Fairfaxes thought of her.

"Oh. Are you two an item?" Nora asked, looking from Tanner to Van and then back again. "I didn't realize. Though I guess it makes sense." Her lips curled up as her eyes met Van's. "I did wonder why he gave you the job of running this place."

Van felt the skin on the back of her neck prickle.

"I gave her the job because she's good at what she does," Tanner said mildly. "As you can see." He nodded at the crowd surrounding them. "I'd call this a success."

Nora's smile faltered. "It all looks lovely," she said, her nose wrinkling as though it hurt her to say.

"It really does. Congratulations." Johnny leaned forward to shake Tanner's hand. "Of course it was all my idea." He smiled as he saw people looking at them, listening in. "I showed Tanner the details, suggested he should make the investment." He chuckled. "Maybe you should name the drive-in after me. Fairfax Drive-In. That has a good sound, doesn't it?" He pushed his chest out, like a self-important rooster.

"I'll think about it," Tanner said, his tone implying he'd do no such thing.

"Van?"

She turned to see Logan and Cam standing there. Tanner's brothers looked more alike than ever, both dressed in dark tailored suits and crisp white shirts, their hair slicked back from their handsome faces. She could usually tell the difference between them without issue. Logan was the one who wore suits and talked about food. Cam nearly always had bruises and cuts from playing football, and was much more casual than his twin.

"Can we have a word?" Logan asked her. "In private?"

She nodded and followed them, shooting Tanner an apologetic glance for leaving him in Johnny Fairfax's clutches.

"Did you find Mom?" she asked as soon as they were out of earshot.

"Yeah. She was in a bar in Shawsville," he told her, referring to the next town over. She's pretty drunk, too. I wasn't sure what you wanted me to do with her. She's sleeping it off in the car."

"She's here?" Van's eyes widened.

"Yep. You want me to take her home?"

Van sighed, pulling her lip between her teeth. "No, it's okay. If you can stay with her until the movie begins, I'll take her home then."

"You sure?"

She nodded. "Yeah, I'm sure." She reached for his arm,

curling her hands around his wrist. "And thanks for going to look for her. I appreciate it."

"Any time. You're one of us." He gave her a soft smile. "Family takes care of family."

Tears unexpectedly came to her eyes. There was something so sweet about the Hartsons. Every one of them filled her heart. "Thank you," she whispered, her voice thick. "I truly appreciate that."

She'd spent most of her life pretending family didn't matter to her. But now it felt like everything. Tanner and Zoe, his brothers and sister, Aunt Gina, and even his dad – they meant everything to her. Her fractured relationship with her mom felt more bearable than it ever had. Maybe things were looking up after all.

She painted a smile back on her lips and walked over to where Tanner was still held captive by Johnny and Nora. "Chrissie couldn't be here," Nora said, all sweet smiles for him. "But maybe you can give her a tour sometime. She did love this place growing up. Said she has a lot of happy memories here."

Van reached for Tanner's arm, her fingers closing around his wool-covered bicep. "I'm so sorry, but I'm going to have to steal him away. We'll be starting the speeches and movie in a few minutes," she said, forcing the smile to stay on her lips as she looked at the Fairfaxes.

"Of course. We can talk later, Tanner." Johnny said, leaning in. "I have a couple of business opportunities I'd like to discuss with you."

"I'll be too busy tonight," Tanner told him. "But maybe another time."

Johnny beamed. "I'll call you next week."

Van blew out a mouthful of air, feeling relieved as they turned to walk away. But then she heard a voice. One she recognized. And it sent a shiver right down her spine.

"Darling! I'm so sorry I'm late."

She turned to see her mom walking toward them, wearing a skimpy white top and tight jeans. Her feet were bare, her soles dark from the earth as she walked toward them. Van swallowed hard, shooting Tanner a look as he stared at her with wide eyes.

"Mom? You were supposed to wait for me at the car." Van reached for her, but Kim somehow managed to dodge her grasp.

"And miss the party? Oh no." Kim was slurring. She looked over at Johnny and his wife. "Nora, how lovely to see you. You look beautiful as always."

Nora said nothing, staring at Van's mom with disgust curling her lips.

"Aren't you going to say I look nice, Nora?"

"Come on now," Johnny said, his voice full of false humor. "We were just off to get some champagne."

"That's lovely," Kim said. "Remember when you used to buy me champagne?" she asked, her eyes looking hazy as she stared at him. "We'd drink it naked, remember? You'd pour it over my tits and –"

"We're leaving," Johnny said, grabbing Nora's arm. "Come on now."

"What's up, Johnny? You embarrassed of me?" Kim called out. "I don't remember you being embarrassed when you were in my bed."

Van squeezed her eyes shut. Please let her shut up. When she opened them again, Logan was hurrying toward them. Or at least she thought it was Logan.

"When I got back to the car she was gone," he said, breathless. "I've been looking all over for her."

"You hear that?" her mom said. "Young guys are still hunting for me." She gave a little chuckle. "I've still got it."

"You never had it." Nora said, her voice harsh. "You're just a dirty slut."

Kim stepped forward, her smile dissolving as she lurched to one side. At the last minute she reached out, steadying herself on Nora's shoulder. "That's what your husband used to say," she whispered. "Before he dragged me to bed."

"Mom! You need to go. Now!" Van reached for her. Kim whipped her head around, her expression full of anger as she slapped Van's hand away.

"What's the matter?" she asked. "You don't want me talking bad about your daddy?"

Van froze. It felt like the whole world did. Her mom's words seemed to drip into her ear, letter by letter.

Your daddy.

Her chest tightened as she looked from her mom, to Johnny then back again, waiting for them to start laughing.

Then her eyes met Nora's. She looked as shocked as Van. Beside her, she heard Tanner murmur something to Logan, but the sound of blood rushing through her ears was too loud to make it out.

"What?" Kim said. "Why's everybody looking at me."

"We should go," Johnny mumbled, grabbing Nora's arm. "Now." He shot Kim a look. "Some people should learn to handle their drink."

Van swallowed, her skin heating up as she realized everybody was staring at her. Tanner and Logan, Nora and Johnny. From the corner of her eye she could see some of the older ladies from *Chairs* watching her carefully and whispering quickly to each other.

She started to shake, her legs feeling weak as mortification washed over her. Johnny Fairfax was her dad? Her stomach twisted at the thought, forcing up the champagne she'd drunk earlier until she could feel the acidity bite at her throat.

She was Johnny Fairfax's daughter, and everybody knew. All the hard work she'd put in meant nothing. She was still Kim's bastard child. The kid everybody looked down on. The one that people whispered about as she walked along the street.

It didn't matter that the dress she was wearing cost more than most people spent on clothes in a year. It didn't matter that she'd organized this whole gala herself. Because they'd never see her as anything other than a piece of trash, just like her mom.

So she did the only thing she could.

She ran.

CHAPTER TWENTY-NINE

*T*anner reached out, his hand missing Van's by an inch as she ran past him. She didn't even look his way. His mouth was dry he watched her kick off her shoes to run faster, her hair lifting in the breeze, like she was some kind of messed up Cinderella.

"I need to go after her," he said, his chest tight.

"You need to put on the movie," Logan said, his voice low. "You've got hundreds of people here, man. And if you don't give them something to do, they're all gonna be talking like crazy."

"This is your fault," Johnny hissed, pointing at Kim. "You and your stupid mouth. You'll be hearing from my lawyer. This is slander."

"It's not slander if it's true," Tanner said, raking his fingers through his hair. *Shit*. He had no idea what to do next. Van needed him, but he couldn't go. Not when this messed up show was still going on around him.

"Can you get Kim back to your car?" he asked Logan. "And this time make sure she gets home."

Logan nodded, his lips pressed together.

"And can you call Becca? Ask her to find Zoe for me. I don't want her hearing about all this... crap... from anybody else." He let out a mouthful of air. "I'll go and get the movie rolling and then find Van."

"I'll call Cam and Gray, too. Let them know what's going on if they haven't heard already," Logan said. "Just keep in touch. Let us know what we can do." He shook his head. "I'm so sorry about your big night."

"I don't give a damn about the night. I just need Van to be okay."

"She will be," Kim said, her voice quieter now. "Van's always okay."

"No thanks to you," a voice hissed.

Tanner looked to his right, seeing Nora standing there with her arms crossed over her chest. She wasn't looking at Johnny at all. He had a feeling the man was going to be put through hell tonight. And he deserved it. This was his fault.

His and Kim's.

"You two need to leave," he said, looking at Johnny and Nora. "Now."

They gaped at him, as though he'd asked them to strip and do a dance for the crowd.

"You heard him," Logan said. "Get out of here. Or I'll make you leave."

"I can't believe this," Nora hissed at Johnny. "Not *her* of all people." Disgust dripped from her words. "Did you know about Savannah?"

"There's no proof she's my daughter," Johnny stuttered, glancing at Nora from the corner of his eye. She shot daggers at him. "Kim slept around. Everybody knows that."

The fire was rising up inside Tanner. He was so damn sick of them all. "You don't deserve her to be your daughter," he spat at him. "None of you do. She's worth ten of you. You see this place? It wouldn't be here without her. Tonight wouldn't have happened if she hadn't taken charge. She's amazing and none of you realize it." He shook his head. "And it's your damn loss, not hers. Now get out of here, and don't come back. Both of you."

He turned his back on them, striding fast across the grass toward the stage, where the orchestra was still playing. The conductor held up two fingers.

Two minutes until he could make his speech and start the movie. Two minutes until he could find Van and check that she was okay.

As the music slowly came to an end, he had no doubt at all that they had been the longest two minutes of his life.

THE OPENING CREDITS started to roll. Tanner let out a huge mouthful of air. Okay, so nobody was actually watching the screen, but right now he'd take it. And maybe turn the volume up a little more to drown out the gossip. From the corner of his eye he could see Nora and Johnny Fairfax striding to their car, Nora wrenching it open, her face full of thunder.

He wouldn't want to be a fly on the wall of their house tonight. Johnny would be lucky to come out with his balls in tact.

With a final glance at the guests who had been drinking champagne and were completely oblivious to Van's real beginnings only moments ago, he walked out of the projector room and toward the refreshment stand, and office that was above it.

When he climbed up the outdoor stairs and opened the office door, he saw Van inside, tidying up the papers that had been strewn across the desk.

"Hey." He swallowed hard. "I made the Fairfaxes leave.

And Logan is taking your mom home." He gave her a half smile. "And not that either of us give a damn, but the movie is rolling, so there's that."

She looked up. Her eyes were rimmed red. And they wouldn't meet his. It was as though she was staring through him.

A shiver snaked down his spine.

He'd seen that expression once before. Years ago. He froze on the spot, as though some invisible hand was stopping him from stepping forward.

"I'm sorry," she croaked, wrapping her arms around her chest as though she was cold. "For ruining your opening."

"None of this is your fault." Finally, he stepped forward, around the desk that felt like a barrier between them. He reached for her and she shrank away, and it felt like a foot slamming into his gut. "Van?"

"Of course it's my fault," she whispered, a sob catching her words. "All of this is. I don't know why I thought it would be different. Why *she* would be different. I was a fool to think it would work out this time. That the Butlers wouldn't come in and ruin everything the way they always do."

"To be fair, you could blame the Fairfaxes, too," Tanner said, but the joke fell flat. Van inhaled a ragged breath and turned her head to the side, but he could still see the tears running down her cheeks.

"I can't believe it." She shook her head. "Johnny Fairfax? Why him, of all people..." Her eyes closed. "Though it makes some kind of horrible sense." She looked up at Tanner. "Do you think he knew all along?"

"He'd been having an affair with your mom when you were conceived. I'm guessing he thought there was a fair chance he was the father."

"And Nora. She must have known *something* was wrong."

Realization washed over Van's face. "That's why she's always hated us."

"Either that, or she's just a bitch."

Van's eyes opened wide. "What about Chrissie?" She put her hand over her mouth. "Oh god, that makes us sisters. Or half ones. Did she know?"

"I've no idea…"

Van shook her head. "She couldn't have. She would have used it to hurt me. She couldn't have hidden a secret like that from me. At very least she would've hinted at it." Her brows pulled together as she followed the thought through. "I guess she just learned how to be a bitch from her mom."

Tanner's lips twitched. "Do you want me to take you home?"

Van shook her head. "I don't know. I have no idea what to do next." Her lips trembled. "What do you do when you find out your dad's the creepy guy you always avoided?"

"I don't know."

He stepped forward again, his arms wrapping around her. But she was still holding herself, her elbows jabbing into his chest as he tried to hug her. It was like embracing stone. Hard, unyielding. She didn't melt into him, didn't sob against his chest. She just stood there, stiff as a bone, as though she was enduring it for his sake.

"Van…"

She pulled her head up, her cheeks shining with tears. "I should never have come back home."

Her words pierced him like a knife. "What do you mean?"

"I was okay in Richmond. I'd built a life. I had a good job. I was respected." Her whole body was trembling. "But here, it's like I'm that kid again and nobody will let me grow up. I'll always be paying for the sins of my mother."

Tanner blinked, trying to find the right words. But he felt like a kid, too. The one she'd rejected. The one who ran away when his mom died. Like his skin was slowly being peeled off, leaving him raw and vulnerable. "That's not true," he finally said. "Look at tonight. All these people are here for you."

"They're here for you, not me. Your friends, your family. Even the good townfolk came because the Hartsons are someone around here. And they support their own." She let out a laugh, but there was no humor in it. "Imagine the talk at *Chairs* next week. They always said my mom was a floozy, and she just proved them right. They're going to talk about this for months. And about me." Another sob caught in her throat. "And Zoe, too."

"Who gives a damn?" he asked her. "Seriously, just ignore them. Their opinion means nothing."

"That's easy to say when you've never been looked down on." Her voice was soft. Almost calm, compared to a few minutes ago. "And I'm glad you haven't. So glad. Because you don't deserve this. Not me or my mom or the baggage that comes with us."

He swallowed hard, as the strangest feeling washed over him. Like déjà vu, except he knew he'd never stood in this room with her before.

But he'd stood in another place, and listened to her tell him she didn't want to be with him anymore. That he needed to go to Duke and live his life without her. That what they had between them meant nothing.

The memory made his mouth go dry.

That's when he knew it. She didn't have to open her mouth for him to know what she was going to say. He could read every word on her beautiful face. It was like watching a bullet careening in slow motion toward its mark. He knew it was going to hit, but the waiting was agony.

"Don't say it," he said, his voice full of gravel.

Her eyes met his, and he saw nothing there. Just a blankness that made his stomach turn. "Tanner, I—" She swallowed hard. "We both know this was a mistake."

"No it wasn't. It wasn't, Van." He wrapped his arms around her tighter. She felt so slight, almost as if she wasn't there.

"I can't do this. Not to you. All these people, they support you, they support the drive-in. If you lose a single customer because of me… I couldn't stand it."

"Look at me," he demanded, tipping her chin until her gaze met his. "I don't give a shit about this place. I opened it for *you*. Everything's about you, Van. All of this. My whole damn life."

Tears streamed down her face. "Then do me the honor of letting me go. I'm no good, Tanner. It's in my blood. I'll never be able to walk down the street without people talking about me. I won't be able to go to *Chairs* without hearing murmurs everywhere I turn. And I'm used to it. I almost expect it. But I don't want that for you. You deserve so much better."

"So what are you saying?" He could feel his heart hammering against his ribcage. "That you're throwing us away for my own good?" His voice rose up. "Again?"

"You heard what Nora said. I'm trash, just like my mom."

He had to lean forward to hear her, her voice was so faint. It killed him to hear her talking like this. But there was something else happening, too. It was like his skin was slowly closing up, as thick as leather to protect him from her.

From the aching pain caused by every word she uttered.

There was a tap at the door. They both turned to look as it slowly opened. Becca was standing there, shifting from foot to foot as a blush stole its way across her cheeks. "Um, Zoe's asking about your mom. Logan's taken Kim home, so I thought I'd take Zoe. I'll stay with her, of course, until you get home."

"No. I'll go with her," Van said tightly, nodding at Becca. "Can you tell her I'll be down in a minute?"

Becca glanced from Van to Tanner. "Sure. Is everything okay?"

"It's fine," Tanner lied. "Thanks for taking care of Zoe."

"Of course." She gave them a brief smile, then pulled the door shut, her footsteps fading as they heard her descend the steps.

"I need to go," Van said, pulling out of Tanner's arms. She wiped the tears from her face with the back of her hand, leaving a smear of mascara beneath them, then grabbed her purse.

"I could come with you."

"No." She shook her head. "I meant what I said. This –us– isn't a good idea."

"So that's it?" His voice rose up. "We're over, just like that."

She pressed her lips together, looking down at the floor. "It's better this way." Her voice was devoid of emotion.

A red hot flash of fury rushed through him, curling through his stomach and burning his muscles. She really was doing this. Messing it all up again. He looked away, trying to swallow down the anger, but it rose up regardless.

She went to walk past him, but he refused to budge, his eyes narrowing as he stared down at her.

"Your walking away and saying it's for my sake? That's bullshit. It's not about me. It's about *you*. You're scared of putting yourself out there. So frightened about what people think that you'd rather lose the good things in life than let yourself be put under scrutiny. So if you want to walk away, do it. But just so you know, I'll never stop loving you." And the thought of that almost broke him. "You might be scared," he told her, his voice raised even louder. "But I'm not. And

I'm not afraid to tell you that you're breaking my goddamn heart right now."

Her fingers curled around the doorknob, her eyes full of tears as she looked back at him. "I'm sorry. I never want to hurt you."

Then she was gone, and he was ready to collapse. He steadied himself on the desk because he was afraid that without it he might fall.

He'd lost her once, ten years ago, and he hadn't known pain like it. But this was worse, so much worse. Because this time he had no idea how they'd ever come back from this.

CHAPTER THIRTY

"Is Mom okay?" Zoe whispered. Van had found her waiting with Becca at the bottom of the office steps. As soon as she saw her, Van hugged her tightly, her legs still shaking from her confrontation with Tanner.

"She'll be fine once she sleeps it off. She always is."

Zoe looked up, her face masked with worry. "Do you think there's something wrong with her?"

Nothing a month in rehab couldn't fix. Van bit down that thought, because she knew it was cruel. Even though everything felt cruel right now, somehow she had to keep it together for Zoe. "She had a bad day. With the letter she got this morning, then seeing that man."

"Mr. Fairfax?"

"Yeah, him. I think it sent her a little over the edge. But she'll be okay, kiddo. She has us."

"Is Mr. Fairfax really your dad?" Zoe asked as they walked to Becca's car. She'd offered to drive them home, and Van had gratefully accepted. The way her hands were trembling she wasn't sure she'd be able to hold the wheel of her own car. Becca promised that one of them would drop it off and put the keys through her door in the morning.

Becca unlocked her car and let them climb inside. It felt weird to hear who her dad was, because neither one of them had ever known. The thought that Johnny might be hers made Van's stomach lurch.

"I don't know," Van told her. "And buckle up."

"I am." Zoe took a deep breath. "Is he my dad, too?"

"No sweetheart." Van squeezed her hand. "He's not." Zoe's dad was one of a few guys her mom had been seeing the summer Van was eighteen. Luckily none of them were Johnny Fairfax. Like Van, Zoe had just accepted the fact she didn't have a father. Van hoped this didn't shake her up too much.

She'd worry about that later. Once she'd worked out how to clear up this mess.

Becca turned to smile at them both. "I'll have you home in a couple of minutes."

"Thank you," Van mouthed. She needed to get out of here. Away from the scrutiny of the crowd, and the loud vibration of the screen.

And Tanner. *Oh god, Tanner.*

She couldn't think about him. Not if she wanted to stay sane. She needed to get home, and make sure her mom was okay. Only then would she let herself wallow.

In her bed. All alone. Without him.

Where she deserved to be.

The road into Hartson's Creek was empty. Nearly all of the townspeople were at the drive-in, no doubt with only one eye on the screen as they gossiped about her mom's revelation. Zoe slid her hand into Van's, her fingers squeezing tightly, and Van squeezed back.

She forced her mouth into a smile. Zoe didn't need to

know any of this stuff. If there was one thing Van knew, it was that her sister needed to be protected the way she never had been. If she managed to do that and nothing else, then it would be okay.

Not great, but okay. Right now she'd take that.

"Here we are." Becca parked behind Logan's rental car. "Home sweet home."

Van looked at the bungalow she'd grown up in. It wasn't hers, though. It was Tanner's. What a damn mess this all was.

Zoe was already pulling the door on her side open, running up the path toward the front door. Van followed her quickly, as Zoe wrenched the door open and ran inside.

"Mom?" she shouted out. Van hurried behind her, gathering her red dress in her hands. Their mom and Logan were sitting at the kitchen table, Kim sipping at a steaming mug of black coffee as Tanner's brother shifted uncomfortably in his seat. As soon as he set eyes on Van, Zoe, and Becca he stood, looking like a man who'd been given a final reprieve.

"Oh, Van," her mom slurred. "I'm so sorry." She put her mug on the table, her hand shaking enough to send some hot liquid sloshing over the side. Her chair scraped against the tiled floor as she tried to stand, lurching to the left before walking to Van and hugging her, putting almost her entire weight against Van's shoulders.

Van stood there, her stomach turning as she tried to decide what to say to her mom. It wasn't okay. None of this was. She wanted to curl up and pretend that none of this happened. "You should go to bed," she said, her voice low. "We'll talk about this in the morning."

"Do you hate me?" Her mom's breath caught in a sob. "Of course you hate me. I hate me. You were never supposed to know."

She was completely aware of both Logan and Becca's presence in the room. They were kind, more than kind. She knew that. Yet having them here was intensely uncomfortable. Even if they weren't judging her, she was judging herself.

"Thank you for all you've done," she said to Logan, before she turned to Becca. "You guys can go now. I'll take it from here."

"I don't mind staying if you need any help," Becca said brightly.

The pure kindness in her eyes made Van want to cry. "It's okay," she said softly. "We'll all just go to bed. Deal with everything in the morning." She was too exhausted to do anything else. Sleep felt like an escape from the awful reality of her life. One she desperately needed.

Logan stood, rubbing the back of his neck the way Tanner always did, and the simple gesture made Van's heart ache. "Let us know if you need anything," he said. "Or I can call Tanner to come over?"

"No," Van said quickly. "It's fine."

"You're family," Becca said, giving Zoe a hug. "We take care of our own. We're always here for you." She kissed the top of Zoe's head. "Stay strong, kiddo."

Zoe nodded.

And then they left, pulling the door closed behind them. Van let out a lungful of air, but it didn't relax her body at all.

"Come on," she said, looking at her mom's tearful face. "Let's go to bed. We'll talk in the morning."

"I'M under strict instructions from Logan to take you home," Cam said as he walked into the drive-in office. Tanner had been pacing the room ever since Van had walked out. He wasn't even sure how much time had passed since he'd heard her steps on the metal treds. Ten minutes?

Twenty? All he knew was that every muscle in his body hurt.

She walked out on him. *Again.* God, he wanted to hit something. He raked the hair from his face and looked at his older brother.

"I can't go. Not until everybody leaves." His jaw muscle twitched. "It's my party, remember?"

"Gray and Maddie are going to make sure everybody leaves. You're too worked up to be of any good here. Let's just go."

Tanner strode to the window on the far side of the office. From his vantage point, he couldn't see the screen, but could see the flashing lights of the movie reflected in the glass.

"Just take me to my place," Tanner said, his voice full of grit. "I need to be alone."

"No can do. I'm under instruction. You're a big guy, but I'm bigger. I think I could drag you if I had to." Cam shrugged. "Just come home, okay?"

Cam was silent as he drove them both back to their father's. Cam leaned forward and turned on the stereo in his rental car, cranking it up so the heavy beats filled the space between them. Tanner leaned his head on the window, his jaw still tight as they drove through the exit, passed the corn-fields, and into Hartson's Creek itself.

When they pulled into the driveway of their dad's house, Tanner climbed out and walked up to the steps, Cam shadowing him as Logan and Becca waited for them on the porch.

Cam gave him a wry smile. "Sorry, dude. Looks like you have a welcoming committee."

"Come on," Logan said, as Tanner and Cam reached the door. "I've opened a bottle of whiskey."

"One of yours?" Tanner asked Becca.

"Yeah. A good one. Retails for a hundred dollars."

He gestured at the kitchen. "In that case, pour away."

They sat around the kitchen table and Logan poured out four tumblers of whiskey, passing them to his siblings. He lifted his glass and held it out to Tanner. "Congratulations on the opening night," he said, then took a sip. Tanner followed suit, letting the bitter liquid coat his tongue before burning the back of his throat as he swallowed it down.

"Was Van okay?" Tanner asked when he replaced the empty glass on the table. "And Zoe?"

"Zoe's fine," Becca said. "And their mom's sleeping everything off. As for Van..." she trailed off, shrugging.

"I asked her if she wanted me to have you call her once you got back," Logan told her. "But she was pretty vehement that she didn't. From the look on her face I'm guessing something went down between the two of you."

Another rejection. He was racking them up. Tanner held his glass out, and Logan lifted an eyebrow. "One more," Tanner told him. "And then I'm heading to bed."

Once filled, he took another big mouthful of whiskey, swallowing it faster this time. Sighing, he looked up at the three of them, his chest contracting as they all stared back.

"We're over."

Cam frowned. "Who's over?"

"Didn't you hear anything tonight? Van and Tanner are in a relationship." Becca sighed. "What were you doing? Stuffing your face with burgers?"

"It's off season." Cam shrugged, then lifted his glass to his lips.

"Who ended it?" Logan asked.

Tanner caught his gaze. "She did." He sighed, remembering their harsh words.

"Oh Tanner." Becca slid her hand over his. He gently pulled away, making her blink.

"You wanna talk about it?" Logan asked.

Tanner shook his head. "No." He was certain of that. "I just wanna go to bed and forget any of this happened."

"You're gonna have to talk some time," his brother told him. "You know that, right?"

"Whatever. Not tonight." The thought of it made him want to hurl.

"Your bed's still made up," Becca told Tanner. "Aunt Gina's old habits die hard."

"Where is she anyway?"

"With Gray and Maddie. So's dad." Logan checked his watch. "They should be back soon. Gray messaged to say they were closing everything up. He and Maddie are gonna drop them off."

Tanner finished his second whiskey and pushed his glass away. "I guess I'll head up before they get home." He couldn't face having to explain himself to them. Aunt Gina would give him the look that reminded him of his mom. Soft, and concerned and completely guilt-inducing. And for his dad, he didn't have a soft bone in his body.

He needed to get over this. Forget the way she made him feel. The way she felt in his arms. How for a few weeks it had felt as though the light had been switched on inside his soul again.

"Good night," he told them. "And thanks."

As he walked into the hallway, he could hear his brothers and sister talking quietly.

"Should one of us follow him?" Becca asked, sounding troubled. "Maybe he really needs to talk."

"No, let him sleep." He was pretty sure it was Logan, though he and Cam sounded almost identical. "He does need to talk, but not after two glasses of whiskey and the night he's had."

That was a small mercy at least. As Tanner climbed the stairs, he felt a wave of weariness wash over him. By the time he'd washed his face, brushed his teeth, and put on the sleep shorts he'd left behind in one of the drawers in his closet, every muscle in his body felt like it was about to break down.

But still sleep didn't come. Not easily, anyway. The bed felt way too empty without her by his side.

CHAPTER THIRTY-ONE

"*I* brought you coffee."

Tanner blinked his eyes open. Logan was standing at the end of the bed, two insulated cups in his hands.

"What time is it?" Tanner croaked.

"Just after six."

Letting his head fall back against the pillow, Tanner sighed. "Come and see me when it's actually daytime."

"The sun is up, there's not a cloud in the sky. It's a beautiful day." Logan pulled the sheets off him, like he used to do when they were kids and it was his turn to wake his brothers up. "Come on, get dressed. We have places to go."

Groaning, Tanner reached for his t-shirt, pulling it over his head. Logan was wearing dark pants and a white shirt, his hair wet as though he'd showered already. "What's got you so chirpy?"

"I'm not chirpy, I'm busy. I leave for home tonight, and before I go I need to make sure you're okay."

"Can I at least brush my teeth?" Tanner asked, though secretly he was touched at his brother's concern.

"Be my guest." Logan grinned. "Though it'll ruin the taste of the coffee."

"I'll risk it," Tanner told him, walking into the bathroom. He closed the door and took a deep breath, rubbing his eyes with the heels of his hands before looking at himself in the mirror. It had been along, unrestful night. Every time he felt himself begin to drift off, he'd jolt awake, the memory of Van's tear-stained face filling his mind, and his heart would race like a thoroughbred until he tried the whole going to sleep thing all over again.

It had taken an act of will not to message her. She'd made it clear she didn't want to talk to him, both in the office, and again to Logan. He wanted to respect her wishes despite all the questions rushing around his head.

Why did she leave?

Why wasn't she willing to fight for him?

Why would she give up something so goddamned amazing?

But he knew the answer to all of them. It had been there all along.

Because he wasn't good enough. And it twisted his guts up so bad.

Ten minutes later, he was sitting next to Logan in the car he and Cam had rented at the airport. His brother hadn't lied about the morning – it was beautiful. The sky was a deep blue already, the sun as golden as Van's hair. Through the open windows of the car he could hear birds singing, as Logan turned left from the main road and into the country.

Tanner frowned as he looked ahead. "Why the hell are we coming here?"

"Because I want to talk to you." Logan pulled the car up right outside the gate. "And this seemed as good a place as any." He grabbed his insulated cup, and Tanner did the same, the two of them climbing out of the car.

"It's locked up." Tanner felt a wave of relief wash over him. The cemetery was the last place he wanted to be. It only held bad memories for him. Of being forced into a black suit. Of Aunt Gina trying to tame his mop of hair with gel and a brush. Of watching a bright white coffin being lowered into the dusty earth, and wondering who was wailing, before realizing it was him.

"We'll climb over."

Tanner eyed his brother carefully. "We're almost thirty, bro. My climbing days are over."

"Take this." Logan passed him the insulated mug he was holding, then grabbed hold of the top of the iron railings, vaulting himself over. Reaching through the gaps, he had Tanner pass him the cups. "Come on, your turn."

"You're fucking crazy."

"Don't swear in a cemetery."

"I'm not in a cemetery," Tanner pointed out. "I'm outside."

"Yeah, well I'm inside and I hear you. So watch your mouth."

Landing inside with a thump, Tanner took his coffee back from Logan and lifted it to his lips. It was surprisingly good. He didn't have to ask his brother where he wanted to go – Tanner knew where his mom's gravestone was well enough. Even if he could barely bring himself to visit her.

He could count on one hand the amount of times he'd been here since he left for college.

"You gonna tell me why we're here?" he asked once they'd been looking at her gravestone for a minute.

Logan took a sip of coffee. "Because this right here is the motherload, excuse the pun."

"The motherload?"

"Where all your problems began."

"Are we back to therapy again?" Tanner sighed.

Logan shook his head. "We're back to two brothers

talking about the worst time in their lives." He tipped his head to the side, thinking. "Maybe not the worst time for you, but it's pretty close."

"Thanks for the reminder."

"You don't need reminding. None of us do. The memories are always there."

"Truth." Tanner shook his head. "But I try not to engage with them."

"And that's your problem. You stuff it all down and think you're okay. And maybe you are okay sometimes. But piling all your problems up under a rug is asking for trouble. You can tiptoe around it all you like, but that big mound of dirt is still there."

Tanner breathed in deeply. "It's old history."

"Old history that's messing up your life."

"What do you want me to do about it?" Tanner asked, his face serious. "Mom's dead. Nothing's gonna bring her back. Not me talking about it, or being silent about it. It's a fact of life. She's gone."

"Maybe you can forgive yourself for not being there when she died," Logan said softly. "That would be a damn good start."

Tanner's chest constricted. "I was a fu— I mean freaking chicken. I ran away because I was scared."

"You left because you were eight years old and had no idea how to deal with Mom dying. And if she was here right now, I think she'd tell you exactly that."

"I didn't say goodbye." Tanner pressed his lips together.

"I know, bro. But she was our mom. She knew you loved her. Heck, you were her little shadow for most of your first five years. You were always the one who made her laugh. She knew, bro, she just knew."

He wasn't gonna cry. He hadn't for years. But his throat was thick with emotion. "I miss her, you know?"

"Yeah." Logan's voice was gruff. "I know. We've all tried to cope with the pain. Look at me, I never stop working because if I do, I'll start to think about everything I've lost. And Cam, why do you think he wants to win every game he plays, even if he ends up in the hospital? Then there is Gray. The way he dealt with the pain was to face up to dad every time one of them opened their mouths. We're all messed up, Tanner. But the first step toward healing is to admit we have a problem. You've spent your whole life trying to save everybody else because you couldn't save Mom."

Tanner blinked. "Who have I tried to save?"

"Van. Zoe. Those guys you worked with who were desperate for the proceeds from your business sale. Let's not forget about all the times you'd throw yourself between Dad and Gray to stop them from hitting each other. You come riding in like a knight in shining armor because it's so less scary than trying to save yourself."

"You think I'm scared?" His thoughts flickered to the previous night. To him accusing Van of being frightened. Surely Logan was wrong. Tanner wasn't frightened of anything.

"Truthfully?" Logan's gaze met his. "I think you're terrified. Of losing Van the same way you lost Mom."

"I already lost her," Tanner said. "She's gone."

Logan pressed his lips together, his eyes crinkling at the corners. Then his phone buzzed. He lifted it from his pocket and unlocked the screen.

"It's Gray. He wants us to come over for brunch in a couple of hours." Logan glanced at his watch. "You up for it?"

"Yeah."

As Logan tapped out a reply, Tanner turned back to his mom's headstone, reading the inscription.

Grace Hartson. Beloved wife, mother, and sister. Taken too soon.

Losing her at the age of eight had broken his heart, but there was nothing he could do about that. Losing Van? That felt like having his soul ripped out. But she wasn't dead. She hadn't even left town. She was only a few miles down the road, and for the first time that gave him hope.

"Bye, Mom," he said, his words peppered with grit.

"You ready to go?" Logan asked him.

"Yeah, I'm ready."

A smile flitted over his brother's lips. "That's good, because I just saw the caretaker pull up. I suggest we get out of here before he realizes we scaled the fence."

Tanner laughed. "If he catches us, I'm gonna blame it all on you."

"Why change the habit of a lifetime?" Logan slapped him on the back.

"I love you, bro." Tanner slapped him back, a little harder.

Logan winced. "I love you, too. But if you hit me like that again, you're dead meat."

"Becca's coming over in twenty minutes," Van told Zoe as she walked into the kitchen where Van was sitting at the table, staring out at the backyard. "She wants to take you out to breakfast."

Her car had been parked outside when she'd gotten up this morning, the keys slid through the mail slot as promised.

Zoe eyed her warily. "Is that code for you and Mom are going to have an argument and you don't want me to be here when you do?"

"Kinda," Van admitted, shaking her head at how observant her sister was. When Becca had messaged her that morning, she'd jumped at the offer because Zoe didn't need to hear the conversation Van and their mom needed to have.

She wanted to protect her, the way nobody had protected Van.

"Okay then." Zoe nodded with a smile. "I hope we go to the diner. I love the pancakes."

"I'm pretty sure you will. It's Becca's favorite place."

Zoe pulled her bottom lip between her teeth, then looked up at Van. "Are you okay?" she asked.

The question made Van's heart clench. "I don't know," she admitted. "But I will be."

"I heard you crying last night."

"You did? I'm sorry about that. I thought I was being quiet." She hated knowing Zoe heard her.

"You don't have to say sorry for crying. Is it because of Mom and Mr. Fairfax?" Zoe patted her hand. "He's not so bad. Maybe he'll be a good dad."

"I think I'm too old to need a dad." Van gave her a half smile. "And anyway, it's not about him. It's more about the embarrassment of it all. I'm so sorry you had to hear it. Sorry that everybody did. Are you worried about people talking about you at school?"

Zoe blinked. "Why would I be worried about that?"

Van lifted the half-drunk cup of coffee to her lips, taking a sip. "Because people say the most awful things. When I was at school, I hated the way everbody gossiped about Mom."

Zoe's brows came together, as though she was thinking hard. "But why does it matter what people say? It's not like anything Mom does is our fault. It's not your fault that Mr. Fairfax's your dad. So why do you look so upset about it?"

Her question brought Van up short. She lifted her head up, considering her sister's question. Why was she so upset? Because people were talking? In Hartson's Creek, people *always* talked. It was practically a town sport.

It wasn't the talking that hurt, as much as it was the judgment. Knowing that they looked down on her because of her mom's choices in life. People like Nora Fairfax and Chrissie. Growing up, she'd worn that judgment like a heavy cloak. Yeah, she'd try to shake it off, ignore it, or even play up to it with all the stunts she and Tanner had pulled. But it was still there, weighing her down, reminding her of where she came from.

"I guess I feel like if I tried harder, mom wouldn't make so many bad choices." Her heart felt tight just saying it.

Zoe's brows lifted. "You sound like she's the kid and you're the mom."

Out of the mouths of babes… Van blinked, because that's exactly how it felt. It's how their relationship had always been. For as long as she could remember, she'd taken on the responsibility of her mom's behavior. Winced at the embarrassment of it, hated the judgment.

But not Zoe. She'd never done that.

Yeah, she'd called Van when Craig left and their mom went off the rails. But not because she felt responsible, but because she didn't know what to do.

Zoe had cried when her friends went to the Maroon 5 concert, but that was because she was missing out, not because she felt they were judging her.

Her hands shook as she picked her coffee cup up again. Tanner had been right last night when he'd accused her of being afraid. Of being willing to lose all the good things that happened to her rather than let people talk about her.

"Are you okay?" Zoe asked. Van blinked, realizing she hadn't said a word for more than a minute.

No, she wasn't. All her life she'd thought of herself as brave. Intrepid. Nothing phased her. Yet the shaking in her body was out of control. The way she'd behaved as a kid had been a mask. Something she'd pulled on to hide the fear and the pain. The same emotions that were wracking her body right now.

She was afraid. So afraid that if she was honest people wouldn't like her. Much easier to pretend she didn't care.

"Van?" Zoe prompted.

Van looked at Zoe, a reassuring smile on her face. "I'm just thinking about what you said."

"Can I ask you something?" Zoe's voice lowered.

Van nodded. "Sure."

"I heard you and Tanner arguing last night. Are you mad at him about something?"

Van's eyes shone with tears. "No, I'm not mad at him." It was true. But she was furious at herself. When her mom had made that announcement last night, she'd withdrawn the way she always did. Taken on the burden of choices two people made before she was born.

"That's good, because I really like Tanner. He's cool. And so are his brothers." Zoe smiled. "And Becca. I love Becca."

"I'm pretty sure the feeling's mutual," Van murmured, her thoughts still filled with him.

There was a knock at the door, and Zoe shot out of the kitchen, wrenching open the front door. Van could see Becca standing there. "I'm almost ready," Zoe said. "I just need to brush my teeth."

"Then get to it." Becca grinned, looking over her shoulder to smile at Van. "I'll wait for you in the kitchen." Zoe ran into the bathroom, as Becca walked into the kitchen and smiled at Van. "Hey."

"Thanks for dropping my car off this morning," Van said, giving her a hug

"No problem. Logan dropped me off at the drive-in at the asscrack of dawn. That guy really needs to learn how to sleep in." Becca grimaced. "But I did get a nice walk back to the house."

You want coffee?" Van asked her, biting down a smile.

"No, I'll get one at the diner. How are you doing?"

"Better." Van nodded. "Can I ask you how Tanner is?"

Becca sat in the chair next to Van's. "I don't know. He was gone when I got back after dropping your car. But last night he was a mess." She shifted on her feet. "I feel really uncomfortable talking to you about him. I hate being in the middle." She blew out a mouthful of air. "We're still friends, right?"

Van's chest tightened. Of course Becca shouldn't get involved. It was unfair to her, and to them as well. "Of course we are. And thank you for being so sweet to Zoe. I know she appreciates it."

"She's a good kid. I like her a lot." Becca smiled. "I hope you get a little bit of peace while we're gone."

"I'm ready," Zoe said, running into the kitchen. "I even brushed my hair. Can we go now?"

"Sure." Becca stood, giving Van a smile. "We'll see you later."

Van nodded. "Thanks."

She saw the two of them out, closing the front door gently behind them, then turned back to the hallway.

Her mom was standing there, fully dressed, her hair spilling over her shoulders as she stared at Van.

Van walked back into the kitchen and poured them both a fresh mug of coffee.

It looked like it was going to be a day for talking.

CHAPTER THIRTY-TWO

*T*anner's phone beeped right as he and Logan walked through the front door of Gray's house. He pulled it out of his pocket as they followed their older brother to his expansive, state-of-the-art kitchen, where the huge glass doors were flung open, the late-morning sun blasting through.

He checked the screen. Just a junk email. Tanner swallowed down his disappointment.

"Coffee?" Gray asked.

"Give me a vatful," Logan said. "This guy had me up at the ass crack of dawn."

"It was the other way around, dumbass." Tanner lifted an eyebrow, his gaze still stuck on his phone screen. He watched as it slowly faded to black.

"Two coffees coming up. Cam's on the phone in the backyard," Gray said, sliding a pod into the flap at the front of his expensive coffee machine.

"Where's Maddie?" Tanner asked, looking around for her.

"She's gone out." The corner of Gray's lip twitched. "Said

this was 'brother business' and she wasn't getting involved." He held the coffee out to Tanner.

"We're all checked in for our flight," Cam said to Logan as he walked into the kitchen. "I got a car meeting us at the other end. We need to leave for the airport by two."

"Thanks, bro." Logan nodded. "I owe you one."

"What's for brunch?" Cam asked as he pulled out one of the stools set around the huge breakfast bar. "I'm starving."

"Chilli's in the oven," Gray said, passing him and Logan both a coffee, then pouring himself one. "Now we just need to pull Tanner's head out of his ass and we can eat."

"You guys are obsessed with my ass," Tanner muttered, shaking his head.

"I'm obsessed with you not making a huge mistake," Gray told him. "So come on, talk. What's going on with you and Van Butler?"

Tanner sighed, leaning his elbows on the counter and resting his head in his hands. Just hearing her name felt like a stab in the heart. "I'm in love with her."

"So why are you sitting here while she's across town and neither of you are talking to each other?" Gray asked, his brow furrowing.

"That was her decision." Tanner looked up, his eyes catching Gray's. "For some damn stupid reason she thinks I'm better off without her. Thinks all the things her mom has done are a bad reflection of her." He shook his head. "It's not the first time she's walked away from us for what she says is my own good." Tanner's jaw felt so damn tight. "She did it ten years ago before I went to Duke."

"You two were a thing ten years ago?" Cam asked. "Why didn't I know this?" He glanced at his twin. "Did you know this?"

"Yep." Logan nodded. "I know the whole sorry story."

"What story?" Gray asked. "Anybody want to fill me in?"

Tanner sighed and took another sip of coffee. It did nothing to elevate his mood. "I was in love with her ten years ago. We kind of hooked up at the Senior Prom."

"I thought you went to prom with Chrissie Fairfax," Gray said.

"I did. But if you remember, we shared a car with Van and her date, who was my friend, Brad. But he was an asshole and the two of them had an argument and he left along with our ride, so she was on her own." Tanner blew out a mouthful of air. "And then Chrissie got pissed with me because I asked if Van could catch a ride home with us and her dad." Tanner shook his head. "So in the end Van and I were left with each other and… well… the rest was history."

Gray laughed. "Ah, the drama of high school prom. So what happened next?"

Tanner blew out a mouthful of air. "The usual. We dated. We made out. And we both had already gotten accepted to Duke. It was all ahead of us, and we were so damn excited. Then later in the summer, out of nowhere, she came and told me we were over, and she wasn't going to Duke anymore."

"So why'd she break up with you?" Gray asked.

"She said she was thinking about it and she didn't want to settle down. Didn't want to make the same mistakes her mom had made. That she was going to stay in Hartson's Creek and get a job, think about what she wanted to do next."

"Shit, that must have been a kick in the balls." Cam sighed.

"You could say that." Tanner swallowed hard, remembering the way he'd begged her to change her mind. But she was adamant. She didn't want to talk to him, and refused to take his calls. And when he'd turned up at the drive-in, she'd not been anywhere in sight.

It had felt like grief washing over him, making his whole

body ache. He'd lost the girl he was in love with, but even worse, he'd lost his best friend and he had no idea why.

"What happened next?" Gray asked. "That can't be the whole story. It doesn't make any sense."

"That's because it was bull. All of it. I only found out later the real reason she broke it off. Turns out her mom was pregnant, and Van gave all the money she'd saved for college to help out with the baby, with Zoe. And she was too damn proud to tell me, because she thought I'd either try to help her out or stay here with her instead of going to college."

"Would you have done that?" Gray asked him.

"Hell yeah. Of course I would have. I'd have asked you guys for help, or spoken to Dad or Aunt Gina. Done something to make things better for her. It wasn't her responsibility to stay with her mom. She was eighteen years old and brilliant as hell. She didn't have to give up her life for her mom's mistakes."

Gray nodded slowly. "I would have helped."

"I know, man. I know."

"You need to tell them the rest," Logan said to him.

"There's more?" Gray asked.

"Of course there's more." Logan shook his head. "Why do you think the two of them haven't spoken for ten years?"

Tanner's gut twisted. "Yeah, well this is the part where I *really* messed up. And I've regretted it every day of my life. As you know, I went to Duke, and there were a few friends from school there with me. A few weeks into the semester, all the girls came up to visit. I messaged Van and begged her to come, too. Even offered to drive up and give her a ride. I thought maybe she'd change her mind." He licked his dry lips. "But she didn't reply. And when they arrived, that's when I realized it was really over with me and Van. That she didn't care. She wasn't coming, and I had to start living my life without her. And that sucked. I loved her. It felt like my heart was being ripped out of my body. So when somebody opened the first keg up later that afternoon, I started drinking and didn't stop. It felt good. Like I was able to breathe for the first time in weeks."

"Never a good idea." Cam shook his head.

"Yeah, well it felt like it at the time. The whole thing turned into a party. We were dancing, playing beer pong, having fun. Then this girl…" Tanner started laughing, though there was no humor in it. "Damn, I can't even remember her name. She was in my math class, that's all I remember. Anyway, she started dancing with me, and the next minute we were kissing." Tanner shook his head. "Like really kissing. I can't remember which one of us suggested going to my dorm room, but things got a little heated." He lifted an eyebrow. "You can probably guess the rest."

"You slept with her?" Gray asked.

Tanner inhaled sharply. "She stayed the night in my dorm. But the next morning about seven, somebody was banging on the door. At first I thought it was one of her friends checking on her, so I pulled my shorts on and went to answer the door. But it wasn't her friend, it was Van."

"Oh shit," Cam said softly.

"I held the door open a crack, and Van started vomiting words, telling me that her mom was pregnant and she'd made a mistake. That she loved me and was so sorry for hurting me, and wanted us to try again." He lifted his eyes to look at his brothers. They were all leaning in, staring at his mouth, waiting for his next words. "And then the girl walked over wearing only my t-shirt and made it pretty damn obvious what went on."

"What did Van say?" Gray asked.

"Nothing. She said nothing." Tanner swallowed hard. "She just looked at me for a moment, as though she was waiting for an explanation. And I should have said something.

Anything to make it better. But instead I panicked. That's when she turned and ran away." He squeezed his eyes shut for a moment. "When she ran, I froze. I didn't try to explain or chase after her, and I've regretted that for the rest of my life." He'd never forget Van's face as she stared at him. Or the single tear drop that slid down her cheek. And though he'd tried to call, to talk to her, she'd refused to answer.

There were moments you regretted forever. That changed your life in the hardest way. That moment was his.

And it was happening all over again.

"Oh Jesus, Tanner." Gray sighed.

"I know. I fucking know." He dropped his head into his hands. "That was the last time we talked until she came back. I saw her in town a couple of times, when we were both visiting, but we didn't acknowledge each other. She just kept on walking."

And it had hurt like hell every time. Because he knew how much he'd messed up, with no clue how to make it better. So much easier to pretend she didn't exist.

"The sooner you two start talking the better," Gray muttered. "If you did that the first time maybe you wouldn't be here now."

"They'd be married with kids," Logan said. "For sure."

Tanner shook his head. "You're not making me feel any better."

"You want that?" Gray asked. "You want to commit to her?"

"Yes." His response was immediate. "I want her so damn much it hurts."

The oven timer began to beep. Gray walked over, turning it off, then pulled the door open, the deep aroma of chilli filling the kitchen. "Looks like it's ready." He pulled the dish out with a towel and put it on the counter.

"You gotta talk to her," Gray said, lifting the lid. "Tell her how you feel. I know it's scary as hell, but what other option is there? You two don't talk for another ten years?"

The thought of it was like a punch to Tanner's gut. He couldn't do that. Not again. "That's not happening," he said gruffly. "I won't let it." This time he was ready to fight.

"Good." Gray carried some bowls to the breakfast bar, followed by the garlic bread, chilli, and a salad, putting it all in the middle of the table. "Help yourself, guys."

Gray was right on all counts. So was Logan for that matter. He needed to talk, to be vulnerable, to actually fight for the girl who lit up his world. His sunshine girl with the golden hair. For too long he let the memory of pain guide him, but that had to stop.

She was it for him. She always had been. He was so sick of fighting his feelings for the one perfect thing in his life.

And if she rejected him? Then he'd keep trying until they were old and gray if he had to.

CHAPTER THIRTY-THREE

"*I* know you hate me."

Van looked at her mom from across the table. Kim seemed smaller than ever with her shoulders hunched up and her hands cupping the coffee Van had poured for her.

"I don't hate you." Van sighed. "I just hate the way you behave when you drink. And the fact that you lied to me for years about who my father was." She looked down at her hands. "Why didn't you tell me?"

"I made a promise." Her mom was still staring down at her cup. "It was the only way he wouldn't press charges."

"What charges?" Van sighed. "You're going to need to start from the beginning."

"Are you sure you want to know?"

Van nodded. It wasn't about wanting. She needed to know. This was her life. The truth was important.

"I had an affair with Johnny while I was working for him." Kim pressed her lips together. "I guess that bit's obvious. Not that I thought it was an affair. He told me he was leaving Nora, it was just a matter of time. He promised me he'd tell her all about us. And I was twenty years old. Naïve, alone. I believed him. He was older, wiser, and richer." She gave a little laugh. "He told me he loved me. If you'd ever been a foster kid, you'd know how much I needed to hear those words. To have somebody whisper them to me and hold me tight. For the first time in years I felt safe. Enough that when I realized I was pregnant, that I went right to him and told him."

Her mom never talked about her childhood. And the anguish on her face seemed raw. It hit Van right in the chest.

Her mom had been desperate to hear those three little words. And Van feared them.

Especially from the one man she felt everything for.

"What did he say?" Van asked her.

"Told me I needed to wait a bit more. Things kept cropping up. A big business deal Nora needed to approve, a party they were throwing for her parents... every time I thought we'd gotten over one hurdle, another one appeared. It took me months to realize there was never going to be a good time."

Van said nothing. Just stared at the woman who'd birthed her twenty-eight years ago.

"Then one day at church, I heard Nora telling everybody *she* was pregnant. That *they* were pregnant. At that moment I knew he wasn't ever going to leave her. That I'd always be the one waiting around for him. And I got angry, so angry..." She cleared her throat. "I told him we were over."

"But you kept working for him?"

"Yeah. And he spread some story about a guy who kept coming in to see me in the office. Everybody assumed I'd gotten pregnant by an out-of-towner." She pursed her lips together and shook her head. "But that wasn't what got me. It was seeing all the beautiful things Nora was buying for her baby. She would ask me what kind of nursery I was planning, what stroller I was buying, who was organizing my baby shower. And I was so damn jealous. She had everything I'd always dreamed of. A home, a family, a father for her baby."

"So you stole from Johnny?"

"I took what was ours." Her mom looked up, her eyes flashing. "He hadn't given me a dime toward the things I needed for you. So I started taking money out of the business account so I could buy things for your nursery."

"You stole thousands, Mom." It was hard to keep the anger from her voice.

"He owed me." Kim sighed. "I knew I'd never get the chance again."

Van opened her mouth to argue, but it was pointless. Instead, she took a sip of coffee and looked at the woman in front of her. "What happened when he found out?"

"He was so angry. Threatened to call the cops, told me I'd be thrown into jail and you'd be put in foster care. Unless I agreed to leave my job and to keep quiet about me and him."

"So you agreed?"

Kim nodded. "I was never going to tell anyway. Wouldn't give him or Nora the satisfaction."

"You should have told me this years ago," Van told her, breathing down the anger rising up inside her. "I had a right to know."

"That your daddy didn't want you? When was a good time to tell you, Van? When you were six and were going to blab it everywhere? Or when you were a teenager and so desperate for a family you practically adopted the Hartsons? When is a good time to tell a kid their father lives down the road but doesn't want to know them? Believe it or not, I was trying to protect you."

"You were protecting yourself."

"It was the same thing."

"No," Van said, frowning. "No, it isn't."

"You think I don't know how you feel about gossip?

Honey, I know. I've always known. I've seen you wince when somebody looks your way and says something. You pretend you're this strong person, and maybe sometimes you are, but when you get hurt, it kills you."

Van inhaled a ragged breath. Her mom's words were too close for comfort. "I still deserved to know."

"Yes, you did." Kim folded her arms across her chest. "And now you know."

"I would have preferred you'd told me privately," Van said pointedly. "And what about Zoe? Is her father really someone who was passing through town like you always said?" Van had to be sure. There was no way she'd let Zoe go through this pain. Not if she could help it.

Kim looked sheepish. "Yes, Zoe's father isn't anyone in town. And I am so sorry about last night. I should have told you in private. I'm going to stop drinking."

"Sure." Van rolled her eyes.

"I've got an appointment scheduled with my doc. He thinks he can get me referred to a rehab facility right away. He has contacts at a charity."

Van looked up, surprised. "What?"

Kim nodded. "Only for a couple of weeks. But it's a start, right?"

"I guess." Van sighed. "There's something else you need to know."

"What?" Kim's brows knit together as she looked at her.

"When you were pregnant with Zoe, and I gave you that money instead of using it to go to college, it felt like I was dying. Giving everything up because of *your* bad decisions."

Kim blinked, surprised. "You told me you wanted me to have it. That's what you said."

"I lied. I hated you for it," Van whispered. "And I hated me for being so weak to give it to you. It ruined everything."

"No…" Kim shook her head, her brows dipping. "Don't say that."

Van felt her eyes sting with tears. "I was supposed to go to Duke with Tanner, remember? We'd started dating. I was in love with him. We had it all planned out. Three years at college, then we'd head to New York and live there for a while." She pressed her lips together, remembering the day her mom told her she was pregnant. And all those dreams Van had disappeared in smoke. She couldn't leave. Not when her mom didn't have a job or any way to take care of a baby. So Van gave Kim the money she'd saved for college.

And for two years she'd stayed. Until Craig had come on the scene, and calmed her mom down, taken care of her the way she'd always dreamed of. Only then had Van felt able to leave.

"Is that why you broke up with him?" Kim asked.

A stupid tear rolled down Van's cheek. "The first time, yeah. I broke up with him because I knew he wouldn't leave me behind if I told him you were pregnant. He'd have stayed too and I couldn't do that to him. So I told him I didn't want him anymore. That he should go to Duke without me."

"The first time?" Her mom frowned.

Van nodded. "I changed my mind. A couple of weeks after he'd left for Duke. I was going crazy, missed him like I'd never missed anything before. And I realized what a stupid mistake I'd made. So I took your car and drove up to see him. To tell him the truth about why I didn't go."

"So why didn't you get back together?"

"Because I found him with another girl." She licked her dry lips. "Technically, he didn't do anything wrong. We weren't in a relationship. But it still hurt like hell."

Kim gasped. "Oh, Van. I'm so sorry."

"Yeah, well we all make mistakes." Van wiped her cheek with the back of her hand. She could still remember the horror of seeing the petite brunette wearing Tanner's t-shirt and nothing else. Of Tanner's open mouth as he tried to talk and nothing came out.

And the complete pain of knowing that she'd lost the one good thing in her life. And that it was her fault for not telling him the truth. She'd turned on her heel and run without looking back, pride stopping her from ever letting him back into her heart.

Until this year.

"But you and Tanner are friends now, right?" Kim asked, looking hopeful. "You made up? You're working together."

Van had never talked about guys with her mom. Kim was the last person she'd ever ask for advice. Yet this need to get her words out came over her. "We were more than friends until last night." She shook her head. "But I broke it off."

"Why?" Kim's voice was sharp.

Van thought of Tanner's parting words as she left the drive-in office. Of Zoe's as they talked this morning before she went out with Becca.

"Because I'm scared," Van whispered. "I'm so scared of losing the most important person in my life that I pushed him away before he could walk." She let out a sob. "Twice."

It was like a dam had been lifted. Tears started pouring down her face. Her chest was so tight it was hard to breathe, as the memories of last night and from ten years ago came washing over her.

"Oh sweetie." Her mom's chair scraped against the tiled floor. She walked over to where Van was sobbing at the table, wrapping her arms around her, pulling Van's face against her stomach, stroking her hair. "Don't cry."

That only made Van sob louder. How could she have done this again? Messed her own life up, and Tanner's, too. Her whole body ached at the thought of it.

"Look at us," her mom whispered. "Me so desperate

for love I'll take whatever's offered. And you so scared you'll push it away at the first opportunity. What a damn mess."

It hurt because it was true. Every word. She was so scared of feeling pain she did it first. Then lied to herself saying she was okay because she'd chosen the pain rather than having it inflicted on her.

But it didn't matter. Either way it hurt like hell.

And to make things even crazier, here she was letting her mom comfort her. The same mom who'd caused her so much pain to begin with. It made her head hurt.

"I've lost him again," Van whispered. "And it's my fault."

"You don't know that. Maybe you both need to cool off a bit."

"I told him we were over for good."

Her mom stroked the hair from Van's face. "You said that last night?"

"Yeah."

"And did you mean it?"

"No," Van said softly. "I didn't mean it. I was just trying to protect him."

"He's a grown man, Van. He can protect himself." Her mom sighed. "Didn't you just tell me I was wrong for lying to you about Johnny to protect you?"

"Yeah, I did."

"And I was," her mom said. "It was wrong to lie to you. I should have told you the truth."

She looked up at her mom through teary eyes. It felt uncomfortable being soothed by her. As though she was playing a role she was completely unprepared for. Savannah Butler didn't let people take care of her. She was the protector. It was all that she knew.

And it had messed up her life.

That thought bounced around her mind like a pinball,

making her shiver. For ten years she'd paid the price of telling Tanner a lie. One tiny lie.

That had torn both of their worlds apart.

How different would it have been if she'd been honest? If she'd allowed herself to be vulnerable. To tell him that her mom was pregnant, that she was scared, but she still wanted him to go to Duke.

If she'd let herself tell the truth instead of believing she was protecting everyone around her.

"You okay?"

She'd almost forgotten her mom was still there. "Yeah, I'm good."

"Can I ask you a favor?" Kim asked.

Van blinked. "What is it?"

"Will you take care of Zoe for me when I'm in rehab?"

"Of course I will."

"Thank you." Kim's lips curved into the faintest of smiles.

IT WAS past midnight according to the clock beside her bed. After Becca had brought Zoe home, giving Van a big hug before driving away, the three of them – Van, Zoe, and their mom – had spent the afternoon talking. Making plans for Kim's rehab, for Zoe's care, and for Van's next steps. It had been uncomfortable, being honest with them, showing her vulnerability, yet it had felt cathartic, too.

For the first time in her life she was letting the emotion flow out of her. She wasn't sure that she would ever get used to it.

Zoe had asked her what she was going to do about Tanner.

"Talk to him." Van had said, even though the thought of it made her stomach twist. Because he had every right to tell her he didn't want to listen. That he wasn't going to put himself out there for her again.

He could reject her, and she knew it would hurt like hell. But it couldn't be any worse than the pain she was feeling right now. And if that happened, then she would deal with it. Because she'd know that she'd done all she could.

It wasn't the kind of conversation you had on the phone, though. Tomorrow she'd go to his house, knock on the door, and hope like hell he'd open up. And tonight? Well, she'd probably toss and turn in her bed the same way she had last night. She should be getting used to that by now.

She didn't register the slam of a car door at first. Not until she heard shuffling on what sounded like the sidewalk outside of the bungalow. It was probably their neighbor coming home from a late shift.

Van turned on her side, curling her legs up to her chest, and tried not to think about how empty her bed was without him.

And then she heard five familiar notes cutting through the night time silence. A drum beat cut in, sultry and low. Had their neighbor left his stereo going in his car?

She knew the song by heart. *Take My Breath Away* by Berlin. The first song she and Tanner had made love to, during that long, hot summer of the Tom Cruise retrospective at the drive-in.

She'd loved that movie, as schmaltzy as it was. Loved the way Tom looked in his flight jacket, the way he stared at Kelly McGillis like she was his world.

And that sex scene. It had done things to her teenaged body that she didn't know how to deal with. All she knew was that she'd played that song daily over that summer. Tanner had complained about it incessantly.

Yet he'd stored it on his iPod touch, and played it the night they'd let things go too far. Although it had been uncomfortable and awkward and the ground had turned her pretty pink dress black, that night was still the most precious memory she had.

Tanner's kisses, his touch, the sound of Berlin echoing from his phone. The way her body undulated beneath his, as he asked her again and again if she was okay.

And she *had* been okay. More than okay. Until she discovered her mom's pregnancy and everything she'd planned for was torn apart.

The music was getting louder. Berlin was getting to the chorus. She turned onto her other side, waiting for the car door to shut.

But it didn't. Frowning, she climbed out of her bed, padding in bare feet to the window and pulling the curtain aside.

Instead of a car with it's door open, she saw a man standing in the front yard, a large portable speaker held over his head, as he stared at the window where she was standing.

Tanner Hartson.

Her eyes caught his, and she felt it right in the pit of her stomach. She couldn't look away if she tried. He was completely still, his biceps tight with his arms raised up, the song they first made love to echoing out of the speaker.

She went to open the window, but he shook his head. So she pulled her hand back and watched, listening to the song, her gaze caught in his as the memories of that night assailed her.

She knew exactly what he was doing. Channelling his inner Lloyd Dobler. She could remember watching *Say Anything* with him and them both laughing at how awkward the Boombox Scene was.

Tanner looked almost as awkward, though he was doing a good job of hiding it. But how could you feel anything else when you were in somebody's front yard in the middle of the night playing eighties music?

A light came on in the house across the road. She could see curtains being pulled, windows being opened, heads staring out. The neighborhood would be talking about this for a week.

The amazing thing was she didn't care. He was here and he was playing their song and nothing else mattered. For four long minutes, she stood at the window, her body aching for him, her heart so full she couldn't speak even if he could hear her.

And then the music ended. He lowered his arms and turned on his heel, walking away from the bungalow and Van. The next moment, she heard a car door slam and the engine start up. It was only when she saw the Camaro pull away that she let the curtain fall back over the window and walked back to her bed, sitting down and pulling her knees against her chest.

That's when she started to laugh. She couldn't help it. It was so strange and yet perfect. He hadn't said a word and neither had she, yet it had felt exactly like a conversation. Or the start of one, anyway.

She fell back on the mattress, her back bouncing against the springs, wondering what was going through Tanner's mind right now.

Maybe she'd ask him tomorrow. No scratch that, she'd *definitely* ask him tomorrow. But for now she'd try to sleep and dream of Tanner Hartson and his Lloyd Dobler impersonation.

As far as she was concerned, it was everything.

CHAPTER THIRTY-FOUR

"Go now I know you're completely crazy," Becca said, grinning from ear to ear as she stood on Tanner's doorstep. "You're the talk of the town, standing in the Butlers' front yard playing eighties music at one a.m.." She tipped her head to the side, the smile still playing on her lips. "Have you totally lost it?"

"It was a gesture." Tanner shrugged. "Meant for her, not anybody else."

"But what does it mean?" Becca asked. "From what I hear, the two of you didn't even talk. You just stood there, played music, then drove away." She shook her head. "Why didn't you ask her to talk to you?"

Tanner sighed. "Because it was one in the morning. I just wanted to let her know I was thinking about her."

He hadn't been doing anything else. Last night he'd tossed and turned in bed, desperate to figure out how to make things better. His brothers had been right. He needed to change something. *Himself.* He'd messed things up between them twice because of his damn fear of rejection. He couldn't hurt her a third time. He wouldn't let himself.

She deserved to be taken care of. And he wanted to be the man to do it. He wanted to wrap her in his arms and ward off all the people trying to hurt her. The Fairfaxes, her mom… all of them had used and abused her.

But he'd been the worst of them all. Because she'd trusted him back when they were kids. Believed him when he told her he'd always be there for her. But when she'd pushed him away, he hadn't fought for her at all. Because he couldn't bear to risk getting hurt again.

Well this time was different. When he'd seen her at her bedroom window looking out at him, it felt like his heart was finally coming back to life. Her eyes had been wide, her expression soft, and those lips, those damn fine kissable lips, had been parted, singing in time to the lyrics.

When their gaze connected, electricity buzzing between them, he felt full of her.

He hadn't been able to pull his eyes away. Hadn't wanted to. He'd let the music speak for him. She took his breath away. Took everything he had to give. And he wanted to give it to her again. *Forever*.

"You're gonna fight for her, right?" Becca asked. "Because I don't think I could stand it if you give up. Not this time."

"Yeah," he said softly, "I'm going to fight for her." Not with fists or weapons or anything else. This was going to be a quiet fight. Like their four-minute, emotion-filled stare last night, it might not involve words. But it was a fight nonetheless.

He wasn't only fighting for her, he was fighting for himself. And *against* himself. Punching down the little kid in him who'd lost his mom and was afraid of losing anything else ever again.

That kid might be the toughest opponent he'd ever faced.

.   .   .

* * *

"I GUESS THAT'S IT. I'm packed." Kim closed the small suitcase and zipped it up. "Not that I need a lot. Just comfortable clothes, toiletries, and pajamas, that's what it says. No makeup, no food or drink." She gave a wry smile at the last one.

Zoe was with her friends for the day. One of their moms had offered to take them all to the waterpark. Van had jumped at the offer – so much better to keep her sister occupied than have her worrying about their mom.

"What time are you getting picked up?" Van asked Kim. She was biting down the urge to offer to drive her mom. Another thing she needed to get used to. This wasn't *her* problem. Even if it felt completely wrong to be standing here watching life carry on around her.

"In an hour. I've left the directions on the refrigerator. In case you and Zoe want to come see me next weekend."

"We'll come." Van nodded. "Zoe would kill me if we didn't." There was a family session planned, including a discussion about Kim's next steps. "Let me know if you need me to bring anything."

"I will."

An hour later and the house was empty save for Van and her thoughts. Of course they were full of Tanner. Of the way he'd stared at her last night as he played music from his speakers. This was the first bit of quiet she had to process what had happened. She needed to decide how the hell to clear up the mess she'd made.

There was a bang on the door. Her heart immediately leapt. Was it him? Shaking her head at her stupid damn excitement, she walked down the hallway and opened the door to the last man she'd expected to see standing on the porch.

"Johnny?"

There was no way she was calling him Dad. Not least because it sounded kind of creepy.

He shuffled his feet, looking over his shoulder like he was worried he was being watched. "Can I come in?" he asked.

"What for?"

"Because I think we need to talk. And your neighbors are all staring out of their windows right now."

Maybe fear of gossip was genetic. "Okay. Come in." She pushed the door wider and he stepped inside.

"Is Kim home?"

"Nope. Just me."

He nodded, threading his fingers together. "That's good."

She led him to the small living room and pointed at the recliner by the window. "Please sit. Can I get you a drink?" She tried to be civil, even though it was hard to hide the hostility she felt toward him.

"Um, no thank you." He did as he was told, glancing out of the window again. "This shouldn't take long."

She bit down a desire to laugh. This was so absurd and nothing like she thought it would be. Not that she'd spent a lot of time dreaming about ever meeting her father. But in the movies there was always a lot more hugs and tears.

Maybe she should be glad that Johnny wasn't a touchy feely kind of guy. There was no way she wanted him hugging her.

"Okay then. Shoot." She nodded at him.

He cleared his throat. "Um… well… after everything that happened at the drive-in, I wanted to make sure that you're, um, okay."

She swallowed. "I'm fine."

"Nora thinks we should take a DNA test. Just to see if

you're really my daughter." He looked up at her expectantly. "Would you be willing to do that?"

Van looked at him for a moment. At this big man in town who thought he was all that. She could imagine him all those years ago, thinking he was the king of the castle, sleeping with two women, getting them both pregnant. And now he looked chastened. Embarassed. Under the thumb of a woman he'd wronged.

"No," she told him. "I wouldn't be willing to do that."

"Can I ask why?" He lifted his head up, his eyes wide.

Yeah, he could ask. Didn't mean she owed him an answer. She looked at him with tired eyes, wondering why this all felt so damn awkward.

"Because it wouldn't make a difference. You weren't a father to me when I needed one. And now that I know you are, it doesn't matter. You're too late."

He blinked, his gaze dropping to his legs. "You're right. I wasn't there." Another cough. Still not meeting her eye, he took a pen out of his suit pocket, then a small black book that looked suspiciously like a checkbook.

He wasn't going to try to buy her off, was he? Her mouth was dry as he opened the flap, then twisted his expensive-looking pen until the nib came through. He meticulously wrote, then tore out the check and held it to her.

"What's that?" She made no move to take it.

"Ten thousand dollars. Something close to what I owe in child support." He pushed the check toward her. "Take it. It's yours."

She stared at the piece of paper. At his elegant handwriting. At her name written in loops and swirls along the top line. Ten thousand dollars. It made her feel sick to look at.

"I don't want your money," she told him, her voice low. "I don't want anything from you."

"But Nora's worried you'll come for it after I'm gone. I

want to settle it now. Make sure she and Chrissie are looked after." His tone was desperate.

Van's jaw tightened. "You're a piece of work, you know that? Why would I come after your money? I don't want anything to do with you. Not any of you. Once upon a time you might have made my life more liveable." She stood, unable to sit civilly and listen to him anymore. "I know you saw me, running around town on my own when I should have been taken care of at home. And I know you know mom was depressed or drunk or both most of the time. I needed you *then*." She shook her head. "I needed someone. Even if you offered me a million dollars it wouldn't make up for that."

His mouth dropped open. "A million…"

Van shook her head. "Don't worry. I don't want a dime off you. You can tell Nora and Chrissie that your money's safe. And if you want me to sign something stating I have no claim on it, then send it to me. I'll sign anything to get you all out of my life."

"If you're going to be like that about it then I should go." He stood, sliding his pen and checkbook back into his pocket. "You're ungrateful. Like your mom. I gave her a job, a home, and she only wanted more. Nora's right, you're both poison." He pushed his chest out, his eyes narrowing as he looked at her.

"That might be the nicest thing anybody's ever said to me." She walked to the living room entrance, and pointed to the hallway. He walked past her, his shoulders back, his head high. "I'd rather be like my mom than you. Or any of your family."

He pulled the front door open, then turned to look at her. "Yes, well. I'll ask my lawyer to send you a contract."

She was sure he would. Stupid thing was, she'd sign it,

too. Because her pride was worth so much more than this excuse of a father in front of her.

He huffed and stepped outside. That's when Van saw the passenger sitting in his car, with her hair perfectly coiffed as she lifted her nose and glanced at Van on the doorstep.

A wave of fury washed over her. Van pushed past Johnny and almost ran down the steps. Alarm widened in Nora's eyes as Van reached for the passenger door.

"What are you doing?" she asked, as Van wrenched it open.

"I want to talk to you."

Nora lifted her head a little more. "I have nothing to say to you."

"That's good. Maybe you'll listen to what I have to say then." She felt the cool of Johnny's shadow fall over her as he stood behind her, saying nothing. "First of all, you can stuff your money. I don't want a dime from you or your deadbeat husband. I don't want *anything* to do with you at all." She shook her head.

Nora pressed her lips together, saying nothing.

"But more importantly, there's something else you need to know." Van's voice was short. Harsh. "You're the worst kind of woman. One who looks down on others because it makes you feel better about yourself. One who punishes a little girl with hard words and harsher thoughts because you can't punish your husband for being an asshole." Van crossed her arms over her chest. "Well that's over with. *Done.* You say one more bad word about me or my family, and I'll be shouting out about you and Johnny all over town. I'll tell *everyone* about how he left my mom high and dry. How he had almost thirty years to recognize me and never did. And I'll tell them about you, *Nora.* About the way you thought you were better than me because you had money." Van leaned forward, until her nose was only an inch away from Nora's.

"You keep away from my family. Otherwise, I'll make sure you regret it."

Nora swallowed hard, her eyes glassy. She gave an almost imperceptible nod.

Van straightened her spine and let out a mouthful of air, then turned on her heel, almost knocking Johnny over in the process. He quickly stepped back, as though he was afraid she was going to strike him.

Good. She didn't want him anywhere near her.

"Goodbye, *Dad*," she said, her voice full of sarcasm. "I hope you have a happy life. Because mine has been a hundred times better without you in it."

* * *

VAN SLAMMED the door closed behind her and sucked in a deep breath. She was shaking. Enough for her to lean on the wood and let her head rest there for a moment.

She didn't regret it. Not a word. Nora and Johnny had what was coming to them. So why was her body quivering like a bowl of Jello?

Because of him. Right now she should be calling him, sharing her triumph over the Fairfaxes with him. But instead she was alone in her mom's house, aching for the one person she kept pushing away. She couldn't do this anymore.

If she'd just talked to him instead of deciding what was best for them both, she wouldn't be here alone now.

She had a choice. Either, she kept doing things the way she always had and suffered because of it, or she stood tall and admitted that she was afraid. So scared of losing him that she'd pushed him away first.

Last night he'd made the sweetest of gestures. Maybe she

should do the same. But what could it be? She frowned, thinking about the way Jerry Maguire walked into a room full of women and declared himself to Dorothy. Or how Richard Gere climbed up a fire escape despite his fear of heights to woo Julia Roberts in *Pretty Woman*. Actually, he was pretty good at the grand gesture in all his movies. Look at the way he walked into the factory dressed in his uniform in *An Officer and a Gentleman* and scooped the love of his life into his hands.

But where were the grand gestures from the women? Didn't they do that sort of thing? Van frowned, scanning through her memories for a scene, but all she could think of was *Notting Hill*. Where Julia Roberts just opened her mouth and talked.

Maybe that's what she needed to do. Maybe her grand gesture was to be open, to talk, to make herself vulnerable. That sounded damn scarier than anything in a movie.

It was honest. It was real. And more importantly, it's what she needed to do.

Before she got scared off, she picked up her phone and tapped out a message, her hands still shaking.

*I MISS you. - **Van***

HER BREATH RUSHED OUT of her mouth. Maybe climbing up a fire escape was a better idea after all. But then a reply flashed on her screen, and the tightness in her chest loosened.

*I MISS YOU, **too**. - **Tanner***

. . .

THANK GOD. She squeezed her eyes closed for a moment, then opened them again, as another message appeared.

CAN I TALK TO YOU? *Really talk? There's so much I need to tell you. - Tanner*

I WAS ABOUT *to ask the same thing. – Van*

WHEN? *- Tanner*

TONIGHT? *I'm taking Zoe out for dinner, but we'll be back by eight. Does that work? - Van*

YEAH, *that works. I'll be there at ten. See you tonight. - Tanner Xx*

SHE STARED at the kisses for way longer than was healthy, trying to read the meaning of them. She'd see him tonight and the anticipation was already killing her.

* * *

SOME OLD HABITS DIED HARD. Tanner couldn't bring himself to knock on her front door. Instead, he tapped on her bedroom window, his jaw set, his eyes soft, his body ready to be close to her again. The days without her had been like a special kind of torture. Yet it had been necessary. Logan was right about that.

As kids it had felt like Van and Tanner shared a brain sometimes. He assumed she thought the same way as he did. Heck, sometimes he really believed she could read his mind. And when he fell in love with her as an eighteen-year-old, he'd thought it would be easy. They didn't need to talk, they just *knew*.

But that was bullshit. Had been then, still was now. She had her own thoughts, her own needs, her own feelings. And as much as he wanted to know every single one of them, they were hers, and she got to decide whether to share them or not.

Her face appeared at the window, and his breath caught in his throat. Would he always feel this kind of reaction when he saw her? His eyes were drawn to her lips, soft and pink. God, he was aching to kiss her.

You need to talk. The thought sounded a lot like Logan. It made him want to laugh. Van opened the window, holding the curtain aside as he climbed inside.

"Hi." He looked down at her. She must have recently showered. Her hair was damp, tumbling in waves over her shoulder. Her skin was shining, freshly scrubbed clean. She was wearing a pair of soft jersey shorts and a t-shirt, and right now she looked more like eighteen than twenty-eight. "You look beautiful."

"Shut up. I'm a mess."

He grinned because it was so damn good to hear her voice. "Not to me. I want to take a photo of you and make it my phone wallpaper."

"If you do that, I'll castrate you." She lifted an eyebrow. "Just sayin'."

Christ, he was in love with her. He leaned forward,

brushing his lips against her ear. "Sorry, babe, but I'm rather partial to my balls."

Her eyes darkened, and she turned her face almost imperceptibly toward his. Only an inch more and their lips would touch. He could feel the blood pulsing through him, hot and needy.

You need to talk.

Shut up, Logan! He shook his head to get the voice out of his brain. But it was right. So damn right. They were adults, not kids. He had control of his body, even if all he wanted to do was give into it.

"How's Zoe?" he asked, in an attempt to bring things back on track.

"She's okay. Gone to bed early. She's heading to the pool with some friends tomorrow." Her lips curled at the thought of her sister, and he wanted to kiss them again. He curled his hands into fists to stop himself.

"And your mom? Have you heard from her?"

"You know she's gone away?"

He shrugged. "Becca told me. I was surprised when I heard it. I never thought she'd go to rehab."

"Me either." Her eyes met his. "But she's there." She shrugged. "We get to see her next weekend."

"That's good." He glanced at her bed. It was a mistake. Because all the memories of touching her while in bed came flooding back. "Can we go to the kitchen to talk?" he asked her.

"Sure." Her brows dipped. "Why?"

"Because if we stay in here I'm going to need to touch you."

"What if I want to be touched?"

Her words sent a shot of desire through him that was almost impossible to ignore. And yet he had to. They needed to talk. He swallowed hard, trying to harness his willpower.

"You're not making this easy," he told her. "I'm really trying to be strong here."

"I've missed you," she said softly. The way she was looking at him almost killed him. There was a need in her eyes that reflected his own.

"Yeah." His voice was strangled. "I've missed you, too."

She reached out to cup his cheek, her fingers splaying across his rough skin. She stepped forward until her body pressed against his, and desire immediately shot through him.

He dropped his brow to hers, his lashes sweeping down as he stared at her. "Van…"

"I know," she whispered. "But please kiss me first. I need to feel you. Then we can talk."

The wisp of control that was holding him back seemed to dissipate as he stared down at her, taking in her warm eyes, her soft lips, her pink cheeks. She was looking at him like he was the air she breathed. It made him ache all over.

For her.

"Damn," he whispered, sliding his palm up her neck, tangling his fingers into her hair until her head was angled perfectly to his. She overwhelmed his senses. He was full of her. The scent of her strawberry shampoo, the sight of her wide eyes staring into his. He could hear her, too. Soft sighs that made him harder than he'd ever felt before. He tried to remember why he was here, what he was planning to do. But all he could think about were her enticing lips.

Slowly, he lowered his mouth to hers. They touched as she breathed out, warm air caressing his skin. His tongue pressed against hers, and she let out a low moan, flinging her arms around his neck to steady herself.

God, he needed her. She arched her back, kissing him, hot and needy, and he scooped his arms beneath her, lifting her until her legs wrapped around his hips. Carrying her over to the bed, he dropped her onto the mattress, his eyes dark as he went to climb on top of her.

You need to talk, dumbass.

"Get the fuck out of here," he muttered with annoyance.

"What?" Van frowned.

He shook his head. "Not you. It's Logan. He's messing with my mind."

She propped herself up on her elbows, and he tried really hard not to stare at the way her t-shirt molded against her breasts. "Logan's here?"

"Nope, he's in Boston. I still want to kill him though." He sighed, rubbing the back of his neck with the palm of his right hand. "Come on, lets go talk."

"Now?" She sounded disappointed. He felt the same.

"Yeah, now."

She nodded. "Okay. You want me to make you coffee?"

"Coffee would be great." He followed her out of the bedroom, his aching hardness protesting at the sudden change of heart. "And if it's okay with you, I'm going to talk really fast."

* * *

Van sat on the sofa, her knees against her chest, her arms wrapped around her calves, as Tanner took a sip of black coffee.

He'd insisted on sitting in the recliner on the other side of the room. She knew why. Every time they were close they ended up touching each other. They nearly stripped each other in the kitchen as she filled the coffee filter.

Her eyes met his. "Shall we talk?"

"Can I go first?"

Van nodded.

He put his coffee mug down on the table. "First of all, I want to say I'm sorry. Not just for the other night, though that was bad enough. But for every time I've walked away from you. It's happened more than it ever should've. And I can promise you that whatever happens between us, I'll never be the one to walk away again." He looked up at her, his expression serious. "I'm in love with you, Van Butler. And I never want to hurt you."

"Okay," she said softly.

"And we need to talk about what happened between us when you came to Duke. We should have talked about it weeks ago."

"I didn't want to talk about it. It hurt too much," she whispered.

"I know. And I didn't want to either. But maybe those things that hurt are the things we should be talking about. The things that matter to us. And what happened between us matters, Van. Because it ruined both of our lives. It didn't have to, but we let it. Because we refused to talk it through."

"That makes sense."

"Yeah, it does." He nodded. "And I want you to know that girl meant nothing. I was a kid, I was angry, and I needed someone to hold me. As soon as I did it, I knew she was the wrong someone."

"We weren't together then. It wasn't like you were cheating."

"Yeah, well tell my heart that. Because it's always been yours. And I never want to be with anybody but you. I've never stopped regretting that night. Everything about it. It should never have happened and that's all my fault. I'm so damn sorry that I hurt you." He winced at the memory. "But the thing I hate the most is that I froze and let you walk away. I'm never going to do that again."

"It was my fault, too," Van told him. "I'm the one that lied to you. I told you I didn't want you anymore. I think that's why it hurt so bad seeing you with her. I pushed you away. I hated myself for it, and the only person I could take it out on was you."

"I don't want you to lie to me," he told her. "The truth, no matter how painful, is so much better than lies. Even little white ones that you think are protecting me."

Her eyes watered. "I'm so sorry for hurting you. Ten years ago and now."

Those words made his chest tighten. He hadn't realized how much he needed to hear that, too.

"It's okay," he told her. "I'm the one who's sorry. I just want you to let me take care of you. I don't need anything else. I want you to let me through your barriers. For you to be more honest with me than you've been with anybody. Including yourself." He looked down at his hands. "And in return, I promise you that I won't walk away. Not even when you push me as hard as you can. I'll fight for you, Van. Every damn time. Because you're worth fighting for. But you've got to let me in. I can't break down your barriers if you don't help me. And I want to pull them away, one by one."

"I was scared," she said quietly. "So scared that if I let you in you might not like what you see."

His eyes met hers. "I love what I see. I love you. Every beat of my heart feels like it belongs to you."

Her breath caught in her throat, but she didn't pull her gaze away. She could feel the hot pulse of her blood as they stared at each other, the air crackling with electricity. She parted her lips, a soft sigh escaping from them, before she took a long, deep breath.

"I love you, too," she whispered. "So much." She'd never said it before. Not to anybody. For so long love had meant weakness in her world. But now she knew it didn't. It brought a strength that no army could break down. It was solid. It was true.

It was everything.

Tanner took a deep breath in, his eyes flashing. "Say it again," he said, his voice rough.

"I'm in love with you." This time her voice was loud. True. "I've loved you since the first time you knocked me over. And I'll love you until I die. Until we both do. And I pray with everything I'm worth that it'll be curled up together, all wrinkled with kids older than we are now."

He squeezed his eyes shut, then opened them again, his stare dark and full of meaning. "Come here," he said gruffly. "I fucking need you."

He didn't need to ask twice. A normal person would have walked around the coffee table, along the wall to the chair. But not Van. She leaped onto the table, ready to cross it to him, but he stood, scooping her off it, lifting her until their lips clashed together, and she was curled around him like a monkey.

"Enough talking," he muttered, carrying her out of the living room and down the hallway, kicking her bedroom door open and walking inside.

When he kicked the door closed behind him, their kisses slowed. They were deeper, their breathing rougher, as he slowly lowered her to her bed.

This time they didn't talk. They didn't need to. He'd told her everything she needed to know.

He loved her, he worshiped her. He wanted to take care of her.

And she'd let him, with every sweep of his lips and feathered touch of his fingers, lifting her up into a place where words weren't needed anymore.

When it was over, she lay in his arms in a post-sex haze, smiling at him as he softly stroked her hair.

"Can I stay?" he asked her.

"Yeah. All night." She grinned at him. "I'll even make you breakfast in the morning."

He lifted a brow. "What will the neighbors say?"

She leaned forward to kiss him. "I don't give a damn."

Tanner grinned, sliding his arms around her waist and pulling her to his body. "That's my girl," he murmured against her lips. "Now let's give them something to really talk about."

CHAPTER THIRTY-FIVE

"*A*re you ready for this?" Tanner asked, taking Van's hand in his as they walked along the creek.

"As I'll ever be." She smiled at Tanner, but her stomach still felt funny. Like she hadn't eaten for days when she'd just had a second helping of chicken pot pie at the diner. Tanner was carrying their things – two fold up chairs and a cooler with drinks inside, looking completely at ease with himself. He gave her a crooked grin, the corners of his eyes crinkling up, and she felt his warmth washing over her.

Which was a good thing, because summer was almost over, and there was a hint of fall in the air as they walked. The smell of ripe apples wafted in the breeze, and pieces of corn drifted from the fields as the harvest came to a peak. Last night, Zoe had begun to plan her Halloween outfit, even though school had only just gone back.

Or at least it seemed that way.

Swimming pools were closing up, orchards were opening for picking, and the busy summer season at the drive-in was coming to an end.

They wouldn't close up completely. She'd spent the past

few weeks planning their winter program, which would mean opening only on Friday and Saturday nights. Scary movies in October, some long-awaited blockbusters in November, and then their holiday movie season. She smiled at the thought of it.

"You're here!" Zoe said, running over and giving Van a hug. Then she grinned up at Tanner, who put the chairs down and ruffled her hair.

"Hey, kid." He smiled.

"How was your playdate?" Van asked her. Another change, as if this season didn't have enough of them. Zoe was finally being asked over to her friends' house. Probably because they loved hanging out at the drive-in whenever Van invited them over.

"Playdates are for babies." Zoe frowned. "I went to a friends for dinner."

Van bit down a smile. Her sister was growing up. "Did you have fun?"

"Yeah. Milly has this amazing jungle gym. It's as big as a house. We made a den at the top of it and pretended it was a tree house."

"See." Tanner winked at Van. "Not playing at all."

They found a spot with the younger crowd, pulling open the chairs and putting their refreshments on the shared table at the center, before Tanner poured them both a glass of lemonade.

It had been his idea to come here tonight. People didn't stare as much as they used to. Gossip had moved on since that night at the drive-in where her mom had told everybody about Johnny Fairfax being her father. They were too busy talking about the size of Maddie's baby bump – she was at least as big as Regan Laverty was before she gave birth to her little girl, who had perfectly round cheeks that Van had already fallen in love with.

"Hey!" Becca shot to her feet, running over to give Van a hug. "It's so good to see you. It feels like forever."

"We saw you on Sunday," Tanner said dryly. "That was what, five days ago?"

Becca wrinkled her nose at him. "Like I said, forever." She looked around. "How's your mom doing?"

"Good." Van nodded. "She has a job interview next week." There had been ups and downs since she came home from rehab, but she was so much better than she had been. There were still days when she couldn't even get herself out of bed, but she'd kept her word and hadn't drunk a sip of alcohol to try to ward off the misery. She'd even started AA.

"I'll keep my fingers crossed for h—" Becca stopped mid word, her mouth closing quickly as she looked over Van's shoulder.

Van twisted her head to follow her stare. Chrissie Fairfax was standing at the table, pouring two glasses of lemonade. Nora was next to her, though there was no sign of Johnny. When they saw her, they both quickly looked away.

Van squared her shoulders and gave Becca a reassuring smile. They didn't bother her. Not any more. It was funny how they never said nasty things for her to hear anymore. They seemed almost scared of her – more than once when she'd been in the town square she'd seen Nora hurrying away in the other direction.

Van brought her attention back to Becca. "Are Maddie and Gray coming tonight?"

"Yeah." Becca frowned, looking at the watch on her slim wrist. "They should have been here by now."

"They're coming." Tanner nodded in the other direction. Van could see them now, Gray had his arm around Maddie, who was walking as slow as molasses. Still, they both looked stunning. Gray, tall, strong and sexy, and Maddie wearing a yellow-and-white flowered dress, her dark hair flowing behind her as they reached the main group of *Chairs.*

"Did I miss anything?" Gray asked, looking at Tanner.

He shook his head. "Not a thing."

"Good. We would've been here half an hour ago, but we thought Maddie might have been in labor."

Maddie grimaced. "Turned out it was just gas. Gray's face was a picture when I let out the hugest burp."

"It was pretty bad." Gray was biting down a smile.

"Are you okay now?" Becca asked, looking worried.

"I'm fine. I've got weeks to go." Maddie's hand slid over her bump, a smile pulling at her lips. "You should have seen Gray panic though. It's like he's the one who'll be doing all the pushing."

"That wasn't panic. I just like being ready." Gray tipped his head to the side, looking at her through narrowed eyes. God, he was good looking. He and Tanner and all their brothers.

The Heartbreak Brothers. Van bit down a smile at the description.

"Anyway, enough of our problems," Gray said, turning his gaze to Tanner. "If only somebody around here would take the limelight off me."

Becca sniggered. It took Van a moment to realize that every one of them was staring at Tanner. She frowned, wondering what was going on.

"Get off my ass." Tanner shook his head, and Gray chuckled.

"I've heard that one before."

"I've always known you Hartsons were crazy." Van rolled her eyes. "But now you're reaching another level. What on earth are you all talking about?"

"Don't include me in the Hartsons," Maddie said. "I'm still a Clark."

"You're carrying a Hartson, baby," Gray pointed out, looking pleased with himself as he caressed Maddie's bump. "That makes you one of us."

Tanner shook his head at them all, then took Van's hand between his. "Come with me," he murmured.

"Gladly." She grinned at his family. "You're all crazy."

"That's why you love us," Becca told her, grinning.

Stupid thing, but it was true. Since Van had moved in with Tanner a few months ago – officially, that was, since she'd spent most nights with him since they reconciled – it had felt like she was finally part of something. They loved her the way she loved them, and they included her, Zoe, and even Kim in their daily lives. Dinners on Sundays after church, cookouts at Maddie and Gray's at least every other weekend, and of course they all came to the drive-in whenever there was a new movie showing.

Tanner guided her to the center of the grassy field, and climbed up on an empty chair. "Hey, everybody!" he shouted out. The low murmur of conversation stopped, as heads turned to look at him. Van looked up at him, her brows furrowed together.

What the hell was he doing?

As soon as everyone's attention was on him, Tanner grinned, and he took her breath away. She'd never get enough of him. Of that thick, crazy hair, or those eyes that seemed to see into her very soul.

Or his lips. God, his lips. She swallowed hard remembering exactly what they did to her last night.

His eyes caught hers. "I want to tell you a little story," he said, his voice projecting over the field. "About a small girl who smelled of strawberries and looked like the sun. And the little boy who ran into her and almost flattened her to the ground." He winked at Van. "Not knowing that in reality, he was the one who'd been bowled over."

She shook her head. This was so very Tanner. The crowd gathered around them, craned forward to listen.

"And when that kid looked up at the angel he'd almost knocked over, he knew his life was never going to be the same. It was going to be better. Always. Because she was in it."

"Aww," somebody whispered. "Isn't he the sweetest?"

"That girl and boy grew up," he continued. "And they made some stupid mistakes." He raised an eyebrow at Van. "Especially the boy, who turned out to be an idiot. Because instead of putting a ring on the girl's finger, and thanking god for every day she spent with him, he decided to head off to New York and play with computers for ten years."

"A real idiot," Gray shouted out. Tanner rolled his eyes at his brother.

"But then they met again. And the boy realized what a damn huge mistake he'd made. Because this girl was everything he'd wanted. She was beautiful, clever, funny, and for some crazy reason, she decided to give him a second chance." He grinned at Van, and she blew him a kiss back. "And this time that boy – *me* – isn't going to mess it up. He's going to beg her to be his forever, because he knows how damn lucky he is to have her."

"Why don't you say things like that about me?" an old woman whispered to her husband.

"Because I haven't gotten lucky in years," he muttered.

Van bit down on her lip to stop herself from laughing. Or maybe crying. Her whole body was tingling. She didn't know what to do with her hands, so eventually she clasped them together, looking up at Tanner with shiny eyes.

"Savannah Butler. Beautiful, clever woman. Love of my whole damn life." Tanner jumped down from the chair, still smiling at her, and then dropped to a knee in front of her, pulling a ring box out of his pocket and opening it up. "I have something to ask you."

Van's heart started galloping in her chest.

"Will you do the honor of agreeing to be my wife?" Tanner asked softly, looking up at her through thick lashes. "I promise to always take care of you. To kiss you as often as you deserve to be kissed." He slid his eyes to where Gray and Maddie were watching. "And if I knock you up, I promise I won't complain about your gas."

"See?" Maddie elbowed Gray. "That's true love."

"I know, baby." Gray kissed her head.

"Say yes!" Becca shouted out. "Come on!"

Everybody was silent. All eyes were on Van. The old Van would have panicked about what they were all thinking. If they were judging her.

But the new Van didn't care. Not one bit.

Instead, she smiled and looked around, taking in the warm faces of everybody watching. "He's lying," she told them all. "I'm the lucky one."

"You're killing me here," Tanner told her, his lip quirking. "I'm kinda waiting for an answer."

Van laughed, clapping her hands over her mouth. "Oh goodness. Yes! The answer's yes." Tanner started to laugh, too. Grabbing the ring from the box he was holding, he slid it onto her outstretched finger. Then he stood and pulled her against him, smoothing the hair from her face with his hand before kissing her hard and hot.

"Go, Tanner!" somebody hollered, followed by a whole host of whoops and catcalls. The older folk started cheering, and Van's lips curled beneath his before they finally pulled apart.

"Let's make it a short engagement," Tanner murmured to her. "Like really, really short."

She grinned up at him, happiness shining out of her.

She'd never get tired of this man. Of his smile, or the way he teased her, or the good humored way he took the ribbing from his brothers.

They'd be spending the rest of their lives together, and she couldn't wait for it to begin.

"Yeah," she said, cupping his face with her hands, rolling onto her tiptoes to brush her lips against his. "A short engagement sounds good to me."

EPILOGUE

*T*here were three things that everybody in Hartson's Creek agreed on. It hardly rained in November, a wedding should never be held after the last crop of corn was brought in, and Savannah Butler and Tanner Hartson were two crazy kids who never listened to advice.

And still Tanner found himself standing at the front of the First Baptist Church, his hair soaked from the downpour that had caught them on their way in, plastering their hair to their faces.

Not that he cared. Because in a few minutes *she* would be here. The woman who brought sunshine into his life on the darkest of days. She was going to be his wife, and he was counting down the seconds.

"Stop looking at the door," Logan murmured. "She'll get here when she's ready." He was standing on one side of Tanner, Cam and Gray were on the other. He couldn't decide between his brothers who would be the best man, so he'd asked them all.

A loud cry came out, and Tanner looked over his shoulder at Maddie, who was cooing at her baby son. Well one of them, anyway. Tanner was pretty sure that was Marley. Presley, the younger twin, was being cradled by Aunt Gina, who was smiling happily at the babe in her arms. Even his dad looked happy as Presley gurgled up at them both.

Apparently, surprise twins were still a thing. Tanner bit down a grin when he remembered Gray telling him the first thing Maddie said when she got her breath back after giving birth.

"I told you I was big."

That was the understatement of the year. According to the doctor, hidden twins were rare but not completely unknown. Marley – the bigger baby – had been hiding his twin during the ultrasounds, and their heartbeats were in sync, confounding even the obstetrician.

Tanner looked at the church door again, then back at Reverend Maitland who was smiling patiently at them all. From the corner of his eye he saw Gray lean over to take Marley, hitching him up against his wool suit jacket and kissing his fuzzy head. Somebody at the back of the church sighed, making Logan chuckle softly.

"Babies and guys," he murmured. "Ovary exploders."

"How would you know?" Cameron whispered to his own twin. "You haven't exploded anybody's ovaries for years. When was the last time you got laid?"

"Last time you won a game." Logan raised a brow at his brother.

Reverend Maitland cleared his throat, making Tanner bite down a grin. It was so good to have his brothers here with him. It felt like coming home, except he was already here. Every piece of the jigsaw was sliding into place.

The doors finally opened, and Zoe walked forward, wearing a pale green dress that wrapped around her neck and fell in gentle folds to the floor. She grinned at Tanner, and he smiled back at her, watching as she moved down the aisle, scattering pale pink petals in front of her.

Then came Becca, wearing the same color, but this dress was fitted and sophisticated. But Tanner wasn't looking at her. Because behind her was the only person he ever wanted to look at.

And damn, was she beautiful.

Van's hair was pulled back from her face, caught in a low chignon at the top of her neck. Golden tendrils spilled from it, curling around her cheeks and catching the light of the autumn sun. Her eyes caught his, and he felt his chest tighten. This was it. The moment he made her his.

The music began, the organ reverberating through the church as Van and her mom slowly walked down the aisle. With every step she took, his grin widened, knowing that in a few moments he'd be able to touch her, hear her, kiss her.

It filled him in a way nothing else ever could.

Then she was there, her head lifted as she gazed up at him, a smile playing at her lips. He swallowed hard, emotions spilling through him as Reverend Maitland spoke out, welcoming them to the church.

She was beautiful. She was everything. She was his.

He took a deep breath and slid his hand over hers. "Ready?" he murmured.

"Yes." She nodded, her face radiant. "I'm ready."

THE PARTY WAS DYING DOWN. The music was softer now, slower, too, as a few couples swayed drunkenly on the dance floor at the center of the huge circus-style tent Gray had erected behind his house. Tanner was leaning on the bar, Logan and Cam next to him. Gray had disappeared, no doubt helping Maddie with the babies. And

Van was sitting in the corner with Becca, her mom and Zoe, and some of their girl friends, laughing as they talked.

"So Fairfax didn't come," Logan said, ordering all three of them a whiskey.

"Nope. But we didn't invite him. Or his family." Tanner shrugged. "Van didn't want them here."

"She not interested in connecting with him?" Logan asked.

"Doesn't seem to be." Tanner took a swig of his whiskey. "Says I'm the only family she needs."

"Damn, that girl needs a lobotomy," Cam said, winking at him.

"What an asshole, though, pretending he wasn't her father for so long." Logan shook his head. "What kind of man does that? Denies his child? No wonder she doesn't want to see him."

"What would you do if you found out you had a kid?" Tanner asked him.

Logan smirked. "Sue the condom manufacturers."

Tanner laughed. "Logan wouldn't have a surprise kid. He doesn't have sex? He's too busy for that."

Logan rolled his eyes. "Yeah, right. You go on believing that."

"Who doesn't have sex?" Gray asked, walking over to them. "Apart from me, that is. Maddie's already told me we're never having sex again. She's scared that next time it'll be triplets. I told her it doesn't work that way."

"Logan," Cam said loudly. "He's the one who needs to get laid."

"Thanks for saying that in front of Reverend Maitland, by the way." Logan shook his head at his twin. "And for your information, I get plenty. I just don't brag about it like you do." He grinned.

Cam shrugged. "Can't help it. Girls throw themselves at me."

"You could dodge them. You've been pretty good at dodging the ball this season," Tanner teased him. "Just channel that skill."

Gray started talking to Cam about next week's game, leaving Logan and Tanner leaning on the bar. "You think you'll ever settle down?" Tanner asked his older brother.

"Probably not." Logan shrugged. "Not many women like the restaurant business. I work nights, weekends, and holidays. It pisses them off when I'm not around. It's easier when it's casual. No expectations, you know?"

"What are you gonna do when you decide to have a family?" Tanner tipped his head to the side.

"Dunno. All I can tell you is that kids and restaurants don't mix. I guess I'd have to rethink my career choice." He drained his whiskey. "But there's plenty of time for all that. Not all of us need to settle down before we're thirty. Maybe I'll make my millions and have a family when I'm in my fifties." He grinned. "I can be a stay at home dad."

Tanner laughed at the image of an older Logan surrounded by screaming kids. Somehow he couldn't quite see that working. "Sure. You keep thinking that," he said, lifting his glass to his brother's and clinking them together. "In the meantime, I'm going to go and kiss my very real bride, and drag her onto the dance floor."

"You're whipped," Logan said. Was there an edge of envy in his voice?

"Yep. And I'm loving it."

Before he even reached her, Tanner could feel Van's pull. Like she was the sun and he was orbiting her, always trying to push through.

"Hey," he whispered, kissing her bare shoulder as he reached her. "Can I persuade you to have one last dance?"

She looked up at him, her eyes full of love. "Yeah, you can definitely do that." She winked at Zoe, then stood, letting Tanner lead her to the dance floor. He slid his arm around her waist, pulling her close against him, smiling against her hair as her body slotted perfectly against his.

Then they were dancing. His perfect woman and him. They swayed gently to the music, her arms wrapped around his neck, his hand guiding her as they moved slowly around the dance floor.

This was it. The beginning. They had the rest of their lives ahead of them. He dropped his head, pressing his lips against hers, both of them grinning as they kissed.

"I love you, Mrs. Hartson," he whispered, loving the sound of her name on his tongue.

"I love you, too," she said, grinning widely. "Now shut up and dance."

The End

ABOUT THE AUTHOR

Carrie Elks writes contemporary romance with a sizzling edge. Her first book, *Fix You*, has been translated into eight languages and made a surprise appearance on *Big Brother* in Brazil. Luckily for her, it wasn't voted out.

Carrie lives with her husband, two lovely children and a larger-than-life black pug called Plato. When she isn't writing or reading, she can be found baking, drinking an occasional (!) glass of wine, or chatting on social media.

You can find Carrie in all these places
www.carrieelks.com
carrie.elks@mail.com

Three books about strong and sassy women finding love in the big city.

Coming Down

Broken Chords

Canada Square

STANDALONE

Fix You

An epic romance that spans the decades. Breathtaking and angsty and all the things in between.

ACKNOWLEDGMENTS

First thanks always go to my lovely family. My husband, Ash, my children Ella and Olly and not forgetting Plato the pug. You guys are amazing.

I wouldn't be here without my brilliant agents, Meire Dias and Flavia Viotti of the Bookcase Agency. From the beginning of my career they've been my biggest supporters, and I'm so grateful to them.

My editor Rose David and my proofreader, Mich, always work tirelessly to make my words shine. Thank you for all you do.

Special thanks to Marian G for pre-reading and her suggestions on the story. I appreciate your insight!

Kirsty Ann Still is a kick-ass designer, and she hit this cover out of the park. You're so talented my friend!

Bloggers have always been such an important part of my book journey. Thanks to each and every one of you who shows me support in so many ways – sharing covers and release days, promoting sales, reading and reviewing books. You're the engine that keeps the book world going, and I appreciate you so much.

Finally, to my lovely facebook group members (The Water Cooler - if you want to join!), thank you! We have so much fun – you make Facebook a great place to be. You help with ideas, inspiration and most of all you put a smile on my face. Thanks for being so amazing.

Printed in Great Britain
by Amazon